THE
WAR JOURNAL
OF
LILA ANN SMITH

A NOVEL BY

IRVING M. WARNER

PLEASURE BOAT STUDIO: A LITERARY PRESS

The War Journal of Lila Ann Smith

A novel by Irving Warner

Copyright © 2007

ISBN 978-1-929355-33-4

Drawings by Biliana Ally
Book design by Susan Ramundo

Library of Congress Cataloging-in-Publication Data
     Warner, Irving, 1941–
     The war journal of Lila Ann Smith : a novel / by Irving Warner.
          p.   cm.
     ISBN-13: 978-1-929355-33-4
     1. World War, 1939–1945—Campaigns—Alaska—Attu Island—Fiction.
     2. Attu, Battle of, Alaska, 1943—Personal narratives—Fiction.   I. Title.
     PS3573.A7639W37   2007
     813'.54—dc22

                                                2007020732

Pleasure Boat Studio is a proud subscriber to the Green Press Initiative.
This program encourages the use of 100% post-consumer recycled paper
with environmentally friendly inks for all printing projects in an effort
to reduce the book industry's economic and social impact. With the
cooperation of our printing company, we are pleased to offer this book
as a Green Press book.

PLEASURE BOAT STUDIO: A LITERARY PRESS
201 West 89th St., Ste. 6F
New York, NY 10024

The Gatekeeper

I open this gate and invite you into the life and times of 44 real people on Attu Island, June 1942, all part of the historical record of World War Two. I've changed all the names in *The War Journal of Lila Ann Smith*. I've altered some of the facts, also, especially that of the historical school teacher and title character, who was not interred on Hokkaido Island, but on another island, near Yokahama, Japan.

But beyond this gate, the reader is visiting the spirit and times of the real story, and practically speaking, the events themselves, based on my own 25-year long research.

I don't claim to own this story. No one can.

—I.W.

"A great many things keep happening,
some of them good, some of them bad."

—Gregory of Tours, *History of the Franks,* 590 A.D.

Anchorage
ALASKA
Kodiak
U.S.S.R.
Bering Sea
Unalaska
Aleutian Islands
Atka
Attu Kiska
Hokkaido
Otaru
JAPAN
PACIFIC OCEAN

Introduction

Origins

Lila Ann Smith died just a few days beyond her ninety-eighth birthday in August 1979. She was the oldest resident at The Meadows extended care facility at Cedar Falls, Iowa, where I was activities director.

She had been widowed in each of two marriages, both having had produced no children; also, Lila had no known relatives or friends, at least those who survived her. The management arranged her funeral and disposition. Only a few people attended her memorial service; I represented The Meadows, though I would have surely gone anyway.

When I came on staff the year before, she was in full dotage and didn't know individual employees at all. Records show she had been placed in The Meadows by a Mr. and Mrs. A. J. Winters in 1969 when she was eighty-eight. Under the section marked "connection with client," the Winters simply checked "friends." Their contact address proved years out of date and subsequent efforts to locate them were unsuccessful.

So, when Lila Ann died, her unclaimed estate, such as it was, became my concern—one of those unwanted duties activities directors seem to inherit.

Her belongings were few, and it was while sorting through them, I came across *The War Journal of Lila Ann Smith*. It, along with a single newspaper article (see Appendix), is my only source for information about Lila Ann, aside from county documentation.

Lila Ann Smith was born in 1880 to missionary parents serving in northeastern China. She lived through an extraordinary swath of history. To begin, she, along with her family, witnessed the events of the now-forgotten Sino-Japanese War in 1894–95. Four years later came the violent Boxer Rebellion, during which her parents and only brother were murdered. Though she escaped, Lila Ann was soon taken hostage along with four other missionary daughters by a freebooting warlord who eventually exchanged them for military equipment.

Once repatriated to her parents' hometown in Delbert, Iowa, life returned to normal for almost four decades. In 1940, along with her second husband, Osmond (she had been widowed years before), she took employment with the Bureau of Indian Affairs, Alaska Territorial Section.

At the journal's start, Lila was 61 years of age and her husband Osmond two years younger. Her first entry began en route to her new posting as schoolteacher on the island of Attu (the westernmost Aleutian island), September 1, 1941, along with Osmond. He served as a territorial aerographer and radio operator.

After she completed the first school year, the Japanese captured Attu Island and its inhabitants on the morning of June 6, 1942. Within a few days the invaders executed her husband and, though she was beaten severely, she survived. In contrast to these early outrages upon the Smiths, the Japanese treated the resident forty-two Aleut natives with civility and respect.

In September, 1942, after three months of comparatively peaceful occupation, all the villagers and Lila were transported via coal ship to Japan, specifically the town of Otaru, Hokkaido Prefecture. No official reason for this unlikely decision has ever surfaced.

Here the Attuans and Lila Ann spent the remainder of the war under civilian "house arrest." In the ensuing three years, half of the Attuans died due to starvation and disease. The Red Cross arrived at their place of internment in September 1945. At that point, no one knew of the Attuans' capture and survival. Though there are wide lapses, especially in 1945, Lila Ann maintained her journal-writing activities until December 1945. The dramatic survival and persistent care of the journal, despite extreme adversity, demonstrates an extraordinary sense of purpose.

Essentially, Lila Ann Smith left behind nothing but this journal. At first reading, it was clearly a unique document. When she and the Attuans were captured, no American citizens had been taken on national soil by an invading army, then transported as prisoners to a foreign land, in over 150 years.

Despite the journal's special qualities, my attempts to interest archivists over the years were unsuccessful. So, until my retirement, this work languished.

Between 1977 and her death in 1979, when I knew her, Lila spent her days in the fog of advanced age. She was, even then, a tall, stately woman. She had largish facial features, most prominent of which were large, light brown eyes, always wide open. While I knew her, these beautiful eyes were sadly disconnected from her mental processes.

Not so her ears: upon certain occasions, she would listen attentively to music, following the beat by tapping her long, narrow foot lightly against the floor. Sometimes she'd supplement this by keeping time with her index finger against a chair arm, or table. After noticing this, I made it a point to include music in her daily life.

Her journal began on the cheerful note of shipboard adventure and discovery on September 2, 1941. But soon war again overtook her life, as it did all of America, with the bombing of Pearl Harbor. She then records not only life in her new home, but emotions and fears resulting from the imminent threat of foreign invasion.

After the Attuans' capture, and for the next three and a half years, she faithfully journalizes the loss of liberty, life, and finally and most sadly, the heritage of the Attuans. Through callous official acts by the territorial government of Alaska, the Attuans never returned to their island. Wartime events stamped the villagers and Lila Ann Smith with deep indelible scars.

The Manuscript
I feel certain the journal was kept, then stored, with eventual discovery in mind. The handwritten pages, of all sizes, varieties and condition of paper, were tidied up and glued individually into a scrapbook, then numbered. The scattered sketches, demonstrating Lila Ann's sensitivity and attempt to capture the scenes she witnessed, exist just where she left them.

Entries were episodic, and often chatty in a good way, I feel, especially prior to capture. Of course, as war approached Attu and the hope of official evacuation was dangled before them, the tone of Lila Ann's entries changes

After capture, the reportage, of course, becomes somber; the length of each entry decreases for some time. Oddly, after the first week of the invasion, despite their criminal treatment of the Smiths, Japanese authorities showed little concern for Lila's presence amongst the Attuans. Also, during her convalescence from the beatings, the journal has its longest gap in time. When she resumes, we find a different Lila Ann Smith.

Despite the foregoing, or perhaps *because* of it, I took care to transcribe Lila's journal as-is. If I felt a note was in order to clarify content or bridge wide time gaps, I bracketed and italicized my comments. It is my view, and I hope that the reader will come to agree, that the voice and eyes of Lila Ann Smith were a unique and fortunate alignment of time, person, and circumstance. She moves her journal beyond a war-and-survival account to create an intimate testimony to the calumny and delusion that is warfare.

The Journal of Lila Ann Smith

<u>Tuesday, September 2, 1941. Aboard the *Northern Supplier*</u>
This is the third day aboard the good ship *Northern Supplier*, our humble transport to Attu Island, the village of Chichigof, and my Aleut charges. All these names! And this exciting mission.

The weather, thus far, has been beautiful, and this morning we entered the Shumagin Island Group at a stately seven nautical miles per hour. After these many days aboard, it is almost incredible to realize it is 1,200 more miles to far-flung Attu. Mr. Smith declared that at this rate, "Your little papooses will be grown before we reach there." Such impatience from the masculine set is to be expected, but I, by contrast, am happy with our progress.

There are numerous souls aboard the *Supplier*, a hulking tramp freighter cut full-cloth from adventure books. In fact, there presently are eighteen "civilians," all but six of us bound for Dutch Harbor.

For passengers, meals are group affairs, served by our cook and waiter, a good-hearted chap who insists on being called Sidemeat, a most extraordinary sobriquet. Suppressing a laugh, I declined referring to a fellow soul thusly, and being informed of his given name, opted for it. So, to me, he is Louis. His great ebony features grew quite pleased when he said, "I ain't been called Louis since I left Passagoula before the Great War."

Captain Eustace Winston is the master of the *Supplier*, an elderly salt familiar with all the bays, inlets, and waters of Alaska, and particularly the Alaska Peninsula and Aleutian Islands. Since we came aboard in Seward, the Captain is not a frequent sight, instead the chief mate, Mr. Arlo, seems to superintend everyday affairs, especially the unloading and loading of cargo at every stop, of which there are many.

We are aboard the "milk run," though Mr. Arlo in his somewhat crusty manner opines that the beverage is more likely raisin jack than milk. His reasons are based in the natives' overweening craving for alcoholic beverages. Though Aleuts and Eskimos are discouraged—actually disallowed—from having strong drink shipped to them, a similar prohibition does not exist on the ingredients for *biwok*, local parlance for home brew.

Though I suppose northern seafaring is not a gentle life, I still feel that Mr. Arlo's words are perhaps too severe. The people I see at dockside are sober and happy. The villages have such names as Chignik, Perryville, Ivanof, etc. Each welcoming party is filled with joy to see the *Supplier*—for in some of the smaller towns, we are the last boat prior to the holidays.

Our next stop is Sand Point in the Shumagin Islands. I cannot express my excitement at being at sea. After three months in Anchorage, and a year at River Station [*Lila Ann and Osmond Smith worked for the Bureau of Indian Affairs, and were stationed at Three River Station from 1940 through mid-1941*], even the comparative confines of the *Supplier* are a great improvement, especially for Mr. Smith. The poor man could never fully enjoy Three River Station. But, his sense of *purpose* is immeasurably better now, and in truth I can say we both have high hopes for our new and unique posting on Attu.

September 12, 1941. Aboard the *Northern Supplier*
One would think shipboard life is conducive to keeping one's journal, but it is not, perhaps [*more*] due to my own lack of discipline than events. Oh! Progress toward our new home is so arduous. We've spent the last two days anchored before the village of Akutan, a tiny native hamlet located on an island of

the same name. But, an Aleutian Island, no less! My pallet is so brimming with new "colors" it is daunting to know where to begin!

Since my entry of September 2, much has happened, not the least is Mrs. Lieskof giving birth aboard the *Supplier*, a loudly protesting seven-and-a-half-pound boy-child! She is a lovely Aleut woman of advanced age for a new mother. Mother Lieskof came aboard at the village of Pavlof, en route to Unalaska where her sister and oldest daughter live.

Upon coming aboard (in view of her advanced *expectant* condition!), Mr. Arlo was not happy, and voiced same, but Mr. and Mrs. Lieskof assured him the baby wasn't due for "long time now," in that strange abbreviated way of speaking these Aleuts have—with a beautiful melodic touch as well. Well, the baby was early. So, flouting Mr. Arlo's stated ship policy about not giving birth at sea, baby arrived while we were at anchorage in a remote bay after a violent late summer storm. "Late summer storms, Mrs. Lila, they don't last long," Third Officer, Mr. Kokkahiko, assured, but then we sat on anchor for almost *four* days!

But I shall go back to our stop at Pavlof Village.

For some reason (seemingly!), almost half the village came aboard for transport to Unalaska, but after long parley, with Mr. Kokkahiko representing the captain, it was determined only four souls had the price of passage, two of which were Mr. and Mrs. Lieskof. One would assume that, so publicly denied passage, those excluded might be humiliated, but they were not. Instead they joined those in the longboat (there's no dock at Pavlof), waving goodbye as cheerfully as if they'd never planned on going in the first place. Quite remarkable.

The storm was my first sea tempest, and it was frightening. Most of my fellow "civilians" (Mr. Smith so coins our fellows) were sick, save the villagers from Pavlov. The *Supplier* began to rise and settle into the seas which were building rapidly. Mr. Smith urged me to stay in my bed, or "bunk" as sea parlance deems it, to prevent the *mal de mer* that so plagued others, including himself.

I, thank God, was free of this; perhaps it was the long shipboard return after my evacuation from China those many sad years back. But in any case, save for the buffeting, I was well, although thoroughly scared. Going *topside* (meaning going *up* from the inner sanctums of the ship, into the superstructure, or on deck), I encountered a somber Father Mordvinof, his black and gray checkered beard ribboning helter-skelter in the wind, his threadbare black habit pressed tightly against him.

Beside him stood Mr. Lieskof, his powerful, short legs planted securely on the deck, smoking his pipe despite our tiny group being on the *windward* side, though in the *leeward* shadow of a lifeboat. (Do I sound like Mr. Melville!) They chatted in Russian(!!), the language of the Orthodox faith [*actually, Old Slavonic, an earlier form of modern Russian*] but politely switched to English in my presence, though neither is comfortable in it. Mr. Lieskof gestured widely with the stem of his pipe and announced, to Father Mordvinof's obvious disapproval, "Big sea now, strong-as-hell winds. Ya! Lots weather." Then he stomped his right foot upon the deck, smiled cheerfully, and opined, "But big-as-hell boat, so we pretty OK, you bet."

Stooping, then turning his back into the wind, he knocked his pipe out—hot ash included—into his hand, scrunched his hand up, and expectorated into it. Then, satisfied, he wiped his hand against his thick, canvas coat and went "below." A most extraordinary maneuver. Father Mordvinof stood placidly during this, then looking at me, lifted his chin somewhat—a gesture southward (?)—and in his thickly accented but correct English said, "So, war with Japan is close."

And it was not a question, but a summation of the conversation he and Mr. Smith had at mealtime the day before. Osmond is sure, as are most, that war with Japan is inevitable. I tried to be more optimistic and switched the topic to Attu, for strangely I already prize my new home, and Father Mordvinof had been there some years before—four, in fact.

But, a tacit man, I have had to *extract* details from him, and was just commencing this when a great winnow of spume and sea water struck the opposite side of the lifeboat, and a bit caught Father Mordvinof in the face, poor man. Dignity lost for the moment, further talk was ended when he politely excused himself and went below, the opposing direction of *topside*, which for some reason is not *bottomside* or *belowside*.

Seaward the waves curled and bowed, the wind had its way with them, sending stray bits of ocean in clouds that dissipated downwind. For the first time there were no *sea pigeons* or clownish *puffins*, the former winging their way from wave-top to wave-top; the latter pattering along the surface, in a great but frustrating panic to become aloft. And always above, the gulls—small and large—wheeling, alert for tidbits.

But these little friends were gone now, perhaps the wind being too violent for them. So, the *Northern Supplier* was alone on these irate seas, with all souls aboard grateful for its old but sturdy hull between us and the deep.

<u>September 13, 1941. Aboard the *Northern Supplier*</u>
I became over-tired during the last entry, fell asleep in spite of the waves, and woke up en route to Dutch Harbor! I am over-joyed to be on our way once again.

I shall catch up, trying to resist verbosity, though without intention of lessening the importance of infant Lieskof's arrival!

Being soundly trounced by the storm, our indomitable ship sought shelter in a haunting wilderness bay. And it was there, in this primordial setting, where infant Lieskof arrived. How many countless Aleut babes have come from the Creator in such untamed, natural surroundings where, at one time, all Aleuts lived unencumbered by civilization?

The mother, whose first name is Fervroyna, or Fern in English, is forty-six years of age, and in a surprise to Osmond and me, Captain Winston broke his long absence from public view for the delivery. Fern's elderly aunt (I'm guessing, for the relationships are confused with language problems) assisted him, with Louis serving as runner between galley and cabin.

Mr. Arlo seemed amused by my surprise at our Captain's unlikely additional duties. "Oh, the Captain's delivered more native babies than old Pocahontas herself." And, it being Mr. Arlo, I've edited his response, for he took opportunity to include rough language about Aleuts, the Captain, and motherhood in general! Osmond, who was close by, protested Mr. Arlo's language used before myself, and the scene became awkward.

Mr. Smith won't have harsh talk before womenfolk, and upbraids any infraction instead of allowing it to pass.

The birth, thankfully, was not prolonged, and soon the Captain had retired to the privacy of his quarters, and the elderly aunt showed us in one at a time to see Baby—father stood proudly beside mother, who looked quite worn, poor thing. And in this tiny cabin, this babe held his first reception for the world!

Four days—three days and four nights—we spent in the tiny bay, on the extreme end of Tigalda Island. I'm told newcomers become discouraged at the uniform (or drab?) appearance of Aleutian islands, most prominent is the complete lack of trees. From the decks of the *Supplier* my first impressions are in contrast to that: the islands seem vast giants in the sea, with—if Tigalda Island is any indication—intricate tangles of coves and bays. Beaches are steep, with the sea grasping at their rocky edges. Ceaseless Aleutian grasses adorn the flanks of the mountains, swaying and rippling in the wind as did the maturing millet fields in Shansi Province.

Osmond has effected "shore leave" for us at Dutch Harbor, and relishes the opportunity to "stretch his pins" and look about. He will take in tour the communication station there. I will accompany Baby Lieskof, mother, and father to the village, for they've extended a warm invitation. I accepted at once—thrilled at the prospect.

In a confidential "Dear Journal" addendum, Himself is smoking again (!!!), after vowing never to "poison" his body with the dreaded tobacco plant. It gives me respectful amusement that he still underestimates the superior function of the feminine olfactories compared to those of menfolk!

September 16, 1941. Aboard the *Northern Supplier*
At the fastest rate yet, the good vessel *Northern Supplier* arrived two hours ago at the village of Nikolski, on Umnak

Island, just under nineteen hours after departing Dutch Harbor/Unalaska. I do understand from Louis, my constant informant for both fact and *scuttlebutt* (read *rumor*, sea-going variety!), that we stopped at a smaller village while I was abed. Louis didn't know the name, but it was no more than a "drop off," shipboard parlance for briefly stopping to unload and take on light cargo and mail.

As I write, we are *departing* (!) Nikolski, and since we arrived just prior to 10 p.m. (or 2200, shipboard time, more about this puzzlement later), I have seen little of the tiny Russian Orthodox hamlet. And now we're departing, and the sun has yet to rise.

Mr. Kokkahiko's *unedited* explanation of our present situation is, "When Captain gets a hair up his snoot about being behind schedule, that's that. Forget everything else."

This explained the canceling of shore-side activities at Dutch Harbor/Unalaska, to the chagrin of those three passengers bound further "westward" (the logical way locals refer to points farther out the Aleutian Chain relative to one's present position). Mr. Smith was irreconcilable about the Captain's reversal. He had earlier assurances for shore time, and demanded to go ashore to consult about official communication issues.

I was not aware of additional functions Osmond had pending, but I would not object, of course. But I do know that the shipping agent guaranteed one thing, but quite another was done. This brings me back to Mr. Kokkahiko's expression regarding Captain Winston's nose. When Mr. Smith insisted on appealing this reversal to the Captain, Mr. Arlo shrugged and gave a typical smirk. Thankfully Mr. Kokkahiko, usually a buoyant, cheerful Polynesian, became quite "gray around the gills"—an expression my father oft used—and said, "Oh, Mr. Smith, I would not do that if I were you."

Mr. Smith is a stickler for keeping to one's word. So, it was only through my unrelenting and repeated invocation for peace and tranquility that Osmond did not protest to the captain, thankfully adhering to the advice of Mr. Kokkahiko.

Louis, using Mr. Arlo's weakness for dumplings as leverage, inveigled from him a worn nautical *chart* ("No, no; not a map, Mrs. Smith! A *chart*," pronounceth Sir Arlo!) of the Aleutian Island Chain. I think they did this in hopes of stanching my constant flow of questions geographic.

When unfurled, it quite takes up half of our cabin wall (aboard a ship, walls are *bulkheads*, a term I do like, for it suggests great strength!) and is not readily decipherable. I only barely follow it, but I'm sure Osmond will interpret for me when his spirits recover from the business at Dutch Harbor.

After breakfast I stood on the *starboard quarter* (right rear portion of the ship—I'm getting to be quite the ancient mariner) and watched Umnak Island, and the unseen souls at Nikolski, fall behind us, its great central mountain rising into a beautiful morning, as clear as spring water. Our sea bird companions cruise and glide around us by the scores, some immaculate white, some a dingy gray; some quite large, others tiny, as black as ink specks against the gray-blue waters. The *Supplier*'s propeller leaves a frothy straight edge that occasionally juts a bit left or right by the sway of the ship. Indeed, the *Supplier* rises and settles in a largish but regular "lump," as Louis calls the vast swelling waves that pass under us.

There are now only three passengers: Mr. Smith, the dour Father Mordvinof, and myself. If on deck, he stands in the leeward side of either the port or starboard lifeboat, hands held behind him, staring placidly at the land. The tacit cleric most certainly would not appreciate being informed how much he looks like a cassocked Leon Trotsky, but he most certainly does.

He is bound for Atka, the second most distant village in the Aleutian Chain, where he'll take over church duties, though I can't be sure, for with him, social talk is rare.

It is difficult to comprehend that after all this time we are still almost 800 miles from our posting at Attu Island. This is such a vast, unceasing expanse of islands. We are, with God's grace, toiling to the very terminus of it.

<u>September 18, 1941. Aboard the *Northern Supplier*</u>
We arrived at the village of Atka just prior to daylight this morning. This is the first Aleut village I've been able to view in full light. I admit to a sinking feeling at the experience.

It was low overcast, the thick rain clouds passing only a few hundred feet overhead; the rain was composed of tiny, chilled droplets. There was a gusty wind, not overly heavy, but insistent, threading its way around and over the *Supplier* as it unloaded freight onto a small barge or lighter, which ferried it to land. In the rain and cold, people worked steadily to complete the necessary duties and return inside to the stovefronts.

Now, unlike our earlier stops, Captain Winston personally observed activities on small platforms that are to the port and starboard of the wheelhouse. A small, roundish man, he was dressed in oilskins with heavy clothing underneath, making him appear even more ovoid. Quite out of region and character, instead of a rain hat he had donned a pith helmet, so he rather looked like something out of the chapters of R. Kipling or J. Conrad.

"Where on earth did he acquire that," muttered Himself, still peevish over Captain Winston's decision in Dutch Harbor. I must admit, Captain Winston did look something of a sight wearing it. But he paced first to one side of the bridge, then passed through the wheelhouse to the other, only to repeat the process.

I looked upon the rather sodden, unhappy appearance of Atka Village, located on the island of the same name. All the old wooden buildings, quite small and frail at this distance, seemed huddled together more for protection than common society. The church, its smallish cupola and Byzantine cross prominent, are the universal emblem of the Orthodox faith.

So it was not a sight that buoyed one's spirit. I could see the Atkan people: Some (just a few children) around the houses, others—adult men—unloading the freight at the shore-line. And it was this overall mood that seemed somehow matched to Father Mordvinof's departure. A launch came alongside, its small motor's laborings muffled in the thick weather, and by the time I reached the rail and looked over, the craft was shore bound. Since Father Mordvinof was looking *aft* (to the rear!) and the others in the opposite direction, he saw me at the same moment I saw him.

I hesitated. Would such a person wave "goodbye"? But, *I would*, so I waved very conservatively, and he surprised me by raising his arm, then wagging it back and forth—an odd, railroad-signal gesture. But, nonetheless, a sign recognizing the moment.

Oh, *good fortune* to you Father Mordvinof, may the good feelings and words of Christ always serve you and your flock lovingly.

My father was not unlike *this* Father Mordvinof. He was such a good human being, a devout pastor, but unlike mother could never laugh. I recall, those many years ago, once asking Father, "Father Dear, why don't you laugh as much as Mother Dear?"

"Because, Daughter," and absolutely without any smile whatsoever he pointed out to me, "the Laugh Fairy bit her and not me. Didn't you know, child?"

<u>September 19, 1941. Aboard the *Northern Supplier*</u>
According to our chart and Mr. Kokkahiko's information, we are 195 miles farther west toward our new home, "which isn't that bad a day's run." Mr. Smith does not share our Second Officer's view, and shakes his head at the *Northern Supplier*'s matronly gait. He points out that it is little more than eight miles per hour. He has taken charge of our chart and busies himself with calculations diverse. This has improved his spirits considerably.

A remarkable incident happened, or at the least, remarkable to *this* newcomer. It was in the middle of what had been the darkest of clouded nights, and averse to such gloom I retired early. I awoke some two or three hours later, for a restlessness again disturbed my sleep. I grow anxious about my unique and new teaching responsibilities, and the closer I draw to Attu, the more unsettled I become.

In any case, I could not go back to sleep. To access the galley—open at all hours—one has to exit our cabin (or *stateroom*, which is, according to Himself, anything but stately!) via the *hatch* (salt-talk for door, and makes me think of chickens! Anyway, Lila Ann, to the point!). Outside, it was no longer dark, but the sky was brimming with stars and the generous wedge of a three-quarter moon. I could see wonderfully in all directions, and as the ship moved with the incessant swells, the stars seemed to rotate, stop—and then return to center, quite making my head spin. On land, one never experiences this disorienting strangeness.

This was my first experience approximating a queasiness, though it ceased when I looked toward the horizon rather than straight up. But, taken with this novelty, I would again look up, become queasy, and then look away to recover.

The sea shone with the glow of the moon, and was a rolling plain of ghostly light. But cold drove me into the galley. There I poured piping-hot black tea Louis has waiting in a massive thermos. I sat, drinking my tea, marveling about this strange night, and drifted on to what my new young charges might be like. Then I had quite a surprise. Captain Winston entered, wearing a floor-length robe (actually its hem almost dragged, like that of most monarchs), each foot adorned with worn carpet slippers, then lastly reading glasses hanging about his neck. He too drew himself a large mug of tea (I had been vain enough to think Louis kept this supply solely for me, thinking myself the only tea drinker aboard!) and poured an extraordinary amount of sugar into it. To all the world, our Captain looked as if he'd just come in from listening to *Amos and Andy* on the Philco.

Stirring in the sugar, he turned and looked at me, nodded a silent hello, and said he hoped Mr. Smith was not still angry with him for keeping everyone aboard at "Dutch," a short way veteran Aleutians hands use when referring to Dutch Harbor. I demurred to repeat the word "angry," and demoted it to "disappointed," then I surprised myself, blurting out that I was surprised he knew.

He put the spoon down, sipped, nodded his approval at his blend, and said, "Mrs. Smith, I know everything that goes on aboard. That's my job, you see." Then he bade me goodnight and exited, hems, slippers, and all. What a curious fellow, our Captain. But I can't help but like him.

<u>September 20, 1941. Aboard the *Northern Supplier*</u>
Today a navy plane circled the *Supplier* which labored some-what in rough seas—not a storm, but then again, not calm. "Sloppy, Mrs. Smith; we call this weather sloppy," advised Louis. I breakfasted without poor Osmond, who again suffers from queasiness. So he was not on deck when, toward midday, the plane circled just several hundred feet above us. I could see the blinking signal light, and Mr. Arlo on the platform adjoining the bridge signaling back with his light. They did this awhile, then the plane left.

In the galley, I asked Mr. Kokkahiko what the plane wanted, and he just shrugged and said they had "wanted to know if we'd seen any Japs about." For reasons unknown, this caused a chuckle on his part, and I became more curious than before.

Because of the troubled seas, the *Supplier* made only 125 miles this day. Will we ever get to Attu Island?!

<u>September 21, 1941. Aboard the *Northern Supplier*</u>
It is late on in the day and I'm in improved spirits. Perhaps our better-than-average rate of travel (203 miles in 24 hrs!!) has made our destination more real, immediate. Also, Osmond is much improved, for we've been traveling in the leeward side of the Rat Island Group. Blessedly shielded from the southerly seas, the motion of the *Supplier* is far less. When Osmond suf-fers, I attend him—and though I'm without *mal de mer*, I hate to see him so miserable.

He is curious about the plane that circled yesterday, and quite inexplicably asked Mr. Yost if it had any messages for him. Mr. Yost, of course, responded in the negative, and that was that. But we could see he thought the query unusual.

Osmond points out that the long, low island to the south is Amchitka Island, quite unusual (compared to almost all of its neighbors) for its flatness and lack of steep mountains. Near shore, extraordinary flocks of sea birds gather, feeding and building their resources for the coming winter, I would expect. I wish I had a book telling me more about the bounty of sea life, especially the birds. All are unlike any land birds I'm familiar with, and except for the sea parrots, or puffins—and of course the gulls—I'm unfamiliar with all.

In any event, these acres of birds—rafts of birds— part before the oncoming *Supplier as* a floating mat of bog weed might, some of the birds pattering off in a frenzy, their wings beating the surface of the sea, others just paddling off, or suddenly diving—almost daring to be ingested by our propeller. (It seems this way, at least, to this newcomer.)

But I'm no zoologist, and save for great creatures like sea lions and porpoises, behold all in ignorance. One thing absolutely true is these seas teem with life, and surely the waters beneath contain bounties of food.

"The Lord provideth for the innocent creatures of the forests, skies, and vast oceans," Father used to say. During the Shansi famine I finally asked Mother about the incongruity of Father's words during those cruel times. She told me that Father did not include humans amongst the innocent, even infants. She herself did not opine pro or contra regarding his view.

September 22, 1941. Aboard the *Northern Supplier*
This close to our long-awaited destination of Attu Island, an ugly incident has occurred, bringing to light another facet of Captain Winslow's personality.

Earlier in the day. I was on deck, trying to decide which island was which. Mr. Kokkahiko approached, and told me gently but firmly to go below, and limit myself to our stateroom until he called on me. I saw several of the other crew members scurrying here and there, and knew something was wrong. Mr. Kokkahiko, seeing that I feared for our safety, assured me it was nothing connected with that.

In the stateroom, Osmond was abed because the motion of the *Supplier* had resumed, though not as bad as before. When I told him of events, he was curious beyond words, but knowing he couldn't go out, took a sly way of gleaning information. He opened our single porthole, first the inner hatch, which is solid metal, then the outer, which is thick glass.

At once, we heard shouts of protests—language of quite exceptional vileness. "Put a pillow over your head," Himself advised at once, but showing unstoppable curiosity, I *did not*! The shouts continued—then a veritable chorus of outcries. Then a moment of silence, followed by one voice repeating twice an awful invective, promising revenge for some outrage.

Then it was over.

"It might be mutiny."

And initially Mr. Smith's assessment seemed likely. Yet soon came a knock on our door, and it was Mr. Kokkahiko, and without comment we were again free.

Osmond and I went on deck, but though apparently the hatches and such had been hosed down, nothing appeared unusual. No one would answer Osmond's queries, and I knew that Louis would be my only chance to find out what happened.

I could not talk to Louis alone until midafternoon. Carefully, he looked about, took me into the non-perishable locker, sat us both down on cases of tinned groceries, then confided: Two of the engineering staff—*oilers*—had broken into cargo and stolen liquor bound for non-natives up north. They had become intoxicated. But only one, named "Zebra," was caught, but would not confess his co-conspirator.

In full fury, Captain Winslow had the hapless man dragged to the deck in manacles, and sprayed with ice-cold seawater until he informed on his mate. The other guilty one forthwith joined Mr. Zebra, and he too was sprayed liberally. They are confined for a period of 48 hours, until the ship is clear of Attu.

"The union will hear of this," Louis added, and, putting his great ebony index finger to his lips, said, "and you heard nothing from me, Mrs. Smith. Not a whisper."

Osmond gathered this additional tidbit from the "deck boss" (Edward): evidently the pilfering had been ongoing—the two men imbibing on the sly—until the abundance of their forbidden cache overwhelmed Mr. Zebra, and he went on a toot. Osmond explained that corporal punishment was nowadays out of bounds for a ship's master, and the men could prefer charges when they returned to Seattle some months away.

The excitement made me momentarily forget that we were within a day's run of our new home. As I write these lines, it is estimated we will arrive in Chichigof Harbor on Attu at 7 a.m. It will be difficult to sleep. Even Mr. Smith paces, and more than anyone looks forward to our return to dry, motionless land!

September 28, 1941. Chichigof Village, Attu
Six days have elapsed since I arrived, and the first time I felt free enough to dedicate time to these pages. I've been extraordinarily busy!

We arrived on the morning on the 22nd September, which was a Monday. Since this day is Sunday and the villagers are at worship in the Chapel of the Dormition of the Mother of God (more on that exotic name later), the children and their families are temporarily absent from my life.

There is much to write, yet putting events into some sort of organization, according to Himself, is not my strongest suit.

And he's quite right! But I'll start on Monday—the day the *Northern Supplier* finally arrived in Chichigof Harbor. The name of this far-flung village was borrowed from this bay (Chichigof Village). We dropped anchor here not eight hours after the unfortunate business of Captain Winslow's unlikely disciplinary actions. Suffice it to say, the crew wore long faces when unloading procedures began.

For myself, even prior to dropping anchor, I took in the sight of my new home with nothing less than excitement. I know seasoned Aleutian veterans view Aleut villages as "peas in a pod," as Louis expressed it. There's a huddle of small, whitewashed wooden structures close to the shore, ready access to water being key to village life, of course.

Even from the ship, I could make out the distinct footpaths between the tiny houses, and the larger buildings somewhat removed from the houses. There are no roads or vehicles, motorized or horse-drawn.

The church, central to all Aleutian villages, is conspicuous from all else by its cupola, with its distinctive cross at the top. This holy marker's unique design (an added small, diagonal board below the main crossbeams) marks it as a citadel of the Orthodox faith.

Without ceremony the village chief, Alexi Chirikof, scaled the chain ladder up the *Supplier*'s side and was introduced to me and Mr. Smith by Mr. Kokkahiko. Alexi was all smiles, looked us up and down, and announced (I only approximate the strange syntax!), "We have waited for you so long now that you are here." Then he pumped Mr. Smith's hand once, then twice, but executed a more gentle exercise with me. Himself and Alexi were conversing about the status of his equipment, when two smiling faces appeared from under the handrail, and immediately shinnied onto the deck—from where, I know not.

One, a boy in midadolescence, looked me up and down and asked, "You our teacher now?" And as I responded in the affirmative, the far smaller fellow of not more than ten or eleven years of age "surrounded" me by making two complete circumnavigations of my person. And then they began in that strange Aleut tongue for a few moments until Alexi— laughing—commanded them good naturedly to speak English. "You guys talking to your teacher, for goodness sakes, you know."

Then, contradicting his own request, they *all* spoke Aleut— breaking out in peals of laughter, leaving Mr. Smith and me looking left to right. Alexi shook his head and explained to me, "They never see any woman in their life so tall. But I say they'd only seen one other white woman and she was smaller than Anna. That's their oldest sister's name. These two smiling guys brothers." And this is how I met Zephryis and Alfred Tschigorin, scions of Attu's House of Tschigorin!!

At this point, Mr. Kokkahiko saw the boys and boomed, "Did I give you permission to come aboard!?" And they shrank behind Alexi, shyly looking out at this huge Polynesian man. With Alexi smiling on, Mr. Kokkahiko reached down and slowly withdrew a dime from Zephryis's ear. And this sleight-of-hand (and its product) were overwhelmingly well received. More laughter, while the little chap admired the dime, front and back.

I hear the greatly revered chapel bell ending the service, already! I know the little ones (eleven of them!) will be here soon, and if I can prevent Mr. Smith from shooing them off, my time will not be my own. I *must* close. But I could never begrudge the children my time, Sunday or otherwise. I was so terribly late getting here (twenty-one days!). I tell Mr. Smith, who is always very *ordered* regarding time and place, that I owe them the extra time.

He states that my lack of resolve with "urchins" results from never having children of my own. "Therefore, Mrs. Smith, you take each urchin to your heart, and become quite permissive," yet he smiles, for Himself knows he can do little to prevent this.

<u>October 5, 1941. Chichigof Village, Attu</u>
Has it really been a week since we visited?!

If my goslings learn as much as I have during this last week and a half, I'll set records as a teacher. Did I say I had eleven students? Well, one day I have eleven, the next fourteen, then the following nine—and so on.

Before shoptalk, I suppose I should discuss the "shop" itself. I've set up my school in the village's largest building, which was originally meant to be a school. Subsequent to its construction some years ago, it was used for numerous purposes, one of which was a fur warehouse. Fox-trapping is the

key industry here, and even as I write, the men of the village
are preparing for this season's activities. These activities
explain the variance in my daily student body, for the boys
close to "trapping age" (as Alexi Andreanof puts it) are
learning this business of preparing traps, etc.

I was cleaning the schoolhouse trying to reduce the aroma
from its former use when I met my new friend Anfesia Korovin,
who prefers the simpler "Anna." We are a pair! I tower over the
tiny young woman, for she can't be over five foot, a quiet little
wren, not much more than a girl, despite her advanced state
of expectancy. She is the young wife of Mike Korovin, a most
positive, pleasant Aleut gentleman at least twice her age.
"Anna is my big happiness," Mike explained to Osmond, who
only barely hid his mirth over the ironic word play.

Indeed, my new neighbors and hosts, the Aleuts, do not
say or do one thing when meaning another. Coyness or device
is not their way. If they feel something positive, they come
right out with it, especially if there is humor attached. My
height is a constant point of village pride, for it seems I've
become all seven wonders of the Attu world. I'm nearly equal
to Himself's six-foot, though a tiny notch under it. Even in the
European world, I'm a "tall drink of water," as dear late
Emmett [*her deceased first husband, Emmett Hastings Slater,
1875-1919*] used to tell just about anyone. To Emmett, like the
Attuans (but unlike Himself), my stature was a source of husbandly pride. "Women are not supposed to be tall, my dear.
Especially taller than their spouses," I would oft remind, but
Emmett remained quite impressed.

The surnames of Chichigof Village are part of my everyday
vocabulary. There are six of them, not including our own, of
course. All of them are Russian in origin, which is the second
language of the village. English is quite rudimentary here,
but the villagers are proud of what little they speak. English is
their "American" language, which identifies them as citizens,
they feel.

So, I have also begun English language lessons for adults, three afternoons a week.

I'm so *awfully weary* that Himself has convinced me that I must take this entire Sunday off, and I have. "You are fifty-six years old, and cannot work without rest." Why is it that Osmond, who is an absolute fanatic about dealing strictly in *truth,* cannot deal with my true age?

"Well, my *word*, Lila Ann, you don't *look* sixty-one, so don't complain, my dear," Mrs. Wolfe, our BIA [*Bureau of Indian Affairs*] supervisor, told me, "and men are off balance about being younger than their spouses."

Today, just after sunrise everyone heard a plane flying above the clouds—thick, dark banks of them that pass right overhead. Above this was the sound of the plane. "It is multi-engined," Mr. Smith commented, and listened attentively until, after fifteen minutes or so, it was gone. He nodded and when Peter Andreanof and Walter Sergief walked over to the teacher's residence (a tiny, two-room wood-frame house, identical to the rest) wondering if it was Japanese. Osmond, of course, will include this in his daily radio dispatches to AMCS [*Alaska Military Communication Service*] Dutch Harbor/Unalaska.

He is so happy that it makes *me* happy—to see him feeling so needed in a key location regarding our national defense. At Three River Station [*an Athabascan Indian village on the U.S. side of the U.S./Yukon Territory boundary; according to the 1940 Census, its population was 145. It would be 2,100 miles east of Attu*], he felt entirely ill-used, I'm afraid.

October 6, 1941. Chichigof Village, Attu
Oh, I hate to talk (or write!!) shop, but most of the classroom materials provided by the Bureau [*Bureau of Indian Affairs*] simply aren't appropriate for my duties. Language is such a

problem in the village, and I mean for *me* (!) not the villagers or their children. They do *fine*.

All the children are in widely different levels regarding language. For instance, the Chirikof children—two boys and two girls—can barely make themselves understood in English. However, the Andreanof children do better in English, but cannot write it. (Oh, I didn't mention that the Chirikof twin girls can *write* English!)

Then there is little Anna Tschigorin who speaks and writes English almost to her age level (thirteen years). I've promoted her to Chief Tutor, a post of which she's quite proud.

So, with the actual number of students varying each day, *and* their different language levels, there is a confusing mix in the possible number and type of skills. (I'm hesitant to apply the term *grade*, herein.) This is far different than even Three Rivers Station, and certainly any one-room school teaching in Iowa or China.

True enough, Mrs. Wolfe cautioned me this posting would be quite unlike any others in the Territory of Alaska, which is how Himself cautiously refers to our home of now approaching two years. "Wife! This is not the United States, but United States *Territory*, you see. And for good reason."

Osmond considers this posting as adventurous in nature as any in darkest Africa, and won't hear of any comparisons I might venture with my years in China. He claims China is the oldest and most sophisticated of civilizations. "They don't chew raw blubber and run around naked in sweat houses in China."

But I'm digressing again—from classroom chat to raw blubber! Lila Ann, how your mind wanders, as Father would say, though never in a critical way.

In truth, I tire more easily and do feel my age. Since arrival, my life is filled with getting our school off to a proper start. One example: I've only recently diminished the scent of a fur warehouse from it. My "sea chest" of school supplies is

almost as priceless as my first aid "station" I've brought via
Nurse Garrison. Her one-week medical training leaves me completely ill at ease in the healing department. Yet she quipped,
"If you treated Chinamen blisters and such, you can do the
same for Aleuts, so don't worry, dearie."

Mother was the nurse, of course. She had the healer's touch
despite never having so much as an hour of training. Our mission was "healing headquarters" for miles around in Shansi
Province. Mother was of the kindest and most gentle nature,
which makes her and Father's fate even that much more
unkind. "The Lord's way, at times, is impossible to fathom."

When I am tired, memories best left alone do come forth.

❧

<u>October 18, 1941. Chichigof Village, Attu</u>
My student body (!) has settled down, for the men have left
for fox-trapping. They shall be gone until January. Though this
might be considered by some wives and families to be a hardship, it is a way of life to our Attuans, and they forbear without
any complaint. So, I have *eleven* full-time students, and three
afternoon adult students.

A routine has set in, as it has for Himself, who under the
tutelage of Peter Tschigorin the Elder—a youthful eighty-one—
has taken to learning about our island home. Mr. Smith, if I
may air this gentle observation, has maintained a policy of
some distance from our native friends since coming north from
Delbert [*Delbert, Iowa, birthplace of Osmond Smith and Lila
Ann's parents, Paul and Miriam Howland*] eighteen months
ago. This first was evident in Three Rivers Station with the
Athabascan folk.

And just as it appeared he might continue in the same
manner here, he was "adopted" by the "Elder" Tschigorin, who
took to (initially, by walking in and sitting down uninvited)
posting himself nearby, smoking his pipe and observing

Himself at the radio. I try and not see the connection between Elder Tschigorin's endless supply of tobacco tins (he's the village tobacconist) and this new relationship. Though bent with age and no longer able to trap, the Patriarch and Himself set out when the weather allows (this is *not* frequent!) for purposes of geographic and nature familiarization.

It makes little difference that neither speaks the other's language, for both are men of few words anyway. So they communicate readily via gestures and facial expressions. Mr. Smith is rapidly learning of life along the seashore. "Old Peter is truly a resourceful individual," Osmond tells me, which after nearly eight years of marriage, I've learned is his highest form of praise.

The weather has settled into being awful, with plentiful rain and wind, low clouds whirling in overhead, and always the sea in Chichigof Harbor frothing away in one state of emotion or another. The temperatures, however, are nothing compared to Three Rivers Station, which by this time last year was falling, often, below zero degrees, especially during the lengthening nights. In Chichigof Village, temperatures actually are warmer than they would be back home at this time of year. As yet, there is no snow or ice in the village, and only traces high in the mountains.

Still, even with the temperatures somewhat above freezing, a moist, angry sea wind makes it intolerable within a minute if one goes out without the very warmest of clothing.

<u>October 25, 1941. Chichigof Village, Attu</u>
During morning class all came to a stop when another plane was heard flying directly overhead. This brought everyone out of their houses despite the drizzle and chill. Though out of view above the cloud layer, all could tell it was circling repeatedly. Mr. Smith identified it as "single-engine," then dashed to his

radio set to, I assume, make talk with it. Meanwhile it kept circling, its engine sounding not unlike that of my uncle's elderly
Ford back in Delbert.

All the adults and children stood listening, and the lonely
sound of its engine was mournful—a drone, becoming quite
loud as it passed directly overhead, then fainter as it grew distant. Also, it was getting lower—probing downward cautiously, I fancied, as a person might when entering a strange
dark room.

There are steep mountains around much of Chichigof
Harbor, and I was concerned for its safety. Then, after one of
its passings, it resumed its course, climbing away, then
returning I assume to wherever it came from. And one can't
help wondering where such a frail craft might come from, or in
fact go to?

All this time, the villagers stared steadfastly up into the
clouds until it was gone. Class did not settle down to business
until well after midday repast, and then all questions were
about this novel visitor and (especially with the older children)
the concept of flight. Surrendering to this distraction, I
decided to create another! For the first time in six months, I
took out my flute, and while they gathered around, looking at
me (and it) in wonder, they listened to my humble interpretation of a medley of church songs.

<u>November 2, 1941. Chichigof Village, Attu</u>
Today ends with my severest challenge yet, my first serious
medical emergency. This function in my new post has been the
source of great anxiety, yet was part of the agreement with
Mrs. Wolfe at the Bureau. Her cheerful voice still rings, "Oh,
you'll do just fine, Mrs. Smith, after Mrs. Garrison's fast class.
She's taught dozens of Bureau teachers to be fine medics. Even
those with terribly weak stomachs."

When it came time, though, I'm afraid the outdated first-aid books from my old friends at MMS [*Mennonite Missionary Service*] were more helpful. In brief, Heratina Chirikof burned her entire left forearm severely in her daughter's kitchen. This was something far different than a cut or sliver of wood. I made it to be a "second-degree burn," via the photographs in my book, and acted accordingly.

The poor thing was in terrible pain, and though I feel so terribly inadequate, I *think* her heart wasn't doing well, plus she went into shock, the latter of which I am familiar with from those years ago at Bethel Mennonite. Anyway, I administered my first injection ever—of morphine sulfate. It was nothing less than astounding—the amount of comfort it afforded almost within seconds.

Then I treated the wound precisely as directed, and was so *relieved* to find everything required in Nurse Garrison's "treasure chest," as I've now deemed it. Tiny Annie Korovin, who has become my close friend, functioned as my nurse—so tiny and frail, but with nerves of *steel*. Also, she was able to comfort poor Heratina, who wasn't in any condition to speak her limited English, of course.

Albert Chirikof—the patriarch of that clan—is fox-trapping on Unalga Island and cannot be contacted; however, Heratina's two daughters—Mary and Annie (the latter now an Andreanof)—are in attendance. Mary is more involved than Annie, for there are bad feelings between the latter and mother for marrying in defiance of her parents' wishes. When Albert is home, she cannot and will not visit her parents' tiny house.

As I write, Heratina is resting in our "front room," the first patient-occupant of my officially designated "hospital" cot, partitioned off with privacy blankets. Annie Korovin is watching over her. Himself is posted at the radio, as is his late-evening practice, unless he's reading. The church "Reader" (I gather this is a kind of lay-deacon, since Chichigof lacks a priest), Philamon Ivanof, and his wife Lena were the latest of the villagers to visit poor Heratina.

I will relieve Friend Annie [*for virtually the remainder of the journal, this is how LAS will refer to Annie Korovin*] at 11 p.m., then the remainder of the nightwatch is mine.

Just prior to Mary Andreanof beating frantically on our door to report her mother's accident, I was absorbing another less urgent bit of news delivered by Mr. Smith. As if a week-plus had not elapsed, he dryly informed me that the aerial visitor of the 25th October was undoubtedly launched from a Japanese submarine. "And its job is reconnaissance, I would think."

Confident of Mr. Smith's knowledge of such things, plus his twice-daily presence on the radio "network" with other Territorial Stations, I don't doubt its veracity. With habitation being so distant from Attu, what other credible explanations are there for such a small craft?

This news is most unnerving.

Since early summer, there has been considerable talk and written speculation about the inevitability of war. Himself is convinced of this, and maintains his view publicly during discussions. Though I don't agree, I maintain a silence, for it is a wife's sacred duty to support her spouse always.

It was not Scripture but Mother who taught me wifely responsibilities decades back. And true to form, she taught by example. Many times she confided to myself, and even once to Joseph [*Lila Ann's younger brother*] that we should (at least until the situation subsided considerably) avail ourselves of numerous offers of evacuation by friends and sympathetic officials alike.

I was even more convinced than she was, my Chinese being far better than anyone else's. I remember the rising terror of it all. But Mother absolutely adhered to Father's views and subsequent decisions on the Boxers. [*The "Boxer Rebellion," China 1899–1901; a nationalist reaction against foreigners, including*

*missionaries, many of whom were summarily executed in the
summer of 1900, including LAS's parents and brother.*]

How repugnant and tragic are my memories of Asian wars;
hence, *I must not believe* all the nonsense about it. I pray
nightly to our Savior to spare us from the calamity of humans
killing humans.

I can only think that Himself spares me news, knowing
some of my background; hence he fears raising old anxieties,
which in the end he probably judges would do little good.

November 27, 1941. Chichigof Village, Attu
Today is Thanksgiving, a holiday not celebrated in Chichigof
Village, but we maintained the tradition in the Smith household. Since it is a national holiday, I explained to all my students—both child and adult—on Wednesday, how as a nation
we celebrate Thanksgiving.

Actually, several had heard of it, but confused it with other
holidays celebrated by non-Orthodox peoples. (Mike Korovin
associated it with trick-or-treating!) Then several villagers
(including Philamon Ivanof) thought we might be celebrating
the start of Orthodox Advent, which begins tomorrow. Sweet
confusion reigns!

To Osmond, this is a special event, for this is the first *con-
gressionally* mandated Thanksgiving, fixing it on the *fourth*
Thursday in November rather than Mr. Roosevelt's *third*.
Osmond, of course, is no admirer of our current President, so is
especially thankful for *this* Thanksgiving!

On this day, he carefully arranged events to be climaxed
by standing the community flagpole upright. He and three of
the men had been crafting it for over a month, and now our
proud new 45-foot-high mast with flag atop it (brought here
at Mr. Smith's initiative) flaps noisily in the perpetual Attu
winds.

Though perhaps the villagers do not celebrate our national holiday, they certainly identify themselves as Americans, for only the Elder Tschigorin was born a Russian citizen. But all are proud of their "Americanship," represented by the Stars and Stripes. Still, the essential Russian nature of the village remains.

Lena Ivanof became so enthused about our new flag and matters patriotic she brought her photograph of "Our Mr. Roosevelt President" during our Thanksgiving/Flag-raising ceremony. During tea and cakes afterward, Himself came over to me; behind him Lena Ivanof beamed. He gave me a small photograph in a frame, and said with great irony, "Here, Mrs. Smith. Our President."

In the frame was an old photograph of Czar Nicholas II. It was with effort I maintained my presence of mind.

<u>November 30, 1941. Chichigof Village, Attu</u>
This first Sunday after Thanksgiving found me melancholy. As is my practice on the Sabbath, I read Scripture in the morning. While on their way to chapel, Heratina and Mary stopped in, and the former's recovery from her burn is pleasing to me.

The Orthodox chanting of the faithful reaches our tiny house. Himself works at the radio sets. Out the window, the sea is a dull metallic gray. Flocks of sea ducks chatter; the wind carries their conversations to me.

The mountainsides are brown, all the green—so iridescently green upon our arrival—gone until spring.

In the early evening Osmond tapped me on the shoulder while I was reflecting on what we might have for dinner. Going proudly to the radio, he turned on a speaker and from it, albeit very weakly, came the unmistakable sounds of Mr. Gilbert and Mr. Sullivan. "The BBC from England! All the way from tomorrow."

We sat together listening, and the melancholy magically lifted from my shoulders.

December 9, 1941. Chichigof Village, Attu
The world has changed since my last entry. Sunday, December 7, Japan attacked Pearl Harbor in the Hawaiian Islands, destroying our fleet and killing thousands. News reports contradict one another.

The United States has declared war on Japan and Nazi Germany and Congress has granted it. Mr. Smith called the entire village to meeting this morning and announced events. Families, of course, have great anxiety over their menfolk who are out trapping.

Mr. Smith has exchanged dozens of official transmissions with Dutch Harbor, which relays bulletins from Anchorage and Seattle. But with his electronic gift and talents, Osmond's "telegraph station" picks up reports from all over. "We must now go onto a war footing. We are at a strategic center here."

There was no school, yet through the day I was besieged with questions from the children about events. I answered as best I might.

I retired early thinking to read Scripture, but could not. Scripture didn't help four decades ago, and it won't help now. I feel blasphemous thinking that.

"Jesus wept" are the words that have been with me since Sunday.

December 21, 1941. Chichigof Village, Attu
I have not mentioned how satisfying I've found teaching sewing to the women. On Saturday afternoons our "sewing circle" meets in the craft corner of the schoolhouse. Though the

women are clever seamstresses, their knowledge is limited, and I flatter myself that my years of teaching sewing have their benefits. My electric Singer is a marvel to all, of course, the only other two in the village being treadle-powered, with all their notorious quirkiness. We have a fair supply of outing flannel, Indian lawn, bleached and unbleached muslin, blue denim, and sewing accessories provided by the Bureau's Education Provisioning Services.

Over the cutting table we have many fine talks, but I've absolutely made it a practice to keep Saturday afternoons *war-talk free*. Lord knows, it plagues us enough on most other days. It was inevitable, though, that my birthplace and first two decades in China would come up, for the Attuan women-folk are intrepid question-askers! The syntax of questions (even after translation!) often invites a smile, though I do not. All people have a powerful instinct to detect when someone is "staring down their nose" at them. I won't harbor that in myself or others.

"And is China place this good place, too?"

Attuans are deliberate talkers, so the time required for me to parse through the strange word order to understand the query is not noticed, thankfully.

Indeed, my responses pass back through that dubious process of translation; the translators usually are Friend Annie or Anna Tschigorin. And what lexical voyages my responses travel! Some into Aleut, others into Russian—others yet into a mixture of both—back and forth we all talk, laugh, and ges-ture through these comfortable and educational afternoons.

A powerful tempest blew through Saturday night and into Sunday morning. Chichigof Bay was lashed to its angriest state. Gulls, poor things, were blown into buildings and killed. Spray lifted from the waves, was picked up by the vastness of the wind and hurled landward. The mornings, when light is arriving so late anyway, remained darker longer, as if the sun itself was impeded by these winds.

The Attuans struggled to Chapel, braced almost double into the wind, some of the little ones almost being swept from the grip of their parents.

But the deafening clamor of the wind is beyond words. This is a land where winds reign without challenge.

<u>December 25, 1941. Chichigof Village, Attu</u>
Christmas was celebrated quietly by Himself and me, the only two who will observe "American-style" Christmas on this island! It is a Thursday, and the children were confused when, on Wednesday, I announced there would be no school; however, the adult men were relieved when Mr. Smith cancelled this week's "military preparedness" exercises, which Himself has decided fall on each Thursday.

When Walter Sergief stopped by to chat, Mr. Smith was quite short with him, announced we were celebrating the Savior's birth and would not be available, save for emergencies. I wish he had not done that, but Osmond is inclined to shortness in situations where he perceives disrespect or ignorance. His view of Orthodoxy remains someplace between those two points. Osmond's Mennonite roots are long and deep, though untended and oft scoffed at by himself, save for the Essentials. [*The central tenets of Mennonite doctrine are divided into the Essentials and Non-Essentials.*]

My dear late Emmett's disposition was far different, of course. He would have been perfect for missionary or foreign teaching service had he lived. Far better than myself, surely. Yet I hasten to amend, that I cannot help but admire Himself for tending to his aging parents and managing Delbert Commercial all those years despite his dreams for a wider life.

He craved foreign adventure. And instead of lessening his frustration, his growing interests and skills in wireless communications only enhanced it. "I listened to the world, and how I marveled, Mrs. Slater," was one of his first statements when he began "calling" on "that homely widow cousin of yours" (how *strenuously* Osmond apologized for his mother's ill-timed words!). In a quiet manner, Osmond is a good and devoted man, quite passionate about his beliefs, which he defines and holds tenaciously.

January 1, 1942. Chichigof Village, Attu

We suffered the entry of 1942 quietly. The first pair of fox-trappers (Mike Korovin and Albert Chariot) returned home the day before. Ostensibly, they returned for Christmas, six days hence, but the troubles due to the war contributed, for Friend Annie is quite far along now in her pregnancy. Also, Old Albert (to differentiate from *Young* Albert, who is his oldest son) had heard of wife Heratina's accident.

Though New Year's Day, it is also a Thursday, and because we use one calendar and the Attuans another it causes confusion at times. This was one of those instances, for the men put in an appearance for a regular military preparedness class. So Osmond went ahead with the class, to which all males from fourteen on up are invited. Since the events of December 7, the classes have taken on a more serious overtone.

As for me, I became a student, under the instruction of Friend Annie, Lena Ivanof, Anise Sergief, and Fekla Andreanof, in the art of *starring*. It is a much-anticipated Orthodox Christmas activity when villagers, carrying a Holy Bethlehem Star aloft on a pole, go house to house caroling. The aforementioned ladies are the honored keepers of the star, responsible for it looking absolutely its best on Orthodox Christmas, January 7.

Each village, they tell me, has a traditional star, kept in storage for all the year, until the day of starring approaches. "Our" star is eight-pointed and a grand four feet in diameter.

In the center is the nativity scene—all of this, joyfully hand decorated with crafts produced by the village seamstresses and designers. The design of the star itself allows the outer portion of the star to revolve, while the center stays stationary.

I find myself already captured by this new Christmas spirit, despite already having celebrated "our" Christmas, as Himself has come to call it. For it is the village's Christmas, their view of our Savior's birth. The spirit and celebration of this wonderful event is the same, regardless of calendar or language.

There is snow now, though not a great accumulation. Narrow, bare footpaths thread this way and that between the houses, and from the village to the schoolhouse and church. It is cold, to my mind, all the time, and Osmond devotedly attends our stove, a small affair which burns both wood and coal—several tons of which were landed from the *Northern*

Supplier. That day feels distant to me now. Was it a century or a day ago?

Though I experienced joy in teaching (first) the Athabascan people of Three Rivers Station, and certainly on Attu, still I have to soon inform Mr. Smith that I *must* return to Delbert after the end of this school year. I must choose the right moment. I'm hoping that Mr. Smith's thirst for foreign adventure is now somewhat quenched. Mine was some four decades plus a year ago.

Iowa is as proximate as I want to be to this new war. Once you have seen one war, there is absolutely no necessity or forbearance for repeating the experience.

❧

January 4, 1942. Chichigof Village, Attu

Friend Annie has gone into labor. I can't decide if I'm assisting Fekla Andreanof or she is assisting me. We seem to be vying for the position of assistant midwife, though her seven children [*to my* none] absolutely render her more knowledgeable, despite my short course in midwifery from Nurse Garrison!

"Slow and sometime now and sometime go," Fekla advised me in her strange English, shaking her head and crossing herself when out of Friend Annie's sight. Thank goodness!

I sit and dampen Friend Annie's face with a moist cloth and we talk through the 3rd and all through this day, an awful length of time. It is only during this time that Friend Annie confided that she'd lost a child three months prior to my arrival! His name was Gregory. Such a strange, silent, uncomplaining people.

It is late evening of January 4, and Friend Annie's labor has slackened noticeably. Fekla relieved me during the late evening, with Heratina and Annie Sergief, all conversing merrily in Aleut, and quite (including Friend Annie) at ease. Very impressive.

At home, Himself is in deep commune with Maestros Edison and Marconi, as he puts it (!), so I retired and got out my tiny memorabilia box, as I do each year on January 4.

It was precisely forty-one years (January 4, 1901) ago at Bethel Mennonite when the Boxers led by that awful Mr. Fung Lo battered through the front gates, overwhelmed our brave and protesting resident staff, then seized father, mother, Joseph, and me, and committed their atrocities.

Mother and Father had assumed that by 1901, after five years of war and uprising throughout the province, that Bethel Mennonite had gotten through the worst of it. Since I was Father's typist, I recall how relieved I was for all of us when he elaborated on the Mission's safety in his annual report to MMS [*Mennonite Missionary Service*]. It brings on bitter moments thinking how wrong poor, well-meaning Father had been.

We have been invited to village Christmas Eve services and I have accepted, for up to this time, I wasn't sure how appropriate my intrusion would be within the walls of the Chapel of the Dormition of the Mother of God. Himself has quietly declined, so I will represent us on this, our first Orthodox Christmas. And since it will probably be our last such exotic celebration, I will mark it indelibly in my memory. These are special people whom I shall never forget.

January 19, 1942. Chichigof Village, Attu

Events, plus my own procrastination, kept me away from these pages. The temptation is to seize upon the recent, and work back, but I shall follow my tradition, writing from earlier to later.

Now having written that, I've ordered my thoughts!

Just eight hours prior to Christmas Eve services, Friend Annie was delivered of a baby girl—Titiana Irini Korovin. To be born on Christmas Eve is considered a propitious sign of God's grace upon the new infant. Fekla and I attended; birthing went well after those first few days of on-again, off-again labor. And by well, I mean *quickly* (!) for (since these *are* private lines, I will write plainly!) Babe Korovin almost scooted out untouched onto the bedding despite awaiting hands.

Husband Mike became increasingly beside himself with a combination of joy and stress; hence I compelled him to sit beside their old kitchen range and take a capful of Miss Whitson's Bromide of Chamomile, a remedy from my own personal stock!

I shall never know this day's equal for its pure humanity of life. For not many hours later saw everyone proceeding toward the Chapel, including the new mother and child, the former swaddled with her infant in quilts, carried by a proud but dazed father.

I could not approve of this, but kept my peace as all Attuans—if anything—thought it even more a part of commending our Savior's spirit for mother and child to attend. In a way, I imagine it is.

The service began at 7 p.m. and lasted for a little over two hours. A chair was provided for me, the guest, and for the new mother, thank goodness. We sat side by side. A third chair was provided for Elder Tschigorin who has not been well of late. Philamon Ivanof, as Reader, presided. Everyone else stood, the men on one side, the women on the other.

Though St. Ann's Catholic Mission was only six miles distant from Mennonite Bethel (those many years ago), until this time I have never attended a Catholic or Orthodox service. Himself comments that they are one and the same, yet his classification of world religions is rather general, I fear. For, of course, they are different and either would take offense at a suggestion to the contrary.

Ritual chanting is a greater part, it seems, of Orthodox tradition. And the thirty-seven people in Chapel all chanted so beautifully in the ancient tongue of the church which even

Philamon cannot understand, for the conversational Russian of the village (being of a more modern vintage) is different.

Candles, icons, and vestments abounded, and since the electric lights were not used and the sun had long set, the interior of the tiny chapel was cloaked in the ancient shadows of candlelight. The scents of church incense and candles dominated, and with the intermittent chanting, it was all new and intriguing to me.

It was indeed a fine and devout Christmas service.

February 1, 1942. Chichigof Village, Attu

One would think that living 718 nautical miles from the closest human habitation, life would be so leisurely I could easily keep up, but not so. Our daylight regime is one available excuse for Lila Ann!

"Sunset" comes rapidly in Chichigof Village, occurring in the teacher's residence when Osmond turns off our tiny generator at precisely 9:45 p.m. on weekdays and at 11 p.m. on Saturdays and Sundays. Since my last entry was on a Monday, my muse halted abruptly when I was cast abruptly in darkness at 9:45 p.m.! Usually I prepare for this predictable event by lighting one or two candles, my preferred alternative. I had not that evening.

I will *not* operate those hissing air lanterns of which I strongly disapprove. "What was wrong with the old-fashioned oil lanterns?" I ask. It is a sore point between the Smiths. And Himself will elucidate about progress, but to no avail! I wish a return to this warm, yellow, tranquil light.

Then suddenly there were *exciting events*! On the morning of January 20, the *Western Flyer* pulled into Chichigof Harbor with the remaining Attu menfolk. Trapping had been a disaster, due largely to the heavy snowstorm, yet goods and such (including *mail*!! and our Bureau merchandise and grocery order!) were shuttled between the boat and shore via small craft. *Commodore* Deery, owner/operator of the *Western Flyer* and district fur agent for San Francisco Consolidated Pelt and Clothiers (CPC), was in command. With him were four crewman, all Chinese. Quite unexpectedly, I was able to converse in my old linguistic friend, Cantonese.

Only now, twelve days later, has our quiet village settled back to normal.

The arrival of mail, the speaking of Chinese, and recalling my sorely missed translation responsibilities with Beacon Light Press [*imprint of the Mennonite Missionary Services, defunct since 1956*], and all my friends there, has made me heavy of heart.

And I'm brought low thinking of my cousins Mary Margaret and Pamela, and their darlings, my grandcousins (!) and, always, Uncle Thomas. All thousands of miles away in Iowa. Uncle Thomas reminds me so much of Father, though as siblings they were starkly different in world-view.

Yet, in his letter, Uncle Thomas's hand was steady, and he assured me his health was fine, but he would miss me "more than any of the other ne'er-do-wells and bounders" on his grand ninetieth birthday picnic on May 8. The entire War Memorial Park, gazebo, and hall have been reserved for it.

It is late. I don't know which is wearier, my heart or my hand.

February 2, 1942. Chichigof Village, Attu
It was a church holiday this day, and as is often the case, I found out when the children didn't appear for school, and I espied village folk bustling in preparation for the celebratory doings after chapel. That the Smiths are invited is assumed and they are expected by these hospitable friends and neighbors!

I still had much stock and inventory work to do, so I utilized the time well. It is our last merchandise boat until June. Two of Mr. Smith's weather mechanisms were broken in the sweeping, flaying winds of the last two days, and he's busy at his repairs. Usually, especially in the evening, he's affixed to his headphones, monitoring a world busy with the madness of war.

The most recent winter tempest is almost spent. Yet its winds persist, hitting school and residence with stiff slaps, as if angry with us for staying up so late.

This late a.m. found the Smiths unpacking foodstuffs and stocking our pantry. Having steeled myself, I informed Osmond of my desire to return home at the conclusion of our contract in June. He thought at length, and replied, "I do feel useful here, Mrs. Smith." Though he never opposes me, depriving him of this new sense of mission raises feelings of guilt.

Our manner of "discussion" is tacit, meaning we *don't* say more than we must say. This usually is sufficient, but not this time, so I persisted.

"Husband, I do, too, but I have spent enough of my life away from home."

He finally responded, "Yes, I know." And it was settled.

I almost celebrate the thought! I could be home in time for freshly picked sweet corn and the 4th of July picnics!

February 7, 1942. Chichigof Village, Attu
There has been a week of more or less continual events marking a Holy Week in the Orthodox Church [*Week of the Publican and Pharisee*]. Now, flush with fresh supplies, the dinners and such are especially grand. The villagers are fond of Commodore Deery, and cannot remember a world without him or his firm. Just a day before the Commodore's departure,

Himself braved this giant of a man (despite great age, he's at least six and a half feet tall!) to ask him the source of his imposing rank. At the time, we had him as dinner guest.

"My rank!? Why, Mr. Smith! From islands of the same name. [*The Kommandorski Islands to the west, across the international date line, a possession of Russia.*] There's not a seafaring trader living who dares venture there, save me. Not nowadays with the Bolsheviks about, the scum."

The villagers have numerous heroic stories about Commodore Deery and his surprisingly tiny and frail *Western Flyer,* not very much exceeding seventy feet but famous for its capacious cargo hold. At this point of the winter, Attuans had run out of flour, sugar, tea, coffee, and other necessities, and the *Western Flyer*'s biannual arrival replenished that "at a rate of $23 per hundred-weight for the Territorial Government, and $28 for the village, taken in the form of 'green fox pelts,' " Himself points out with the knowledgeable sigh of a longtime store manager.

After turning over the company's "share" of the furs, the entire village only had a half-dozen pelts remaining for future barter.

CPC owns the village warehouse (referred to as a store) and residence, and contributed an unknown quantity of money to build this schoolhouse and teacher's residence. The Commodore, who years ago usually spent two [to] three months a year here, possesses every inch the commanding air as he walks house to house, greeting each family in his hail/hearty way. Now over seventy years of age, he allows a younger company agent to set up shop at the end of each trapping season.

The *Western Flyer* and its owner set sail for the Kommandorski Islands on January 24. This year, he left no one on Attu due to the war.

<u>February 8, 1942. Chichigof Village, Attu</u>
The entire village is celebrating this special week with
marathon sessions in the chapel. Only now are our storeroom,
pantry, and supply shed stocked and inventoried to Mr.
Smith's satisfaction.

Something of a melancholy still persists post arrival and
departure of the Commodore, et al.

It had been almost three years since I'd spoken the language of my childhood, and then only intermittently with Mr.
and Mrs. Jong Tu over in Centerburg [*Centerburg, Iowa, headquarters for the Midwest Mennonite Assembly*].

It was strange once again struggling to converse in
Cantonese, ghastly to see how out of form I've become. Yet I'm
now the eighth wonder of the world to Friend Annie, and to all
the villagers, especially the children.

Two of the four Chinese crewmen were working in the
storehouse, and hosting quite an entertainment for the young
ones. The children surrounded the Chinese gentlemen, larking
with them re: their exotic language, who themselves were
enjoying it.

Mr. Wo pointed at objects, and Mr. Fong would announce
their names in Cantonese, and I (was it vanity, or the desire to
enhance the novelty?) pointed at myself, and said "old
woman" in their language. From there, it became quite an
event. "Mrs. Smith, and the Chinamen Vaudevillians!"
announced the Commodore.

Osmond is not at his best in reflected light, but according
to Mrs. Hilton's *Christian Marriage,* unions require patient and
proper management respecting each other's personalities.

My entire China background is unsettling to Mr. Smith and
never discussed or referred to between ourselves. And when
this topic arises and he's present, a *difficult air* results
between us for a day or so afterward. It soon passes.

But finding me speaking with our visitors in Chinese occasioned his first openly critical comment after we retired to

quarters, something about vanity before others. But as Father often professed, "Silence, Lila Ann, is golden." And adhering to Father's wisdom was never a poor choice.

<u>February 22, 1942. Chichigof Village, Attu</u>
Time, of late, has gotten away from me.

Perhaps it is because I'm uncertain about who will succeed me, or if indeed *anyone* will succeed me, that I've narrowed all efforts to teaching. I had become quite the socialite out here, but have settled back to *work*. Another benefit of becoming absorbed in my responsibilities with the children is avoiding war talk.

Because I do not speak Aleut nor understand much, I'm spared most discussions about war. Probably this language gap would not persist much longer, I fear, because of my *magpie-like* (Uncle Thomas's coinage!) linguistic inclinations, with me since childhood. Yet when Mr. Smith is present, the men speak as much English as is manageable, which for the most part is better than the women's, save for the older gentlemen.

And now there is talk of *evacuation* of the village to points east, possibly even the mainland of the U.S. I assume this is nonsense, for what sort of prize do these isolated isles offer Japan? Himself has added a second military preparedness day, to wit, Mondays in addition to Thursdays. He is training village men into a "little military force," and much to everyone's pride and amusement, leads them in marching drills.

So, submerging myself in the *literacy* of the children is by far a more substantive occupation for myself. The children benefit from my new resolve, and progress is very satisfying. Anna Tschigorin has become my assistant, and with her help, even the "kindergarteners" (I use this in an age and skill sense!) have learned their letters and sounds.

This weekend is another Holy Feast Day, and there have been so many of them, I've lost track. Himself observed, "I'm beginning to think I joined up with the wrong church, Wife! This one is bursting at the buttons with festival days."

Osmond has thrived in this village, and if it weren't for my powerful, intuitive force urging me home, I would relent about departure. But I cannot. For this, I feel a bad wife.

March 7, 1942. Chichigof Village, Attu
It was suggested by Himself that I stay in too much! Osmond is the out-of-doors type, hiking and exploring everywhere—even making maps, etc. I am not.

My formative years were spent in compound living, the rule for missionary folk in western Shansi. Weeks passed without leaving the compound save with Father and Mother for brief trips; longer journeys he and she took without me.

Upon coming out after Oberlin [*Oberlin College, which then specialized in Oriental languages and missionary training*], Mother had brought climbing roses, and all the walls surrounding the three-acre compound were dense with them by the time I could remember. All our gardens were inside, as were our livestock, save for the sheep. So life, in the main, took place inside the compound.

I am contented with a small area.

So today I put on the heavy rain gear and went afield with Friend Annie and Heratina. The purpose, I thought, was for collecting grass for basket-weaving, a skill in which Aleuts, particularly the Attuans, are unrivaled. But I had not understood, for grass had already been cut, sorted, and stored for a type of aging process in several locations, actually old *barabaras*, once the abodes of Aleuts prior to aboveground wood structures.

It must have been dreary, spending one's life beneath the sod, but certainly it afforded accessible primordial shelter from the insistent and terrible winds and storms.

So, heavy with bundles of natives grasses, we walked back, me out of breath, laboring along, Friend Annie and Heratina moving lightly up and down the paths, skirting patches of snow, which has been light this year, they say.

At Heratina's we sorted the grass and I listened, for the talk between the women, while Young Albert Chirikof sat and looked on, was in Aleut, of course. It was the first time I understood Aleut beyond a single word: It was the expression, "We're all in danger," or something close.

This was repeated. Young Albert laughed, and shook his head. There is little shelter from war talk. This is contrast to the last days of the rebellion [*Boxer Rebellion*]. Father would allow no talk around womenfolk concerning the developing ugliness.

I asked Friend Annie if I could learn to make Aleut baskets. She, and Heratina, seemed shocked I would ask. Annie responded that if I needed a basket, she would be glad to make me one, of any size. When they understood I wanted to learn for the sake of learning, they seemed confused, but consented.

March 15, 1942. Chichigof Village, Attu

The Sabbath found me at my homework, which would have met disapproval in earlier years. Now, my interpretation of acceptable activities on the seventh day has expanded, as it has with Himself.

I work at my weaving, and it is arduous.

Actually, rather than weave, I *prepare* for weaving with my assigned roll of grass which will make up the warp. These must be twisted together, many lengths of cured grass to form one strong warp, constantly keeping one's fingers wet so the grass doesn't break. After tutoring I'm now allowed to do this without immediate supervision, though Friend Annie did stop by to carefully check my work. Strand by strand I struggled along. An ancient activity.

It blows hard, though perhaps no harder than usual. Himself, though, went out slogging about in it with Mike Korovin and Young Albert who helped Elder Tschigorin along. All were bundled and "slickered up" against the rain and cold.

Today is an extraordinarily low tide and Elder Tschigorin had vowed to show Osmond one thing or another regarding animal life, storm or no, I presume.

In the evening, Himself without warning brought out a beautifully crafted brooch that he'd laboriously gift-wrapped; it is a jeweled grasshopper with dearest, tiny ruby eyes. I, of course, wept at this kindness—this expense. He'd purchased it in Anchorage last summer. From out of nowhere came another of his secrets, a jar of strawberry preserves from home!

I am sixty-two years of age this day.

March 24th, 1942. Chichigof Village, Attu

Today came official query via wireless concerning our tiny village's state of mind re: thoughts on evacuation. It was addressed to all Department of Interior teachers at Aleutian posts. The issue about the response brought division between Mr. Smith and myself, for I found him composing a rejoinder to it as sole author in my name.

Earlier, I had been upset by the dispatch's subject matter, which arrived during Mr. Smith's morning wireless schedules. He was over an hour getting the message to me, and I had already convened school and was involved with my children.

So I could not contemplate a response until midday, and by that time Mr. Smith had convened a meeting with the first and second chiefs of the village, Alexi Chirikof and Peter Andreanof respectively. In view of the village's "military preparedness" training, they concurred with Mr. Smith that evacuation would not be necessary. By this time, school was dismissed and I found things as described, meaning Mr. Smith in process of composing the response.

I despaired over being so excluded and retired to our sleeping quarters. The response was sent before I read it, under my name, with Mr. Smith's beneath. Sensing something amiss, Osmond came in and carefully read me the response to Juneau via Dutch Harbor. I was so angry I would not risk words to openly disagree with both the sense of the response and the method of gleaning the village's feelings. For at that point, the horse, as Father used to say, had departed the barn.

What sense in arguing the past.

Osmond, though, spoke confidently about the content of the message. Finally I managed *some* response.

"Osmond, in the future, do not affix my name to messages that are your effort entirely."

He was surprised.

"You are upset, Wife?"

"Yes, I am."

And that was as much as I would manage.

March 25, 1942. Chichigof Village, Attu

Things are uncomfortable in the Smith household, and of course the entire village is buzzing about evacuation and the coming possibility of Japanese invasion. The children were all in a state, overjoyed with the possibility of going to San Francisco to see (and possibly live in!) Commodore Deery's house and to visit China and Anchorage on holy days.

So, the day turned into a geography lesson, which for all (save three of the eldest children) was not done to great effect. Perhaps it eliminated *some* confusion.

All nine Attu households are on the verge of packing.

Heratina worries about her tea things, for she has an elderly samovar, more valued than any other item in the Chirikof
household.

After a confusing day, Mr. Smith has retired to the generator shed to work on one thing or another, though I know he's
angry with the village and me. He cannot understand the
nature of our neighbors' frightened response, nor my views
expressed last evening. My anger he sees as a vote of no-con-
fidence and said so at noon. He speculates that my views were
"sensed" by the Attuan women, thereby explaining the menfolk's sudden lack of resolve to stand fast.

These villagers are a people unfettered by *almost* everything that plagues "civilized" folk. They don't know war nor
had they been curious about wars and warfare. So, of course,
confusion reigns.

Mr. Smith has not seen war, but is a student of military
matters, and a zealous and loyal member of the Iowa State
Militia. He volunteered unsuccessfully to be involved in the
Spanish-American conflict, and of course the Great War in
Europe. Chance, thank God, spared him that.

Having seen two "wars" in person [*in addition to the
Boxer Rebellion, Lila Ann Smith's family were witness to
events in the Sino-Japanese War of 1894–95*] and been
involved and fallen victim to another, I cannot state I see any
reasonableness in them. Wars are begun by fools and suffered
by innocents.

<u>March 28, 1942. Chichigof Village, Attu</u>
This weekend marks the end of Lent and is the week leading up
to Easter Sunday, easily the most important holy day in the
Orthodox faith and therefore for the Attuans. I am once again
thankful for the supplies, no matter the expense, making it
possible for all households to properly celebrate this time.

I work steadily warping and woofing under the artful eye of Friend Annie on my first basket, and I've been making a frightful snarl of it. But she is a patient tutor and so young! Also, she is very observant yet with a great sensitivity to one's feelings. If it weren't for dumb fate I might have had a daughter or even granddaughter (!) like Friend Annie. (But I was fortunate to survive when my family and others were not.)

Friend Annie knows things are askew between Mr. and Mrs. Smith. She does not dream of asking, but instructs me patiently. Today, she explained about today's religious signifi- cance—the Saturday of Lazarus—-and how it plays such an important part in the church year. Then she asked me about war.

Knowing how I felt, she resisted asking until today. Also, we were alone; Heratina and Lena had just left, and Annie knew her question wouldn't result in runaway war chatter in two or three languages.

There was no reason to withhold from my dear friend per- sonal facts. A less painful means of informing would be to take out my scrapbook with the article [Des Moines *Register, 6/15/1905, "Lila Ann Howland, China Survivor," the almost exclusive source outside of this journal for her China years, 1880–1903. See Appendix*] but her reading skills are yet quite basic, though making steady progress.

So . . . I took a deep breath, and explained that a long time ago, I had lost my parents and brother during a war in China and only survived after suffering as hostage of a bad man who used womenfolk for ransom "or trade, like fox pelts."

"Four of us were traded for a shipment of military rifles and other materials, provided by my government to free us."

Annie's response was to cast a glance with her ink-black eyes into the corner of our residence, and I knew she was looking for the "Holy Corner," present in all Orthodox houses.

Anytime, during conversations—or often just during a significant moment—Attuans will look to this Holy Corner, a tiny
alcove in the upper corner of a room. There burns, always, a
tiny candle before one or two religious icons. It is their way, I
suppose, of saying "Praise the Lord," as some in the Protestant
denominations might.

This quiet practice is a most winning and salubrious part
of their faith. It may be the darkest night, yet inside the room,
this tiny area will glow, casting peaceful, kindly shadows.

But to return: Friend Annie, not finding such a nook in this
household, looked back down at her work and said, "I tonight
at church give thanks to Lord Jesus for your survival, and pray

forgiveness for the evil men who did those bad things." And she began to quietly weep, poor soul.

For those old troubles, my tears are long spent.

March 31, 1942. Chichigof Village, Attu

The week of approaching Easter (which for once is a holy day that seems to be shared by all Christendom) saw a great village event, the taking of a vast "fatted beast" in the form of a sea lion. This will provide village-wide feasting for the Holiday, plus meat for weeks, even months, beyond.

Though all shared in the joy of this event, I could not bear to watch its preparation and all sundry activities. Himself was quite impressed, and grabbing our Brownie hurried to take snaps while light persisted. As is our pattern these past nine years of marriage, our differences have not been discussed, but simply experienced a sort of *evaporation*. Mrs. Hilton's *Christian Marriage* does not list this as a method to resolve problems, but it seems to work for Mr. and Mrs. Smith!

While villagers said prayers of thanks beside the poor animal, I marveled at its immensity. It had been shot and towed by boat to the beach just below the school. Work went on well after dark, the village's single wheelbarrow put to its best advantage. From our back window, I can see the comings and goings, the laden vehicle preceded by a villager carrying a lantern. On the beach, working away, lanterns bob to and fro as work is done.

For me, despite the sad but clearly necessary demise of Mr. Sea Lion, I welcomed the respite it brought. War talk and an overall nervousness about events and news ceased for the day.

The results of the Territorial Standard Examination were less than satisfying. "Well, Mrs. Smith, I wouldn't put much stock by it. Remember, these people are only a generation or two away from paganism and savagery."

I was so shocked when Mrs. Wolfe presaged her explana-tions about the "TSE" by this blunt view, I even shared it with Himself those many months ago.

Now, seeing the results, I too wonder why I administered it, for scoring was a sad process. Only Anna Tschigorin scored close to standard. But paganism and savagery as causes are much further from my mind than the absence here of a teacher before, and probably after, my meager one-year effort. I feel the guilt of abandonment.

It is unfair that such uncomplicated souls go without basic education in letters and figures. And for savagery? In my view, lack of civilization's ugly *snarls* in this village is an admirable trait, not the least bit accidental. I view this as a hallmark of civilization, which survives because of their devotion to their ancient, Byzantine faith.

If this be "savagery" I pray for it to become widespread.

April 3, 1942. Chichigof Village, Attu
It is Good Friday. People go to and from Chapel. The bell, a very special bell from Russia, rings from its place in the belfry with sonorous clarity, calling the faithful. I cannot understand the goings-on peculiar to the Russian Orthodox faith. The Attuans do not have *missionary zeal* for their faith, and if one doesn't ask about their faith, they do not foist the topic upon you. I have been hesitant to ask, at times.

I celebrate Good Friday with a reading from Scripture to myself, for on religion Himself is more *no* than *yes*. This does not mean he does not believe, rather has allowed "the formali-ties" to lapse.

This is partially due to his mother, Mrs. Edna Smith. Uncle Thomas, who remembers Uncle Winslow quite well, says unkind things about the "Widow Edna." Even Father, bless his hard-working soul, wasn't prone to generosity when alluding to his eldest sibling's wife. She was a difficult woman, with uncommon zealousness in her religion. And son Osmond did not benefit, in my view. That we are cousins made our courtship impossible until Aunt Edna died. [*In summary, Osmond Smith was the youngest son of Winslow Smith (1834–84), and Edna Smith (1833–1929), therefore Lila Ann's first cousin.*]

"Never did a woman have less need to live ninety-six years" was a most improbable and scandalous statement Uncle Thomas aired at the funeral reception. "You've been imbibing, Thomas!" was all Aunt Sarah managed as a reproach. Lila Ann found herself *almost* laughing.

I've been gossiping. Unusual for me. But Easter week is the time of memories, and I miss family so badly that floods of such "gossip" (present in any large family, mine and Himself's *especially*!) sneak out from my memory's "nooks and books," as Father used to say.

I feel like a debutante with a full dance card, we have so many invitations spread over tomorrow and Easter Sunday. "We'll eat so much sea lion, we'll bark," Osmond vouches. His humor has returned and I've assured him we're equal to the social task before us.

To see the villagers in their finery is wonderful—the women lift up the hems of their skirts as they pick along the muddy, slushy paths between the houses, and up the longer path to the Chapel. The children have been *stuffed* (pimiento into olive) into the best clothes their mothers and grandmothers can manage. They are almost at once dirtied to the accompaniment of frantic, scolding Aleut.

I have been invited to one of the Easter services (there are several that day) and I have accepted, of course.

As if to celebrate our Savior, the Attu days are noticeably longer, and the weather slightly improved, I think. Today I saw a tiny bird, beautiful frail soul, and I think it a new arrival

from the south, a faithful sojourner looking to the new spring
without thought or care about mankind's strange problems.

April 12, 1942. Chichigof Village, Attu
The week following Paskha, which is what the Russian Orthodox
call Easter, finds the faithful recovering. Now, according to
Philamon [*Philamon Ivanof, the church Reader*], the most vital
part of the church year is past. During a "teatime" visit to the
Smith household by Philamon and wife Lena, I voiced curiosity
about their faith. I'm presently writing letters in anticipation
of the arriving ship. In his last letter, Uncle Thomas wondered
what sort of "paganism" we were dealing with out here, and

though he intended levity, I felt I might become better informed.

Though warming to the task of responding, gentle Philamon's English, I fear, left something to be desired. The Attuans' style of English is earmarked by a strange syntax, logical to the speaker but not the ordinary listener, yet it is musically intoned. Friend Annie was not here to "translate," so my confusion was obvious. Becoming impatient with Philamon, Lena began to *translate* (!!) for her husband in the difficult places. But the dear lady's translation only clouded things, for her English is poorer than husband Philamon's, though she is not of that opinion. Since Lena is "chairman" of their household, Philamon gallantly yields to her in matters of earthly substance, including linguistics!

My "catechism" turned into a very chaotic time, I'm afraid, and though ostensibly busying himself at the radio "station," Himself struggled against smiling while our session ran its course over "Russian Tea."

The navy ship *Barracuda* will arrive "within the next two weeks," and though it is evidently a semi-secret mission, Osmond informed the village, for naturally there is no way word could escape Attu save through his radio set. So everybody readies their catalogue orders and mail to Atka [*farthest west village in the Aleutians save for Attu, at that time*] and distant villages.

From what I've learned, the Aleut language differs quite markedly once one leaves Attu and moves east. Also many traditions differ to some extent. Most of the Attuan women have close relatives in the more eastern villages, for often men must negotiate away from Chichigof Village for a wife. This makes adjusting to married life for Atkan women or those Aleuts even farther east, difficult.

"Lonely times were with me all the time when I first be here," Lena explained, for she was born in the village of Nikolski, almost eight hundred miles directly east. What a strange *protracted* geography they endure out here, islands strewn across this giant of a northern ocean. God seems to have placed the Aleutians in a line, like stepping stones from one portion of the planet to the other.

April 19, 1942. Chichigof Village, Attu

Yesterday Tokyo was bombed by the Americans This, in its own way, is even more dramatic war news than the bombing of Pearl Harbor. Osmond says wireless reports about the level of damage our planes did are a swirl of conflicting accounts. Yet most speculate that the Aleutians must have been the likely departure point for the bombers. [*General Jimmy Doolittle's B-25's, however, took off at sea from the USS Hornet, the first operational launch of heavy bombers from an aircraft carrier in history.*]

When he told me, Osmond was as excited as he becomes during a Huskers ball game back home.

"The fat is in the fire now, Wife!"

The villagers talk of nothing else on this Sunday, and evacuation buzz is quite reinvigorated. There is as much worry and tension concerning the Japanese as there was about the Boxers those many years ago in China. There is an irony, though.

In Shansi Province the Japanese were at the same time feared and respected. When Father and Mother came out from Oberlin in 1879, through circumstances not of their own choosing, they were delayed nearly a half-year in Nagasaki, Japan. Father came to admire the Japanese, and during the troubles leading up to the [*Boxer*] rebellion, always championed the Japanese spirit as being honor-bound and steeped in the discipline of obedience.

During the rebellion [*1900*] we prayed for the arrival of the international force. In particular, I recall how we hoped it was the Japanese who would reach us first. Sadly, no one reached us. Now, save for this irony, all that remains in my heart is sadness.

No human wickedness undermined my faith more than wars, especially during my marriage to Emmett. He so ardently wanted children. In fact, twenty years elapsed before I resumed praying to a God who would permit such agony to fall so heavily upon innocents.

April 22, 1942. Chichigof Village, Attu

Outside events are catching up with this poor village. Osmond found out late this day that the arrival of the *Barracuda* has been put off another two weeks. Furthermore, in a following dispatch, that evacuation of *all Aleuts* from the Aleutians has been approved in Juneau and Washington, DC. Though a date has not been set, Mr. Smith speculates that evacuation will take place prior to the end of the school year.

Evacuation is necessary, even to Osmond who initially opposed it, but it won't be the *Barracuda* who will do the moving, for "I'm sorry to inform, my dear, that it is a submarine. I thought you knew from its name?" Of course, he had not included that information earlier; hence, the villagers all thought a vessel on the order of the *Northern Supplier*, or at the least the *Western Flyer,* would be arriving.

Communicating the concept of a submarine to our friends, he thought, might have resulted in more confusion. I will not argue with this assessment, for in fact this vessel cannot evacuate us. So the community question will be, "When will evacuation take place?" As I write these lines, the village is as yet uninformed about the *Barracuda*'s delay and the seeming certainty of evacuation. There will be much dismay and worry on the morrow.

At this moment, I decided to err on the side of *saying something*, rather than *not*, because save for the most conspicuous facts, I'm unsure how many details Himself knows about my background in China. So I told him that under no circumstances would I ever tempt fate again by remaining in a war zone, that I had stood by powerless as my father made that mistake. His response to my declaration quite surprised me. "Wife, during your captivity, what did those yellow devils do to you?"

At this moment, with fears of war at hand, I was even less inclined to narrate events forty years past. "They held me captive, Osmond." Which is the truth. After all, what can be stolen from another person more blasphemous than their freedom.

I feel a severity returning I thought long absent. It is a harsh fact, but there are conditions where thinking first about oneself is necessary to survive. This lesson was cruelly opposite to all I had learned. Mother and Father were selfless souls and held compassion as a Christian Essential. "There is no room in heaven's kingdom for selfishness, Daughter."

I hear these words even now. They bring a calming sensation like that when Father's warm tenor was right next to me.

April 26, 1942. Chichigof Village, Attu
It is late Sunday, and for the last five days it has been hectic in this village, no other word for it. All families prepare for certain evacuation, and rumors abound, though Mr. Smith and myself are cautious about disseminating information received via wireless. That source of information is *anything* but certain. In fact after the misinformation re: the *Barracuda* and the necessary corrections needed, it only increased the anxiety for all the Attuans.

Frankly, *my* anxiety rises.

Initially, the date for evacuation was only several weeks hence, then that was canceled. Through Thursday and Friday, this seemed to have changed once again, until by Saturday both the date and the actual decision to evacuate were all quite "up in the air," and Osmond had become quite frustrated. Finally, by Sunday morning he declared, "They must be planning to evacuate us first, as we're closest to Japan."

Friend Annie and infant are my special people, of course, and she frets about what outside life will be like, having never experienced that. How will it be for her baby? Will there be good and proper things to eat for them? Will there be soldiers and such?

Packing, then repacking, has turned into a community effort for the womenfolk, and I pitch in, for truthfully, the Smith belongings are not that extensive. During these activities, I try and answer each question. Yet I can't predict what life might be like after evacuation if I don't know where we will be moved.

Finally, by early Sunday evening, Osmond received reassurance we would indeed be evacuated. Also there was news for us.

"One thing sure," Osmond informed me sadly, "evacuation also fixes our fate." And handed me the Territorial Schools directive to all teachers—that the school year will officially end the day of evacuation. Subsequent to that our employment will cease.

So we will return home.

To think that I might be in Delbert within the month almost overwhelms.

May 2, 1942. Chichigof Village, Attu
Yesterday at sun-up, the submarine *USS Barracuda* arrived, several days early. The captain was Lt. Senior Grade Herb J. Wintergreen. Just months ago, he and his entire crew had been reservists, never dreaming they'd be sailing "Arctic waters," as their first officer, Lt. Higgins put it.

This was their first Alaska village, in fact their first Alaska landfall, and the entire crew swarmed the village, taking photos and looking every bit tourists. They had mail—almost a ton of it for Alaska destinations—and indeed Osmond and I helped sort through it all until finding the two modest-sized sacks for Attu Island.

Himself was not impressed with the tiny craft's military preparedness—not at all what he expected. "In a way, the *Northern Supplier* was tighter run."

However, they seemed military enough for the villagers and myself, of course! With the villagers, the deck cannon especially marveled, and the gunnery officer desired to demonstrate, but Captain Wintergreen demurred. "Ammunition is a problem," he explained to me. "They stopped making that sort back when they invented steam power."

They were a joking sort of crew, and prior to their departure a mere five hours after arrival, were an immediate hit with all including myself.

"It looks like the *Monitor*, doesn't it?" bragged the Captain about his ungainly craft. "Ugly as a plug mule and harder to steer than a cow." In the tiny, unnerving quarters below, Chief Engineer Lt. John Herbert showed Osmond and myself the dedication plate, polished to a high gloss. "USS Barracuda. Bath Ironworks, 1922."

"Second oldest sub in service!"

And he and his Chief Petty Officer seemed inordinately proud of this mark.

This was too short a visit. They were an optimistic sort, just precisely what we needed. About evacuation, Captain Wintergreen assured all it was at hand, though he did not know details.

His sure, matter-of-fact demeanor bolstered everyone's spirits. I cannot help worry about them, young men all, to enter war activities in such an extraordinarily homely and ancient vessel. I pray for the best for all the family and friends whose hearts ride so heavily with the *Barracuda*'s good-natured crew.

It is sad to see good, upright men employed for such dark, cheerless purposes.

<u>May 10, 1942. Chichigof Village, Attu</u>
This is Mother's Day. It is no surprise that Attuans not only do not observe this day, but don't know about it.

During an "unpacking/repacking" social at the Ivanofs (these have become popular throughout the village's nine houses as evacuation anxieties yield to everyday demands; also they give focus to villagers' endless enjoyment of chatting, of which I've become enamored, I'm afraid!), I began my effort to introduce the "Mother's Day concept" and it failed utterly.

Philamon thought immediately I meant the Orthodox "Mother-of-God" day, which he explained is celebrated at a different time of year than churches in the "village of Iowa."

Despite my explanations, our Mother's Day discussion became entangled in this cultural net. Language gaps made explanations about a secular holiday vs a religious holy day almost impossible. Finally I yielded to Philamon's resolve that today is "Iowa and San Francisco's Mother-of-God Day," but the Orthodox world's occurs "most best" in late August.

I must shoulder some responsibility for this virtual *soup* of languages: When there is a difficult word or term (and this is not infrequent), all my adult village friends must hear the word in all the languages *they* know, plus those *I* know. This is popular parlor amusement, especially when I render it into Chinese, though French is a close second!! English and Aleut are judged to be without entertainment value.

This evening I observed my annual remembrance of Mother by reading a few of her favorite psalms. Osmond remains *flinty* due to officialdom's neglect in passing on coherent information throughout the week. Fact is, there is nothing firm concerning evacuation, despite his requests to Dutch Harbor, Juneau, and Anchorage via the wireless.

Knowing my Mother's Day ritual, Osmond allowed a most extraordinary observation. He had put on his coveralls prior to changing the generator oil, when he volunteered a rare bit of information: he said that every Mother's Day while she lived, Aunt Edna [*Osmond's mother*] received a card from his eldest brother Hubert. "'Throw it away,' she'd say." And after this fair rendition of Aunt Edna's warbling contralto, Osmond allowed a rare ironic (?) smile.

I recall that neither he nor Aunt Edna ever mentioned Hubert after he abandoned his family for a life of adventure. His absence forever altered Osmond's life. Prior to today, the closest he ever came to mentioning the prodigal was by implication. "I was the dutiful son," he observed a few months prior to our marriage. And he was.

Though in our family, there was occasionally mention of Osmond's "inflexible" nature, yet it is his sense of unswerving loyalty and decency that I most admire.

May 20, 1942. Chichigof Village, Attu

It is nigh impossible to sustain any discipline at school because of the impending evacuation. It is made worse because of the uncertainty of its time and manner, and has made our lives very awkward. I can't help but harbor some resentment for both the Territorial and military authorities; after all we are the ones potentially in harm's way, yet remain so markedly uninformed.

The children can't concentrate on schoolwork, and at the drop of a pin will begin asking questions about all sorts of things, none of which is applicable to lessons, save for geography.

Furthermore, the village has nearly run out of staples, and soon our household will also. It has been almost five months since Commodore Deery's *Western Flyer* left us, and of course, unlike years previous, there's no late spring boat planned.

This has raised a thorny situation: Aleut people, like the Indian people at Three Rivers, think nothing of asking from us what they were so wont to conserve.

I don't mind so much this attribute but this situation has raised difficult scenes between Osmond and the village women, for it is the womenfolk who come around asking.

"Wife, haven't you told them the story of the grasshopper and the ant!"

I must remind Himself that the villagers are endlessly openhanded and give anything they have to anyone in need. He feels that if someone becomes a profligate giving to a profligate, it indubitably spreads the original folly about.

"All is uncertain now. It *is* war. There must be conservation."

To Osmond, this is absolutely sensible, and he logically points out that our larder is not the village store.

So I have become reduced to sneaking out flour, sugar, and rice from the storeroom which we had so amply (I thought) provisioned. But after almost a month of this, we too are low. And when our staples are spent, Himself will know the truth.

"*Balls of Fire!*" is the expression that comes to my mind, very much in the manner of Emmett [*Lila Ann's first husband*] when he was hopelessly frustrated. He would puff out his cheeks like a chipmunk, look upward, and speak this invocation. He was such a funny man; I believe he could make a statue laugh!

<u>May 22, 1942. Chichigof Village, Attu</u>
Current events develop at an uncomfortable pace, and fate has reached into our household with a somber hand.

Himself, though of a placid nature, cannot hide "something brewing" from me, and since he was not forthcoming about the matter, I asked what troubled him. I supposed it the situation with supplies, or bad news about evacuation, but I was mistaken.

"I was talking to Oly two or three schedules back. Seems ASC is asking for full-time radio operators."

The wireless community is quite fraternal, and via the radio, the operators speak of each other as next-door neighbors might, which in their world, they are. Mr. Oly Halston is one of the wireless operators at Kodiak, the name of an island and community proximate to mainland Alaska.

If Osmond volunteered, he'd be stationed remotely, and there might not be accommodation for married operators. I would then return back home and, like other "war widows," wait. When I asked about his age, he said it didn't matter, that the need for operators was urgent.

I've long known of his urgent and unrequited wish to serve his country. This is his third war.

He was barely of age for the Spanish-American conflict, but of course Aunt Edna refused to sign the papers. He was a few months under the maximum age for the Great War [*WW I*] but enlisting would have devastated the family business, for his father had died and brother Hubert was long gone.

I am in an emotional and mental uproar over his possible service. I don't know *what* I think. I would naturally miss and worry terribly about him. How might Mr. Smith do, even in a quasi-military situation? His tenure with the Iowa National Guard was ruined by that terribly corrupt Colonel Bates, and Osmond withdrew from that with a bitter taste in his mouth.

Since there are yet uncertainties, we left off discussing it further. Yet I know poor Osmond wants my approval and blessings.

May 24, 1942. Chichigof Village, Attu
This is Pentecost! It seems dozens of Sundays have passed since Easter, though it has only been seven. There is no resolution to

the continuing evacuation uncertainty. Perhaps it is to relieve this that I consented to Friend Annie's invitation to join her and others on a day trip tomorrow.

On her way home from worship, several of the women stopped by, urging me to join them. She and Heratina guaranteed immaculate weather for the outing. Indeed, the villagers have an uncanny way of anticipating what little fair weather occurs.

Since I am a poor "out-of-doors girl," I was hesitant to join such hardy individuals rambling about this rough terrain. But Lena assured me they would watch after me.

"No mens peoples. Just us."

So I have consented, for a positive byproduct of my adventure would be Anna Tschigorin's solo debut as Chief Tutor. She is now a mature thirteen years old, the joy of my teacherly vanity. She has consistently exceeded all expectations in language, and is every bit ready for high school. Also, she is a lamb, and is wonderful with all, never basking in her skills, rather, a modest young lady.

When she told Philamon [*Ivanof, reader of the church*] she wanted to be a priest (!!), Philamon and Lena were torn between pride (she is their dearest niece) and anxiety. The first because she's such a credit to them, but next because females cannot be priests, and they haven't the heart to tell her. Aleut adults, almost without exception, give their children what they want, and in my experience do not spank.

If all children turned out like my dear little Attuans, it would bring an end to the tired saw, "spare the rod, spoil the child."

May 28, 1942. Chichigof Village, Attu
It is almost three days since my outing, and even breathing still hurts me! Oh, how every muscle in my body screams and complains. My writing muscles hurt!

Osmond applies "horse liniment" twice daily to my wretched old limbs. "Wife, you are no Shirley Temple!"

By this, I suppose, he means at my age I should not be cavorting about the countryside.

And thankfully, during the long day of activities, I didn't *feel* all that badly, hence enjoyed it completely. It helped that my companions were patient with one so slow and unused to such activity.

"Binni" Chirikof was our expedition leader, amongst the oldest women in the village, and by far the shyest. She was born on Attu, I think a decade after myself, but due to the rigors of living here, this has earned her the title "Old Binni."

She is without any English, and cannot look at me directly, and when she does, smiles and looks down, poor thing.

"Binni too bad used by storekeep."

Which is "Heratina dialect" for Binni being taken as mistress by one of the CPC [*San Francisco Consolidated Pelt and Clothiers*] storekeepers many years back and sorely treated. He brought her to one of the other Aleutian fur stations for several years.

We began very early, and our destination was a lake. We must have appeared quite an exotic column of Amazons! Eight of the village women, including myself, filed out of the village, up the steep mountain behind it.

Having climbed this familiar slope, we descended until we returned to the seashore. Now all terra incognita to me!

After picking our way along the rocky shore, we came to a narrow, steep gorge. A rough trail ascended paralleling a fast-running stream that "spoke" with more vigor than Mr. Fenimore Cooper's "babbling brooks." We took this.

Though these islands are without trees, they don't suffer for lack of profuse flora. The grasses of the Aleutians are giants—tall, imposing, well over *my* head. Even on a fair day, as this was, they are laden with water, and oilskins are required, or one would get soaked. During a rain, acres of these grasses are bent with their burdens of water. It is one thing to look at this expanse of grass from afar, but a problem to wend your way through it.

If a visitor looked from a distance, I suppose we would have made an unusual impression! Here we were, deep in the grass, utterly out of view, all these chatting feminine voices interspersed with not infrequent laughter.

"Up inside house too long now!"

Friend Annie was exuberant at her day's liberty. For indeed, she and baby were both present, the latter swaddled snugly and carried on her back, with an oilskin mantle over all.

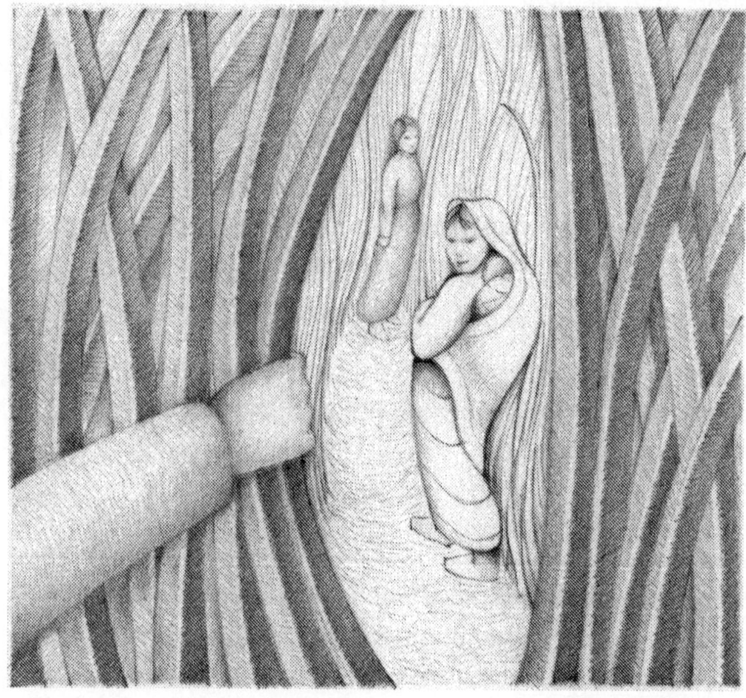

I understood from the onset that our destination was a lake, and at mid-morning, I wondered what had become of our lake. But no complaints, Lila Ann! I was the slowest wagon in the train and felt properly humbled.

At the head of our column, "Old" Binni was anything but old as she moved up those steep, grass-cloaked mountainsides. And indeed these slopes are beginning to assume that incredibly green hue—a brilliant Sherwood—I first saw last summer cruising by the Aleutians aboard the *Northern Supplier.* It is a green that shimmers with intensity, so brilliant I cannot recall seeing its equal elsewhere in nature.

Birds scattered before us, and I again lament my omission of not bringing some sort of book along, as for the most part I don't know their names. One is sparrow-sized, but with far more beautiful garb; Friend Annie does not know its name in English, only in Russian and Aleut. But they thrive in this lush "grass jungle," especially along the higher slopes. As one advances high up the mountainside, the grass gives way to ground-clinging lichen and moss-expanses of terrain with great rocky outcroppings.

It must have been not too long before midday that we *finally* reached the lake, a small unassuming body of water without garish shoreline, but a welcome sight. I was pleasantly surprised to see our destination was a small shelter, something of an ancient lean-to, built alongside a stream that fed the lake.

Here we made ourselves at home. A fire was deftly started; hot tea and pilot-bread were served. I sat, my skinny old legs so relieved at this rest. Now it became midday; the sky almost cleared of clouds and the sun burst through. On this island, a completely clear sky is a wonderment, perhaps even a miracle!

Attu is God's great land of clouds, and they rarely depart. Though now a few were visible, by and large the sun forced its way. And at once, everything turned into a fantasia of steam— as might a hot pudding placed on the kitchen sill. The grass, the rocky shores of the lakes, this eternal *wet* turned to vapor and was drawn upward. This ethereal mist rose heavenward, and all of us looked on in awe. This lake, so shrouded, struck a visual portraiture without equal in my memory.

Taking me by the hand, Friend Annie, Old Binni and Mary led me up a narrow path to the edge of the mount. And here what I saw further struck me mute! Beyond, below—everywhere (!!)—was the sea, intensely blue in the sun, yet at our backs, and slightly below, was the lake, its waters much darker; hence against its surface those phantom sun-mists stood out markedly.

And now these spirits—feathery tongues as it were—of ether spilled over the summit, then coiled and wove down the slopes. with the air currents. The mountain's rocky flanks leading to the sea were now adorned with these white, drifting garlands.

From our vantage point, in any direction, we could see for an infinity—seaward was a grand fjord-like arm of the sea, which, as all do out here, joined with the open ocean itself. Both sides consisted of steep mountains which closed in, until at the head of the bay all was rocky, imposing mountains.

Look at what I've done! I've written forever, and have only begun to describe this miraculous day. It is hopeless. It is almost one in the morning. Behind me Himself snores, my dubious lantern hisses away, and I absolutely refuse to pump it.

And more to the point, I cannot keep my eyes open. Old Prof. Shafford [*Oberlin College English professor, 1893–1928*] would be *stunned* to witness this exposition by his most hesitant "poet," as he described all his acolytes, despite our lettered inadequacies.

I must continue later to relate this most outstanding day.

<u>June 1, 1942. Chichigof Village, Attu</u>
There are warnings from all quarters of impending Japanese attack, both "on the net" (wireless) and official. The continued neglect regarding our evacuation has elevated tensions in the village, and I'm afraid I do little to soothe.

Mike [*Korovin, Friend Annie's husband*] and Young Ivan Tschigorin noted ship activity during the last two nights, hearing ship engines after dark. Osmond is exasperated at the inexplicable delay and made himself something of an "airways nuisance" with his queries about every schedule.

Yesterday, he, Walter Shergief, Mike, and Young Albert [*Chirikof*] hid supplies, etc., a half-mile away from the village, a part of Osmond's "defense plan." During village "preparedness Tuesdays/Thursdays," Osmond has devised a "retreat and defense" scheme.

Villagers ask, "Why would anyone invade here?"

And this evening, on the heels of this stressful business, Mr. Smith again broached the possibility of his service with the Territorial Signal Corps. Given developments, I knew it was on his mind.

In the fortnight since he brought this up, I have remained at odds with myself. On one hand, I should be a dutiful wife—and citizen—supporting my husband. Yet after this nearly two years of service, have we not done enough? My upbringing was one of service to others. It was my family's entire charge in life. "The world has more than enough Takers, Lila Ann." These were Father's words, which were my mother's beliefs also. Their memory is ever present. Yet our family, for after all my family *is* Osmond's also, has given much that is irredeemable.

I'm crestfallen at how I failed this test of inner resolve.

"Husband, when I return to Iowa, I suppose I might endure if you stayed behind, but frankly I would prefer so very much if you were with me."

I cannot say he was surprised when I said this, nor might I conjecture how he *felt*. However, he did say, as I knew he would, "Well Lila Ann, if you prefer it, then indeed it will be."

June 3, 1942. Chichigof Village, Attu
God help us all, it has happened. At 6 a.m. this morning, dozens of Japanese warplanes attacked Dutch Harbor,

inflicting serious damage. There were many deaths and injuries; navy and civilian ships were sunk, as were aircraft on the ground. Evidently, unlike Pearl Harbor, there was at least *some* advance warning, and resistance was mustered minutes before the attack.

Osmond spent the day and evening at his station, and our house became quite a *terminal* of activity, even moreso because ours is the only pantry with coffee and tea. Finally, Mr. Smith lost patience regarding the chatter, and in abrupt terms announced, "For pity's sake, I can't hear myself think, let alone anything else."

Now, village emissaries are sent at modest intervals. I cannot blame our neighbors; all are close to distraction, as I am. Yet there are no signs today of Japanese activity here. Toward evening, Osmond concluded, "Well, they've passed us by. Dutch evidently was a bigger fish." And, for the first time, I see he is relieved, for we've been provided with enough excitement.

He has decided to run the generator through the night. My first wartime duty was as *Messenger Figure*, going from house to house to make sure everyone kept light-sure curtains over their windows. I took this opportunity to smuggle out tea, dropping some at each house.

Now, without exception, all families are completely packed and eager for evacuation.

[*Mr. Smith was unfortunately incorrect about being passed over: On the morning of June 6, 1942, 1,200 Japanese troops under the ultimate command of Rear Admiral Sentaro Omori invaded Attu Island, taking possession of the entire island, including Chichigof Village. Many eyewitness accounts are on record. Though there was shooting, there were no fatalities, save for the " male Caucasian and aerographer on*

duty there." The Japanese invaders killed Osmond Smith within twenty-four hours of the attack, and at the same time, Lila Ann Smith was severely beaten during interrogation or otherwise roughshod military treatment. The villagers were unharmed during and after the attack, save that a female villager was struck in the leg by a stray bullet. Both she, and eventually Lila Ann, had their wounds treated by a Japanese doctor.

The village was occupied, put off-limits to Japanese troops, and the villagers confined to their houses for the initial several days. After this, they were given limited but adequate access to ordinary fishing-and-gathering activities. The occupation then became a daily routine.

There is an understandably long hiatus in Lila Ann Smith's journal, after which time she resumes entries.]

<u>July 24, 1942. Chichigof Village, Attu.</u>
I occupy a nook in Friend Annie's house since my discharge from the infirmary. The Japanese infirmary, of course. This journal was amongst the few Smith items saved by Annie and Mike, hidden beneath their floor—such cleverness from innocents.

I have difficulty breathing because of the ribs and my foot is not mending properly and aches. The other injuries have healed, but a certain fogginess of thought prevails, due, I think, to the large quantities laudanum given.

All my Aleut friends are well, thank goodness. I should write *Thank God*, but not so. No superior hand could possibly have participated in these disastrous developments.

In China calamitous events developed at a slower, more predictable speed. I cannot testify whether sudden is better than gradual.

<u>August 2, 1942; Chichigof Village, Attu</u>
I am embarrassed to be a burden to my friends. Until last week, I had to be helped everywhere. Usually by Annie or Mike [*Korovin*]. Anise Sergief's leg has healed, our village's only bullet wound from the events of June 6.

She speaks proudly of her "war wound," even showing it to other women. It has become a group event. Poor Anise was struck by a stray bullet. Sadly, however, during the days following June 6 all bullets were not stray.

The villagers are allowed to go about their business on a somewhat revised basis. The commander of the occupying Japanese forces is one Senior Colonel Oshima who all must bow to whenever he passes.

This confuses the villagers.

<u>August 16, 1942. Chichigof Village, Attu</u>
The translator, a corporal who will not inform anyone of his name, will not relay Philamon's request for a Wednesday evening exception to the strict 6 p.m. curfew. This is an Orthodox holy day. [*This would be Transfiguration Wednesday, a fixed Russian Orthodox holy day, always occurring on August 19.*] A security wire encircles the village houses, after curfew no one is allowed outside, and *certainly* not beyond the wire boundary, which forms a kind of compound. Armed guards man an entranceway always.

So when Philamon appealed to Sergeant Ota for an exception, he was pushed to the ground and screamed at. All were horrified, for Philamon is their church reader and respected.

Since all know they murdered Osmond without cause, Alexi [*Chirikof, village chief*] cautions them repeatedly against further appeals. After 6 p.m., travel between houses is quite clandestine but the young men do it with alacrity, acting gladly as couriers.

<u>August 20, 1942. Chichigof Village, Attu</u>
At no time am I permitted out of Annie and Mike's house, save for hobbling under the scrutiny of a guard to and from the outhouse, helped without complaint by Friend Annie.

There she is, with responsibilities for infant Titiana, yet with always time for my needs.

My lovely village friends cannot understand why our occupiers single me out for such total confinement.

"It is better than an abandoned *barabara*" [*traditional underground Aleut residence*]. This where they kept me initially. Friend Annie says I was so confined for at least two weeks and she thought me dead. Even the infirmary was better than living underground.

<u>August 22, 1942. Chichigof Village, Attu</u>
Though I cannot understand a word of Japanese, my Chinese
enables me to read their writing somewhat. In the infirmary I
discovered this, for close at hand were various medical materials with writing upon them, and once a magazine was left
close at hand.

At Oberlin I remember Professor Yu discussing this oddity.
He was such a gentle spirit. I do so remember fondly he and
Mrs. Yu sitting with me during a church baseball game, and
being so beguiled about the goings-on, even more than I.

I find it impossible to reflect on any of my present captors
without experiencing such un-Christian thoughts it is alarming.

I'm sure that, like poor Osmond, I shall never set eyes on
Delbert again. Oh, how Osmond strived to leave this place.

<u>August 23, 1942. Chichigof Village, Attu</u>
Today is the second day I read stories to the children and it has
done much to improve matters. They again asked questions
about *events*. This time I managed *not* to weep. It is vital I not
do so before the children. They are curious and ask questions,
as youngsters must do.

<u>August 25, 1942. Chichigof Village, Attu</u>
There are regular inspections of all nine houses and today an officer
they call "Mr. Ugly" in Aleut (thank goodness!) found our story-
book and confiscated it. "NOT PERMITTED," he shouted in English.
"No matter," I shot back, "I shall just make them up, then."

He and the translator jabbered about this between themselves,
and I thought I might be in for a beating, and too late regretted

my indiscretion. But no. Mr. Ugly gave me back the book, curtly
bowed, and left with Mr. Translator scurrying behind!

How odd.

August 26, 1942. Chichigof Village, Attu

This journal is a thorn. If found, it would certainly be confiscated with disastrous consequences for the Korovin household.
I keep it in a small compartment Mike made for me beneath a
floor plank. "This is dresser drawer!" He is a thoughtful, clever
man. Looking at it, one would never guess its presence.

At first, my journalistic intentions were to share my Alaska
adventures for folk back home. I have kept journals previously.
Most friends and relatives enjoyed my parlor readings, or at least
seemed to. I was certain they would after my experiences teaching.

As for my sketches, although I enjoy making them, I fear
they aren't of much quality. In lieu of a Brownie camera,
though, they will have to suffice. I only hope any reader will
bear with me in my attempts.

I strongly suspect that my time remaining in this village is
short. About my dear friends, and my students, I pray they're
left alone. Strangely, but gratefully, our captors seem to view
the Aleut people differently than if they were "Americans." In
fact, "Corporal" Translator (since he won't share his name)
refers to me as "American Prisoner," and the villagers as "liberated Japanese subjects."

This seems a fortunate confusion of fact.

August 27, 1942. Chichigof Village, Attu

The doctor had me brought to the infirmary. Through Corporal
Translator, I asked what was going to become of me and as I
expected, this was not translated. "NOT PERMITTED," in the
inevitable raised voice.

"Your foot has not knitted properly," the doctor then said in perfect English, though with a strong accent. *All these weeks and he speaks English!* Immediately, the translator repeated, "The Doctor says your foot has not knitted properly."

I looked with unconcealed surprise at the doctor and asked why he had a translator when his English was so good. "NOT PERMITTED," roared Corporal Translator. The doctor smiled, while fitting my foot with a brace.

With Corporal Translator walking smartly ahead, a sentry to each side of me, in case she were to become rowdy, I was escorted back to the housing area. At Annie and Mike's door, Corporal Translator barked, "The doctor prescribed limited exercise outside the abode once a day."

And then my escort departed.

<u>August 30, 1942. Chichigof Village, Attu</u>
I was witness to my new family's courage and devotion to their faith. It was a most stirring occasion.

August 28, a Friday, was their "Holy Momma's Day," as Philamon and Lena worded it for my edification, a great day of religious devotion celebrated in an evening service. This time, instead of asking, they just all—with Elder Tschigorin in the lead (for it is village tradition that the eldest precede)—commenced a processional. Elder T. was followed by Chief Alexi and Philamon, carrying a small crucifix. All else followed, save myself. I watched events from Anna and Mike's house.

They proceeded toward the Chapel of the Dormition of the Mother of God, the newest structure in Chichigof village. The name of their beloved chapel adds special emphasis to this Orthodox holy day.

When the confused Japanese guards at the "wire" were confronted with this unannounced event, the sheer number (forty+) of villagers, I suppose, was enough to cause the guards to step aside.

But soon a corporal strutted into view, espied this breach, and at once shouted—*barked!*—an order, to stop this defiance of the Imperial curfew. But Elder Tschigorin and Alexi were already by, and since our former Czarist subject's hearing is not what it was, he just shuffled onward despite the corporal following behind shouting.

Confusion. The corporal pushed Alexi, who managed to keep his footing; adding to this rising danger was Sergeant Ota, who ran out of my (former) school strapping on his sword and also barking, I assume, orders. At the moment, one of the guards charged forward, lowering his rifle with its awful bayonet.

Yet, oblivious to this, Elder Tschigorin kept walking toward the chapel, which is some way above the village. Young Zephryis Tschigorin—a twelve-year-old!! and my most mischievous scholar—sprinted around the shouting knot of Japanese, avoided the grasp of the corporal, rushing to the aid of his great-grandfather. (They are fast friends and conspirators.)

I was terrified, sure that disaster would strike, when suddenly the strangest moment developed: As if in a magazine photo, all froze in place, save for "Mr. Ugly" and "Major Spit" (villager sobriquets) who walked into view. They too stopped in place.

So there was our *Life* magazine photo: Most of the villagers behind the wire, a few past it, including Alexi (and Mike!), Elder Tschigorin and Zephryis, all looking to the officers— Sergeant Ota and the others having just completed a stiff bow to their superiors.

The officers scanned the proceedings without apparent feeling. Since Zephryis had taken him by the hand, Elder Tschigorin looked back, and seeing the soldier, a scowl fixed across his hoary, Asiatic features. An endless moment passed.

Then he turned and continued, a terrified Zephryis at his hand.
At once all Attuans followed, filing through the wire, past the
guards and up to the church. Without moving, the Japanese
watched as all filed into the church.

The corporal vented his frustration by alternately cuffing
the two guards (physical punishment of enlisted men is sadly
common) vigorously for a few seconds.

Then all returned to whatever they were doing, and within
minutes soft Russian chanting swelled from the Chapel. The
only Japanese in view were the two guards at the wire, now
somewhat frazzled from their drubbing.

I cannot get over what a mysterious tableau this all was. I
sat at table for a full five minutes, trembling.

<hr>

<u>September 2, 1942. Chichigof Village, Attu</u>
A terrible storm this day. I sat with Friend Annie, drank tea,
and listened to the wind worry our shelter. The Korovin house
is more exposed to prevailing winds than my former residence;
hence, in this strong weather, it talks and growls with many
wooded complaints.

Clouds were black and thick, daylight barely penetrated.
At dark a single yard light cast deep, sad shadows. At the wire,
the two guards huddled, the cold Aleutian rains washing over
them in sheets; the wind plastered their rain ponchos flat
against them. Each watch is two hours, regardless of weather.
All our guards are little more than eighteen or twenty. Children
who fight wars.

Today Mike told me that he, Albert Chirikof, and Peter
Andreanof buried Osmond next to the church. "The Japs did
not allow words but we said them to ourselves."

<u>September 5, 1942. Chichigof Village, Attu</u>
There was a meeting today, in the casual manner of the
Attuans. Chief Alexi, Philamon, and the other older men suspect the "meatballs" (the villager coinage for our occupiers,
after the symbol in their flag) will soon depart. These patient
villagers' keenest quality is watchfulness. Diverse sorts sub-
stantiated this opinion with numerous observations.

Mike, my host, agreed, and all prize him as the village
sage. "He is most smartest," Alexi has oft bragged about his
cousin. Mike spent almost two years with Commodore Deery,
even one entire winter in San Francisco working in the company fur warehouse and going to school.

We have learned—actually our men, who are involved in
work parties—that the Japanese are also occupying the
remainder of the Aleutians, right up to the mainland,
including Kodiak Island. [*They were not. The Japanese only
occupied distant Attu, Kiska, and a few smaller islands.*]

It was agreed that when and if the Japanese left, the village would be entirely abandoned in case they returned. And
that nearby Agattu Island would be the best place to retreat.

Friend Annie and Heratina today observed to me, "You are
understanding of Aleut talk much more."

True. In old age, my God-given knack for language
remains. Father used to tell the Circuit Deacon, "My daughter!
She is the Lord's own mockingbird."

Dr. Norberg [*Professor of Linguistics, Oberlin College, 1893-
1932*] once observed in his inimitable way, "Well, some folk,
Lila Ann, are universal chatterboxes."

<u>September 7, 1942. Chichigof Village, Attu</u>
Reading stories to the children is the finest balm for my own
sanity, and with increased confinement, the children have
become a zealous audience. The women are strapped with the

added duties just to "make ends meet" in keeping a house-hold. The men are sometimes called away by the Japanese to work, and since severe rationing is applied by our captors, the men must hunt even more; this conflict makes homemaking arduous for the women folk. So, in occupying the children, I serve a useful purpose. I cannot agree that abandoning this ancient site is advisable if the Japanese depart, but keep my silence. Also, why would the Japanese have gone to all this trouble to just abandon their prize? In my two walks beyond the wire, I've seen guns and cannons everywhere, construction sites abound.

I'm hopeful my foot will repair. Since I'm now the tallest *Homo sapiens* on this island, I surely must appear to all like a lame stork picking my way here and there.

[*On September 8, 1942, without notice, Lila Ann Smith was removed from the Korovin residence, hence separated from her journal until September 20. Her journal resumes on board the converted coal freighter,* Osa Maru, *sixteen days outbound from the Aleutian Island of Kiska. Unlike the "lost days"— during and after the day of the Japanese capture, which she never reviews—she now seems resolved to keep her journal comprehensive re: a cogent order of events and geography.*]

September 20, 1942. Aboard the *Osa Maru*

In a most astounding development, we are being transported aboard a Japanese merchant ship to Japan for internment. All of us, now forty-one souls since the death of poor Anise [*Sergief*] a week ago, reside in the dark innards of this vast ship.

Since we are the color of the former cargo, which was coal, we are all black as Sambo.

Where to start, meaning how to catch up? More sensible sorts would draw up a list or table, but fools such as Lila Ann are not sensible! But my hope is to remain reliable in my witnessing. I'm confident I have time to catch up.

On September 8 just after nightfall I was (without benefit of a moment's notice) escorted from the Korovin house to the office of "Major Spit," who I think is Colonel Oshima's next in command. Once delivered by the watch, they left me alone with the officer, but soon Corporal Translator appeared. I was told I was being transported on the morrow to Japan. When I requested to remain here with my friends, Major Spit became furious, and shouted, "QUESTIONING ORDERS IS NOT PERMITTED!"

Soldiers at once escorted me out, hurrying me along so I almost had to be dragged. Once again, I was confined in the dank bowels of a former *barabara*. I had nothing save what I wore.

My mood matched my surroundings, and during the two days of confinement, I resolved to remain brave. Without warm clothing or blanket, I shivered miserably the entire time. Once I was given water and rice balls. For "facilities," I made do, as they say. My childhood memorization of Psalms was beginning to enjoy thorough rehabilitation.

Probably somewhere around September 10, in the morning, the door to my warren was opened only for the second time, and under escort, with Corporal Translator walking patiently at my side, I was brought to the infirmary which, praise the Lord, was heated. I was awfully cold for so long.

Here the doctor dismissed Corporal Translator, who went off only reluctantly. Given hot tea, the doctor—one Dr. Ito— watched me imbibe the wonderful drink while he sat at a desk doing paperwork. Then abruptly he said in excellent American-style English, "Never question orders, Mrs. Smith. To a Japanese officer this is unthinkable, and in response to such a transgression, the potential for ugly consequences is high."

He then examined me, replaced my foot brace, and informed me I would be loaded aboard a ship very soon to commence transport to Japan. I was then escorted to and confined in (our) former generator shed, now converted to storage.

Aboard ship I was surprised but overjoyed to find that the villagers had already boarded. When I was lowered into the capacious main hold of the *Osa Maru* (for the long, vertical ladder descending into the hold is virtually unusable by anyone of less than Mr. Fairbanks' athletic prowess due to its damaged state) [*Douglas Fairbanks, Sr., a star of the silent screen known for his daring and agility*], the first face I saw was of Friend Annie.

So typically, she had packed what few things I still possessed—including this journal—with their possessions. Our reunion was tearful, and we were joined by others, including husband Mike. I find it so winning to see such rugged Aleut menfolk cry freely; to the Aleut man, it is anything but "sissy."

September 22, 1942. Aboard the *Osa Maru*

Most are sick and terrified. Our ship has been in heavy seas for almost three days now. My poor companions—my new family, as I see it—though tied to the sea from ancient times, do not benefit from this form of seafaring.

And Friend Annie most of all. The vast iron ship, with us in its center hold, are sorely stricken by the colossal noise and ferocious motion of the great tempest just beyond the hull. One cannot talk nor barely stand.

Friend Annie shelters Titiana in her arms, and I spend much time sheltering them both in mine. Mother and daughter weep, but I resist joining in.

I write this with much tedium, between great pitching, my own script barely visible in the fluid shadows of our single light.

<u>September 22/23, 1942. Aboard the *Osa Maru*</u>
The storm abated hours ago, and we are reassembling our "home" after what was nothing less than a two-day-long earthquake. "Mr. Screamer" (I must again credit the Attuans for the imaginative sobriquet) is our "keeper," our appointed director.

He is a dark, deeply wrinkled little Oriental man. But his age has not impeded his agility: even in heavy seas he would descend the badly damaged ladder—a slip could result in a fall of forty feet at its highest. All would watch Mr. Screamer descend—the notice of his pending aerial antics would be a large supply-bucket(s) lowered on a hand line.

Once down the ladder, he would begin screaming orders in Japanese, gesturing here, there, everywhere. Hence his name. Unlike the screaming of the soldiers, our keeper's histrionics seem to be habitual and guileless.

He eyes the young women, makes a muscle for the children, and chats on in Japanese, first chuckling, then gesturing "topside" and angrily making a fist, then back to chuckling. In short, he makes no sense at all. Then up he goes, and thus his duties are closed.

It is calmer now, and to catch this journal up is a steadier task.

We set sail from Attu on September 11 or 12. The villagers, to a person, were convinced that an island somewhere in that group (about 180 miles *east* of Attu Island) was going to be their new home, possibly Kiska. They had been directed and urged to pack up everything possible to reestablish themselves, short of the houses themselves. They even tried to transport their boats, but at the last minute this was denied by the captain (they assume) of the *Osa Maru.*

I assumed they were correct. It seemed logical to conclude that my Aleut friends would be transported to another island, if for no other purpose than to cease being an encumbrance to the military on Attu. Since I was an American prisoner, it seemed reasonable I alone would be transported to Japan as a prisoner of war.

So I kept the news about Japan given to me by Major Spit to myself.

We reached Kiska Harbor late the following day, and we were bombed by, I assume, the Americans, a horrifying first experience for all. Inside this vast, steel shell, the blasts were especially terrifying.

This went on for a good hour. Shooting, explosions—yells and shouts from topside. The vast metal of the ship amplified all. There were prayers, mine included.

It was several hours after this terror, and perhaps because of it (?) when Anise Sergief began to experience pain in her chest, and could barely catch her breath. I'm sure it was the poor creature's heart, but no matter how much we shouted and tried to gain attention, we were left alone. Two of the young men ascended the horrible ladder, and clinging to the top rung, beat unceasingly on the hold. Yet soon *another* bombardment commenced.

Anti-aircraft gunnery was, if anything, more noisy than the bombardment, and all clung to one another. Having read about the airplane attacks on Shanghai, I was sure our ship would be a prime target. Yet, again, we survived.

Not long after nightfall, we weighed anchor and put to sea; the great rising and settling of the ship would have been a welcome respite, save for my friend's growing fear. At that point, since the men knew which direction we were sailing (I don't know how), I noticed them huddling, discussing this. Friend Annie, Heratina, and Lena tried to keep their fears from the children. Anise seemed to remain stable, though in a poor state.

At this point, I began to suspect, as I'd been told, all of us were bound for Japan. . . .

Our single light is now blinking on and off, indicating its last throes of usefulness. This "catch-up" task is impossible in such light. So, my writing for now must cease. Hopefully Mr. Screamer will replace the light, for this erratic blinking drives all to distraction.

September 23, 1942. Aboard the *Osa Maru*
It is late the same day. Mr. Screamer indeed changed the light bulb during his daily chore of bringing us our supply of water and rice. This bulb is not as bright, but at least constant.

Realization that they were not destined for another island in the Aleutian Chain and Anise's death occurred on the same day, the third day outbound from Kiska Island. There was nothing I could do about Anise; all my medical supplies, of course, were long gone. My knowledge was too insubstantial and I felt awful in my helplessness.

She passed on quietly in the poor light, in a dark corner of this cavernous hold. A pallet had been made on the deck, and she was comfortable. All prayed, with Philamon leading the prayers.

Sergief was an old Attu family, but now they are represented only by her sister Agafia, brother-in-law Walter, nephew John, and of course Strong Ivan.

Anise Sergief was born in Chichigof village in 1898, and was always a joyful and optimistic woman. She was a particularly skilled basket-weaver and had a wonderful, clear singing voice.

During his next visit, Mr. Screamer understood our loss at once. He moaned a little, became uncharacteristically mute. He scrambled topside but reappeared at once with three crew members under the supervision of an officer. While the officer quickly checked Anise, to confirm the death (I suppose), the crew members opened the hatch cover completely. Tossing down canvas, to the villager's horror, they began to wrap and remove the body.

The protestations of Philamon and all others were in vain; the officer didn't understand and nor did he apparently care to understand.

Of course, there were strict Orthodox ceremonies that needed to be performed. All was confusion, yet there was no stopping the removal which took just minutes.

And, I'm afraid, just as heedlessly, dear Anise's remains were callously hoisted up and evidently just thrown overboard.

It was the darkest of nights, rain fell through the open hold, and having made no secret of their harsh actions, the crewmen battened down the massive hatch covers and were gone. Mr. Screamer did not put in a reappearance.

It was the first instance of Mike clearly becoming angry, though Aleut people show anger in a quiet, non-demonstrative way. "What sort of savages?," he asked me several times over, gesturing above. Philamon led the group in prayer. Several of the children came to me, and of course the poor things are scared and confused beyond themselves.

This situation is difficult to explain.

I think it was late that same day—or early the next—when Alexi and Philamon came over to Mike and discussed something very briefly and softly in Aleut. Then Alexi looked at me and, seeing that Friend Annie was asleep close by, asked me, "Mrs. Smith, are they taking us to Japan?" And I had the dreary task of confirming this, passing on to them what I'd been told by Dr. Ito.

Upon close examination, I see that my ink bottle is half empty. I have one remaining bottle of ink to last—how long? So I have resolved to make my words fewer. Paper, I have. Counting and registering my words will, as I was taught those many years ago, make me more aware of economy.

Annie and Mike take my writing efforts seriously and, prior to departing, when I was incarcerated, they carefully included all my writing supplies with their belongings, including my two dictionaries. It seems, quite untypically, that the Japanese did not limit the amount the Attuans could bring, save their boats, as I mentioned. Nor did they inspect what they brought, even though all the Attuans had firearms in their homes, and had been allowed to hunt.

This evening I think Mr. Screamer narrated a joke—or amusing anecdote. At its apparent conclusion, he treated himself to a great laugh, but took affront when none of us understood. Exasperated by, I suppose, our denseness, he flew into a fury of screaming and fist-shaking.

Then, just before exiting, he turned and hurled a final invective, "What sort of people are you? Stupid dirt Chinamen?!"

And this, in wretched but understandable Chinese.

<u>September 24, 1942. Aboard the *Osa Maru*</u>
My dearest Father used to refer to the language of working-class Chinese as "dockside Chinese" to differentiate between that and the more formal variety that was part of our lives in Shansi Province.

This vulgate is the *lingua* of Mr. Screamer, whose name would be more/less best represented by "Foi."

Mr. Foi was dumbstruck when I braved to ask, "When will we arrive in Japan?" in Chinese. I cannot, and would not, wish to truly represent his reply, for indeed "dockside Chinese" is not gentle. That I became (even) capable in it was always a shock to Father and Mother, though little Joseph [*Lila Ann's deceased brother*] would beg me to share tidbits.

But I dared to ask, thereby disclosing a potentially vital skill, because all of us, and especially the children, want to know where exactly we are bound, but more than anything—*when* we'll arrive. It seems to all that we've taken up permanent abode in this dank, dark hulk.

He looked me up and down and essentially said, "In six more days, but I think it could be longer. Where did you learn Chinese?"

When I told him, he shook his head in wonder, and departed via his highly skilled acrobatics.

❧

September 25, 1942. Aboard the *Osa Maru*
Doing this again brings back strong, loving memories of
Mother. All wonder what will become of them in Japan, and
lament the passing of their home. One of the most irreconcilable is Friend Annie, with young Anna [*Tschigorin*] a close
second. I do what I can to console.

I have sworn no entry to be longer than a hundred words,
because of my finite ink supply. And in the manner of Mother,
who was my earliest teacher, I will force myself to write *"more
with less."* Counting was her method of teaching conciseness!

"The best rhetoric is concise, Lila Ann. Which goes against
your nature."

In my primer, I would carefully count each word after my
writing exercise, and include it at the end.

❧

September 26, 1942; Aboard the *Osa Maru*
Our quarters are confining for forty+ souls. We occupy the
center hold of three. Number two hold is our home. It is *stories*
high, which does us little good, but 40 foot long and about
equal to that in width.

We've set up the most basic facilities surrounded by
canvas. We must beg to have buckets taken away.

Left and right, alcoves have been fashioned by most, the
best of which, in my humble view, is ours—that set up by Mike.
One half is lit, the other not.

Being held prisoner for one year [*1/1900–1/1901, China*] has
made me wise in ways my Attu friends are not. Bribery is the
corrupt product of being a prisoner.

❧

<u>September 27, 1942. Aboard the *Osa Maru*</u>
I recall Maybelle White's sly ways, probably instrumental in
our surviving captivity by General Lon Shi *[General Huog Lon
Shi, one time Chinese general, turned freebooter after the
Boxer Rebellion].* "Bribery was employed by Peter to visit
Jesus," she claimed. Maybelle always constructed timely inter-
pretations of biblical passages!

Then, for a sewing needle and a metal thimble, she'd
negotiate a peck of rice! How things change.

The Attuans' belongings are not in hold No.2 with us,
though they have a few with them. Yet how does one bring up
such ugly topics with such innocents?

How could I explain my knowledge of such subjects as
bribery?

I decided on *example*. At the center of our misery is the
almost complete negligence of emptying our privy buckets. I
have two pair of reading glasses, both from old Dr. Hoffman
back home, both with beautiful frames.

In plain view of all, I negotiated with Mr. Foi that our
buckets be emptied once every forty-eight hours, beginning at
once. When he asked if my spectacles' frames were gold, I
feigned confusion, and he made his own assumptions by my
lack of response.

Americans are so inured to the presence of manufactured
items they forget that in other countries, this is not true.

<u>September 28, 1942. Aboard the *Osa Maru*</u>
There is heavy weather—yet another storm. Not the most
extreme we've endured, but sufficient to cause sickness and
the general lethargy.

Today Mike, Alexi, and Young Albert *[Chirikof]* came to
me, and discreetly showed me several items for possible use in

dealing with Mr. Foi. They proved, as I knew, careful observers. Milk is needed for the children and better food.

What lies ahead for them all? I worry so much. Elder Tschigorin, I'm afraid, is giving out.

September 29, 1942. Aboard the *Osa Maru*
Extraordinary seas and I write between lurches. The seas collide against the hull, collapse upon deck, creating pounding beyond words, at least mine.

Our light bulb swings in a sweeping orbit, almost smashing itself against a bulkhead. This is the worst it has been, this nineteenth day at sea. I wonder if this is the end, and God forgive, that it might not be the kindest fate?

September 30, 1942. Aboard the *Osa Maru*
A sudden calm, as if we'd sailed onto a lake. All exchanged looks of, at first, disbelief, then of vast relief and even joy. Most are deafened from the unceasing pounding—voices must be raised.

Mike estimates the *Osa Maru* has traveled 2,500 miles. Since he once sailed with Commodore Deery, I cannot help but think him close to right. His calculation, plus this calm, leads us all to think we are close to arrival. There is a mix of anxiety and relief.

There was a falling-out between the Adreanofs and Chirikofs, the two largest families. I feel like Pandora, because the former negotiated for tobacco with a pocketknife and silver spoon belonging one to each clan, respectively. Supposedly this team negotiation with Mr. Foi was for milk solids *and* tobacco. When it proved to be solely the latter, the Chirikofs (who have more children) were irate, and showed it. A rare situation.

Friend Annie asked why people must be bribed to treat others decently, even children. Mike worries, for she is fearful for her Titiana who has lost weight.

October 9, 1942. Otaru, Hokkaido Prefecture, Japan

Entire *sagas* have taken place since my reunion with this journal two days ago.

We are now resident on the south end of Hokkaido Island, the northernmost large island in the Japanese group. The town is the port of Otaru, which is, we've learned, close to the island's largest city, Sapporo. To me, it appears similar in size to Anchorage, though in appearance nothing could be more different.

We arrived on *our* September 30, which is *their* October 1, this being on the other side of the dateline. The most extraordinary thing, we were not expected (!!), for it seems the military in Attu/Kiska did not notify parties in Japan of our impending arrival, our status—or in fact, *anything.*

Because of this unlikely lapse, we remained on board the *Osa Maru,* and our plight might have remained unresolved if Mr. Foi (AKA Mr. Screamer) hadn't informed a ship's officer of my ability to speak Chinese. Because of some unknown breach of rules, Mr. Foi, poor man, was dismissed from service, and could not serve as interpreter.

We were into the third day of living on board in port when at last a Reverend Wu was selected, an ancient Catholic priest originally from China. (Strangely, in all this time, no suggestion was made about finding an *English speaker!*)

So, with basic communications established, the central issue was the Attuans' overall status along with myself, which added more confusion. Without a virtual *portfolio* of paperwork, the civil authorities declined responsibility for us. But the master of the *Osa Maru* refused to carry us further. At center to his claim was a (for lack of better term) *Bill of Lading*

signed by Senior Colonel Oshima, as one might issue for a load
of coal. This was the *only* piece of paperwork, and on it the
destination was distinctly Otaru.

Things were an absolute snarl with ship and port authorities and municipal authorities at loggerheads. Negotiations
were co-chaired by the *Osa Maru's* purser and the Otaru Port
Authority's superintendent. They took place in Port Authority
office space over tea and countless cigarettes—the smoke
becoming so thick it burned my eyes. I would board and
reboard the ship, depending on necessity, with (usually) Alexi
along to represent us, as chief.

At the conclusion of the fourth day all remained unresolved. Quite unlike him, Alexi told me in Aleut, in which I'm
becoming increasingly able), "This is impossible."

"What did he say? *What language is that?!*" Mr. Osimi
(Senior City Constable) asked through Reverend Wu.

And without "batting an eyelid," as Mr. Twain would
write, Alexi answered in *Japanese*, "It is our language."

At this point there was a high-speed exchange followed by
a mixture of laughter and exasperated sighs. Then, in English,
Alexi told me, "in three months I learn a little," and waited for
peace to return, and Lila Ann to regain some composure!

And so it continued, these negotiations, until I'd traveled
up and down the treacherous gangplank dozens of time, and
suffered the indignity of being lowered and raised into and
out of hold No. 2 by deck-hoist, and never once, God forbid,
with my eyes open.

<u>October 10, 1942. Otaru, Hokkaido Prefecture, Japan</u>
It is immeasurable relief to see the children playing outside,
finally liberated from the confines of the ship. But lest I proceed hastily, I will resume where I left off, while my less-than-
expert narrative benefits by immediacy.

During negotiations, our treatment improved measurably, if for no other reason than that a physician had to be called because of Elder Tschigorin's failing health. A tiny, busy little man named Dr. Nagai demanded that sanitation and lighting be improved at once; also, nutritional needs were elevated with the addition of fresh vegetables and some milk.

Even Elder Tschigorin began to improve.

After dark on the day of Alexi's debut in the Japanese language, the cargo hatch was removed, the winch's engine started, and after much hoopla and longshoring, all Attuans were on "dry" land—the municipal dock. With a single, woefully dilapidated wagon, pulled by two equally woebegone mules, severely overloaded with all the villagers' belongings, we all set off walking behind it, inland.

Elder Tschigorin was allowed a tiny edge on the lowered tailgate, but adults, women, and children alike walked. It was a scene from Mr. Poe, no doubt. It was well past midnight; Mr. Osimi and an assistant constable were our only escort other than the teamsters. Talking was discouraged.

Downtown of Otaru is not pretty. Shops and abodes are as foreign as one might imagine, and the whole dingy-looking. The abodes, for the most part, are plain, old and often covered with tarpaper. There are no dogs; the streets of flagstone were worn. Though there are streetlights, half are apparently out. Our passage along these streets was forlorn, made more so since our destination was unknown.

Since I (and Alexi) were included in negotiations, I knew no agreement had been reached and suspected matters had been taken into someone's own hands. So we proceeded, this strange train of (now) forty-two villagers, plus Lila Ann: Going first was the wagon, creaking and tottering, followed by the Attuans, and with an assistant(?) constable at our rear, and Mr. Osimi moving from one flank to the other, our shepherd, anxious for us to move along.

Bodies were stiff and unbending, being used to confinement in No. 2 hold for twenty-plus days, and progress was
slow. No Japanese appeared at windows or doorways, and
soon we moved from the town proper into a railroad yard.
Close by, a switch engine with a single light moved cars about
in the yard, and I saw several switchmen with lanterns nearby.
Save for a few, the railroad entirely enthralled my Aleut family.

At the edge of the freight yard was our new home, a large
barracks-like building which evidently had been, or was, railroad property. A single-story affair, made of wood, with paint
nearly entirely peeled away, it amounted to a somber sight.

Quickly, quietly, the teamsters and most of our men moved
all the belongings into this building—forming a massive pile in
the front quarter of it.

It was a semi-ruin, evidently long abandoned. There was
actually nothing inside, just one room about 40 feet long by
20 feet wide, with one very small room at the end, which at
one time might have been rudimentary housekeeping quarters—a kitchen of some sort. But if so, all equipment or fur-
nishings were long absent.

Giving us no explanation whether this was permanent or
temporary, and leaving one unarmed constable posted guard
outside, we were left to our own devices.

Though relieved to be liberated from the hold of the *Osa
Maru,* it remained a grim moment. Makeshift pallets were made,
and, absolutely exhausted, most of us found refuge in sleep.

Alexi, Peter, and Mike briefly met, and while Friend Annie
and I were preparing for sleep, Mike said, "I guess we're not
being held by the military or the merchant marine."

Zephryis (called "Zekia") and several of the other boys, too
excited to sleep, asked repeatedly, "What is he doing?,"
meaning the constable outside, whose baton of authority was
a thick bamboo pole painted white. When told he was
guarding us, they laughed. It was the first laughter these walls
had experienced, I fear, in quite some time.

<u>October 14, 1942. Otaru Barracks, Japan</u>
It caused much dismay when it was discovered that all the villagers' crated belongings were pilfered during the crossing on board the *Osa Maru.*

"For three months, the soldiers never stole from us" was the overall lament. All salt barrels (salmon and seal meat) were gone, and much else. The two stoves were not, nor the two kitchen ranges. However all stovepipe was.

And on and on.

Mike has helped me experiment diluting what ink I have remaining, but it tolerates little. Almost all of my diverse writing paper in the Korovins' supplies was taken, including a pencil set.

It has been concluded this railroad barracks is to be our abode for the duration.

We busy ourselves to make this a home.

<u>October 20, 1942. Otaru Barracks, Japan</u>
It is impressive how quickly the youngsters have picked up Japanese in less than four months, and I have resumed classes to at least enable them to keep what English they have. It helps that my story times are in English.

Today John Sergief and Alfred Tschigorin told me they heard (they have discovered how to crawl about unseen under the barracks floor!—this is where their "fort" is located) Chief Constable Osimi talking about me with one of our civilian guards (AKA "Mr. Stick"). "They talked about you, Mrs. Smith. That it wrong to treat you like Aleut guy."

Friend Annie quizzed them in greater detail in Aleut, yet that seemed the extent of it. I'm worried about this, for it might mean my departure. But I keep that fear to myself.

⁊

<u>October 30, 1942. Otaru Barracks, Japan</u>
I have been returned to the railway barracks after being held
for six days in a room adjoining a vast warehouse, part of the
city dock. Four soldiers removed me without notice one
evening nine days ago, the first military we've seen in Japan.

Contrary to Japanese civilians, the soldiers were rude, said
little, and allowed me to take nothing. While departing, a corporal cuffed "Mr. Stick" about the head, then kicked him.

Under such escort, I was walked quickly back to the dock,
and by the time I was incarcerated in the small windowless
room, I was exhausted. I'm unused to walking, especially at
such a pace.

The room was bare; it was unheated. At night, beneath me,
I heard the ocean lapping at the massive pilings. Mixed smells
of oil and seashore reeked.

On the morning of the second day I was given a blanket, a
bucket, and a bowl of rice balls and a large porcelain urn with
water.

Occasionally Mr. Rat would look in. Thank God I am not
like mother, who was *terrified* of them.

After an agonizing five days Reverend Wu and Chief
Constable Osimi called.

"Orders were received for you to be transported by ship to
a prisoner-of-war facility near Yokohama."

I argued with vigor against this, but time and again, Mr.
Osimi through Reverend Wu reminded how unyielding the military was about *anything*.

In short, the issue was closed.

The treatment, the removal from friends, now to be permanent, became too much, and I broke down before them. They
stumbled over each other retreating from the room.

Late the same day elderly Dr. Takata called, escorted by
one of the four assigned military, which I'd learned had been

detached specifically for me. A medical transport certificate was required, it seems.

We began in Chinese. The doctor's was quite good, far better than the corporal of the guard, who only spoke rudimentary Mandarin. Asking the corporal to turn his back, Dr. Takata continued the examination, and absolutely astounded Lila Ann by asking in French if I could manage in that language.

How I had lamented my required Indo-European language requirement at Oberlin, yet I managed to reply "only poorly." He then responded, "Do you want to leave here?" and while the corporal remonstrated the use of a language he did not understand, I responded, "Non, mes amis sont ici." [*"No, my friends are here."*]

Our conversation in French stopped, and without further ceremony, both left, the doctor bowing a courtly European farewell.

That evening, the first indication of changed fortune occurred when I was given water and rice balls. The attendant wore a medical mask, and opened the door only a crack, slamming it shut!

The next morning Mr. Osimi, also wearing a medical mask, escorted me at a leisurely pace back to the railroad yard, and to my friends. Some of the children wept (and adults Friend Annie and husband Mike) to see me, and I them! Then Mr. Osimi nailed a poster to the front door of the barracks with figures meaning "Sickness! Forbidden Place."

Dr. Takata's question at the warehouse, then, was a precursor to this tactic to keep me here. But for how long?

November 5, 1942. Otaru Barracks, Japan
A routine of living in this barracks has developed. We are left almost to ourselves, save for Mr. Stick and his colleagues. A

total of three older men (constable reservists) guard us in shifts, always. The quarantine sign remains.

My ink supply is low and writing supplies non-existent. Most adults remain on the alert for any, or a substitute, as my efforts in my "letter book" have gotten out. Ironically, all consider this *logbook* (!) essential, in what way I or they don't know.

The old bachelor trapper/hunter, Stephan Zacharof, pointed out re: ink for writing, "There much blood. We can bleed ourselves." And he was serious!

"He's just saying that," Mike corrected, but Philamon shook a finger at him and said, "Such talk is unholy," making Stephan sad.

Stephan is an uncomplicated soul who is very confused by all that has happened since June. He is the village's best hunter.

The classes for the children take their minds off hunger. There is not much food.

November 8, 1942. Otaru Barracks, Japan
The first formal church service in Japan was held this Sunday. Philamon had taken along the ceremonial basics. In the "recreation" corner I looked after the three toddlers, Dimitri [*Andreanof*], Titiana, and Edward [*Chirikof*].

The Old Slavonic chanting I found extremely salubrious, even more so than I had on Attu. Poor Osmond had been critical of it. I think of him every day and am sad and angry at the same time.

November 15, 1942. Otaru Barracks, Japan
We had our first scare: three days ago John Sergief, Alfred Tschigorin, and Young Albert Chirikof were apprehended (somewhere) to the west of the railroad yard. They were

caught and held all that day and most of the next. Their parents, and all of us, were close to distraction when Mr. Osimi and two uniformed officials (Mr. Osimi and his constabulary do not wear uniforms, just a small badge) marched them into the barracks, arms tethered behind at the elbows. The boys were clearly shaken.

Mr. Osimi was angry. He lamented his leniency with us, and if such junkets repeated, that would cease. "Departing this building unaccompanied by an official is *forbidden*!"

It was the first time Mr. Osimi raised his voice and the most severe he's been.

After the officials left, Alexi and Peter gathered the men together on the back stoop (the villagers have pieced together a shelter where cooking, etc., is done). In the end, the young men were admonished not to repeat. But, judging from their frightened state, this admonishment was probably not needed.

Today the quarantine sign was taken down and I'm uneasy. The villagers—my fellow prisoners—never knew the sign's significance, and I did not burden them with its meaning.

Food remains meager and the children complain, not understanding it. The adults are devastated by this.

November 23, 1942. Otaru Barracks, Japan

I have spent days on tenterhooks. But the only officialdom apparent are the three changes of shifts per day, with the morning constable bringing rations every second day. To Friend Annie, my anxiety is perceptible, for with every change of shift—approach of a wagon or machine—I become nervous. Also, I'm sure she noticed I've put together an "emergency" bundle in the event I'm given little or no notice of being taken.

Memory serves me well. Being General Lon Shi's prisoner/hostage those forty years ago prepared me for suddenness. We were moved often, always without notice. When I learned the horrible fate of my dear family, I did not care what came of me, and that made it possible to survive the next fifteen months.

Upon return, I told the *Register* reporter a year but it was not.

Is this present repeat of ill fortune punishment because I alone, out of all my family, survived those decades ago, and the things I did to survive? At least I'm now an old woman and my course is nearly run. Yet I hope my fate was not visited upon Osmond. The poor soul only wanted adventure after so many years of dogged duty.

December 2, 1942. Otaru Barracks, Japan

Much has happened, most of it confounding and difficult for the villagers. As regards my own fortune, it seems I will remain at the Otaru Barracks. This brings me great relief.

Any words I might use founder when trying to convey how profoundly mysterious this new existence is to all Attuans.

Ordinary life has become wildly different, and more laborious, especially for the adults. The changes would construct a long list, yet I will detail only the most significant:

Most unforeseen and strange is the requirement that all between sixteen and fifty years of age, male and female, work in nearby clay mines [*Dolomite clay, used in the manufacture of diverse Japanese serving-ware*], which they find abhorrent, strange work. They are paid as the lowest menials. This policy was implemented two weeks ago and the villagers are having trouble adapting to *scheduled* labor, a way of life they've never encountered. I hope they will adjust at a faster rate, for I fear the consequences otherwise.

I have gladly become the *de facto* child-care person for those mothers who must work, which is all save one—Friend Annie.

The bathhouse situation is a second but no less traumatic change. Since our arrival, bathing, as it were, was by sponge and basin type cleaning, but thorough hygiene was an issue. The men (who have become resourceful scavengers) began to piece together a *banya* [*Russian-style steambath, not unlike a sauna*], which is the traditional manner in which Aleuts attain overall hygiene.

Osmond and I, of course, eschewed *banyas*, relying instead on a massive washtub in the teacher's quarters. As Himself said proudly when (repeatedly!) declining offers to *banya*, "We are prudes, and rightly so."

On the day when Mr. Osimi and all three constables abruptly appeared (morning of 16 November) and ordered all of us outside, he explained we were being taken to a bath-house. I surmised a Japanese bathhouse was quite different that what villagers expected, who, to a person, expected some variety of *banya*.

When questions of gender propriety arose, Mr. Osimi assured Alexi and Philamon through the children (who surpass adults in the rudiments of Japanese!) that it would be observed. Hesitancy ceased and all set off—forty-three of us— through the streets at a snail's pace, with occasional sorties by the children, who were chased back into formation by the con-stables, wielding their wands of office.

When we reached what was evidently a municipal bath-house, language failed and rebellion began. The villagers were horrified to see large *vats* of steaming water. "Oh Miss Smith, they are cooking to us!" Though the English was garbled, their meaning was not.

When all learned what was inside the spa, and the situa-tion was relayed person to person in Aleut, at once many wept, especially the women and not a few of the children.

Elder Tschigorin, who had been helped along by Zephryis and Young Ivan [*Tschigorin*] (mostly by "piggyback"), simply whacked his "horse" several times, ordering a return course for home, only to be vigorously stopped by frenetic constables.

Since I was unable to communicate with Mr. Osimi or his men, and the villagers absolutely refused to obey, one of the constables—who has been consistently rougher than the others—threatened, or made to hit, Peter [*Andreanof*] and Old Ivan [*Tschigorin*]. Immediately Strong Ivan [*Sergief*] and Leonty [*Tschigorin*] interceded and took his stick away.

Battle lines were formed; the frantic villagers much like wagons drawn in a circle. They confronted the constables and two bathhouse workers, the men on the outside, women and children in the middle. Strong Ivan had kept the constable's stick and brandished it.

Thankfully Mr. Osimi and Alexi kept their wits, and through desperate gesticulations and shouting, blows were prevented. A very tense stalemate began. Though thoroughly cowed by such desperate acts, I tried to mediate, jumping from language to language, but I'm such a dunce, for I've assimilated very little Japanese. None of the constables or bathhouse attendants spoke anything but Japanese, and what little skills the village children possessed were now buried by fright.

Finally, oh but finally (!) Father Wu appeared in an ancient machine [a *car*] with two men dressed in the same strange uniforms of those who apprehended our wayward boys. Father Wu and I formed a linguistic bridge between conflicting sides. The villagers were told they were not going to be cooked, that the water was just hot. Also, that though genders would bathe separately in their case, they *must* bathe at once. Proper hygiene for internees was not only required medical procedure, but the law!

Mr. Osimi, who despite the presence of the uniformed officials, remained in charge, was confounded to learn that different genders, even of the same family, sometimes did not mix openly without clothes. And *never* with those *not* of the same family.

Mr. Osimi suddenly announced that different genders would bathe separately, but that bathe they must, or food rations would be reduced or eliminated. At that, the stalemate ceased. And the bathing amongst same-gender was an experience of modest embarrassment throughout.

But oh! the water was hot and clean, with straw for scrubbing and even a little soap.

<u>December 3, 1942. Otaru Barracks, Japan</u>
Later the same day of the bathing incident [*November 16*], the villagers became despondent. Everyone wondered: would this sort of humiliation and violence become a regular part of their lives? What sort of people were these Japanese?

Toward teatime, Mr. Osimi, Father Wu, *and* Drs. Takata and a younger colleague, Nagai (who had examined us in October), arrived. Dr. Nagai's nurse accompanied.

Medical examinations began. The younger physician and the nurse worked in an area temporarily made private by blankets. (I don't know if it is my imagination (!), but our involuntary "hosts" seem more sensitive to gender issues.) The Reverend Wu departed after seeing his services were not required. He seems well liked by the Japanese; the poor man is so awfully bent and frail and has a terrible palsy.

Dr. Takata and I sat at tea, and without visible discomfort from any of the constables or his younger colleague, talked in French, then Chinese; ironically, the good doctor was more comfortable in French, and I in Chinese—but either served well to impart information unintelligible to others.

(My linguistic abilities cause great pride in my Attu family.)

I was correct (though he would not identify which disease he'd affected on the records) that Dr. Takata is responsible for my remaining here. He reassured me that the military has a poor memory in non-military matters, and would be unlikely to return.

And my conjectures on arrival were correct: no civilian authority in Otaru, or the prefecture, had any notice or explanation of our arrival. In fact, none have been forthcoming, despite frustrated requests from Constable Osimi. Dr. Takata asked me (!!) if *I* knew why we had been brought here. At this point I explained details of our origins and subsequent capture. He listened keenly, making great disapproving sighs when I came to the loss of Osmond.

After the doctors and constables left, I felt relief. It is so encouraging to find someone with a sympathetic ear.

This distressing day concluded joyously for the menfolk: two bricks of powerful foul-smelling Chinese tobacco (alas! an old adversary of my family) were issued. It was apparent, though, that no other Attuan's delight surpassed Elder Tschigorin's who settled into his pipe with vast pleasure!

In fact, the menfolk sat about smoking and discussing who seemed bravest this day. All agree that the hero is Strong Ivan.

December 8, 1942. Otaru Barracks, Japan

No work in the clay mine today even though it is a Tuesday. It is a national holiday. In fact, Mr. Osimi stopped by and gave us a half-dozen large cans of fish. Our shifts of guards looked at them with envy, but did not attempt to take any, which is a rising tendency I shall reserve for a later entry. Thankfully, the source of this gift yielded it a sort of immunity.

Toward evening, I learned the holiday was to honor the first anniversary of the Japanese victory at Pearl Harbor, declared so by the Emperor Hirohito himself.

I had not thought of the differences in dates, for our December 7 was their 8·

I am feeling unwell. Once again I ruminate about those devastating days immediately preceding and following the invasion. Life is so difficult now for the children and their parents (not to mention unfair) I feel guilty pondering my own misfortune.

December 21, 1942. Otaru Barracks, Japan

I have lost so much weight I've become even more of the "stick lady." But I am "on the mend," as they say. Friend Annie and Mike saw to me, even though their own dear *infant* Titiana continues to suffer from these conditions. She has remained a wee thing, not gaining sufficient weight.

One of the days I was sickest, Dr. Takata stopped in along with his younger colleague Dr. Nagai. I was not up to conversing but they did drop by medicine.

Now, I keep down broth and tea and feel much surer on "the pins," as Himself used to express it.

So, when Friend Annie and Anna [*Tschigorin*] presented me with the box from Dr. Takata, left in their care, my recuperative powers were greatly bolstered. In it were two pencils and a tube of ink-paste, the old-style I used so often years ago.

"The Lord made people essentially good." Father believed this, his most constant principle. Though mother would always nod and agree, I know she did not.

The Lord and the Son *should* be more central in my life and thoughts, and certainly prayers. Prayer was the rock upon which our family rested. Mother and Father had endless faith, which I sadly grew unable to share.

"New" Christmas (Gregorian), 1942. Otaru Barracks, Japan

I am the only celebrant of this Christmas and in addition to general weakness, feel blue. Mr. Gershwin could write a song for me, perhaps. My flute, of course, is gone, along with everything else.

Daily life is routine and predictable. Six days a week, there's work in the clay mines beginning in the morning until mid-afternoon; villagers are escorted to and from on foot by one of our constables. If someone declines work because of their illness or their children, there is only clucking of the guards' tongues and a shake of their heads, nothing stronger. But, of course, no pay.

Once a week a tiny delegation of villagers collects what money they have (usually two of the older women on a rotational basis; children are not allowed along), and are escorted to a general store to buy whatever is possible. Sometimes there's nothing in the store edible or useful. It is apparent that civilians on this part of Hokkaido Island live with food rationing.

On Mondays and Thursdays, official rations, and coal, are provided at the barracks by a jovial, rotund man whose wagon is pulled by an aged mare the children call "Babushka"; he allows them to pet it. The children had never seen a horse.

Alexi and Peter as First and Second Chiefs continue Chichigof Village's structure, with Philamon and Mike serving in important advisory roles: the first for devotional matters, and Mike because he is the recognized sage. I carry on as teacher, with child-care duties added. Also, my "nursing skills," such as they are, do occasionally contribute.

The villagers get along. Having always lived together in close proximity, they are used to each other's imperfections.

As the last day of 1942 approaches I am remorseful over the year's events, and especially the day we applied for an additional post after the indifferent year at Three Rivers Station. Poor Osmond had an awkward time there, never comfortable with Athabascan life. Learning of the Attu posting, he was *eager* when informed he could also serve as part-time aerographer. We talked about it for weeks, Osmond at his most convincing. His life had been *duty to family*, always. I thought then that if we returned to Delbert, he would return with a cloud over his adventure. I had never seen him so optimistic, and that decided matters for me.

It had been a similar situation with the initial application to work in the Alaska Territory Schools in 1939. Then, the events of my young-womanhood were thirty-eight years behind me and not discussed. In fact, few in Delbert remembered them or my parents who had posted to China almost sixty years before. Our family returned for visits three times between 1880 and 1900, once to show off Lila Ann, and the second time the infant Joseph.

Only on the third and last visit did both Father and Mother visit together, 1896. I was but sixteen and Joseph eight. At that point, there was much discussion centered on leaving me in Delbert to finish high school, then go onto Iowa Normal [*teachers college*]. Uncle Thomas and Aunt Sarah were eager to take me in, though Widow Edna [*Osmond's mother*] was also a possibility. The former were, by far, preferred, but even then, my skills and interest were in China, and I begged to return, at least for the next few years.

I've never regretted returning, for my place was with Mother, Father, and Joseph.

I have strayed into autobiography, but it is Christmas, so I allow this indulgence as a gift to myself.

January 1, 1943. Otaru Barracks, Japan

New Year's Day, the new calendar. No fireworks or celebration. It has been snowing heavily, for though Otaru is farther south than Attu Island, this climate seems colder. Certainly, according to Mike, there is more snow. The skies are rarely sunny, like Attu, yet there is not as much wind, and since we are situated in the midst of (by villager standards) a *metropolis,* the ambiance is different. There are noises, smells, and sounds that none were accustomed to, and daily living is more of an adventure for my friends, even now.

Food is an issue, and one that raises the most anxiety as regards the children. The food wagon with "Mr. Babushka" seems a frail tendril, for the amount of food and fuel varies considerably. "What are we to do if Mr. Babushka doesn't come?" Several adults have asked me this in confidence. The visits to the store are unproductive—a few foodstuffs, a little tobacco, and a sprinkling of household items.

Philamon has set aside one corner as the permanent Holy Corner and expands on it for services, which he maintains with admirable devotion. He is the keeper of the *proper* calendar [*Julian*] so Orthodox religious dates are accurately observed.

Work in the clay mines raises health problems; the clay gets in the villager's lungs causing persistent coughing. Overall health declines somewhat, but still holds its own. Or is this wishful thinking? But even Elder Tschigorin, who was so ill upon arrival, is better, though confused by it all. We are adapting to the weekly visits to the bathhouse, thank goodness!

Plans for the upcoming Orthodox Christmas hold out respite to the villagers from these new hardships and strange surroundings. In each other, there is the balm of lifelong familiarity.

January 3, 1943; Otaru Barracks, Japan
Stephan Zacharoff ("Sad" Stephan) has wandered off and is missing. It was early yesterday, a Saturday. There is disagreement over when Stephan was seen last, but it was either going to the mines, or while there. This situation has tragic potential.

His absence was detected late—during the evening head count by the guard "Big Jaw," a most unpopular fellow. Within the hour, Constable Osimi arrived in his machine and began the search for Stephan, taking an agitated "Big Jaw" with him. The far more placid Mr. Ojiwa remained in his place, a constable/guard all, including Lila Ann, prefer to the former.

Stephan is a lifelong bachelor, quite slow of wit and something of a mystery, having appeared in Chichigof Village in a lone native *bidarka* many decades ago. His birthplace was to the west, in the Kommandorski Island group, also home to Aleuts of the same language and cultural group as Attu. This feat of open-water navigation is a village saga.

Stephan never discussed it, except to say it was a long ways, and he hadn't anything to eat, and "just a little water." Mike thinks that Stephan left his home under a shroud of trouble. Because of his commerce in the Kommandorskis, Commodore Deery is thought to know about Stephan, but kept the particulars to himself. Every few years he would deliver a letter, reading it to Stephan, for he cannot. Afterward, Stephan would be even sadder.

Now, he's gone. By closest reckoning he is around fifty years of age.

Kusma, Strong Ivan, and Old Ivan, his closest friends and trapping partners, were denied permission to aid the Japanese in the search. They are most distraught.

Poor Stephan's departure put a shroud over today's service, the Sunday preceding Christmas, this Thursday. Few expect a favorable outcome. Alexi, in a rare address to all as Chief, said, "We must all stay together, so with God's help we may go home together."

❧

January 11, 1943. Otaru Barracks, Japan

It was a somber Christmas, the first substantial sign that the reality of their new, unasked-for home has settled in. There was talk of starring, but none occurred. There was a simple service with singing, in itself a considerable balm to all.

Yet with Sad Stephan still gone, hearts are heavy, especially the trappers'. Aleut men are not conversant about their feelings and situations. This feature of Aleuts is stark, and disconcerted even Osmond, who was *anything* but a magpie. Yet this characteristic contrasts ironically as regards weeping: For Aleut men will shed tears publicly in non-funerary situations, something not common in males of northern European heritage.

However, when Aleut men gather, banter is often absent. A half-dozen will sit, perhaps doing some task, and there will be an occasional word or three, and then all will fall quiet. The archetypal terse Vermonter would be at home amongst the Aleuts, and then some.

There is snow everywhere, and the barracks are cold and drafty, with the men always working and fussing, making it sounder. Two wood stoves were brought from Attu, and a good thing. They do their best with the poor grade of soft Japanese coal. The mountains behind the town, reminiscent of the Attuans' home, shoulder frigid winds that sweep through the town late in the evening.

Infant Titiana's first birthday was celebrated quietly, with Mother and Father proud hosts. From out of nowhere, Papa Mike produced a tiny box of rice candy for this special occasion. "This is my lovely daughter's first birthday present in this world."

❧

January 31, 1943. Otaru Barracks, Japan

A daily routine consists of shoveling snow, going to the clay mines if health permits, keeping warm, and trying to ignore the hunger. Food rations are not adequate. For the first time, I noticed children falling asleep, or just slumping over, during lessons. I've reduced classes from two hours to one hour a day, five days a week.

"I am hungry, Ms. Smith," even Anna [*Tschigorin*] admits. As my assistant teacher and co-child-care monitor, I try and keep her occupied, or at least involved in talk. For, poor child, she is discovering the boredom and erosive nature of "prison-erhood," if Mr. Webster would allow.

To be prisoner is unlike any other experience; years cannot erase either one day or one year of memories of being held contrary to one's free will. A prisoner, once freed, never forgets. They're left with a fear that a morning will come and they will awake a prisoner again.

The one lesson I've retained over the decades is that this, or any form of inhumanity, is *not* God's will.

<u>February 11, 1943. Otaru Barracks, Japan</u>
Constable Osimi and Father Wu arrived riding alongside Mr. Babushka with today's provisions (on Thursdays provisioning occurs in the early morning). Mr. Osimi convened all adults and, with Father Wu translating into Chinese, announced that Stephan Zacharoff was found dead of "exposure" several miles distant. My translation into English wasn't complete before there was weeping, for many (even the adults, now) are becoming increasingly able in Japanese.

Provisioning was then completed. No further explanations were given, and when asked about Sad Stephan's remains, Chief Constable Osimi just shook his head and went off. Father Wu told me (in Chinese) that he doubted any ceremony was performed, a harsh fact.

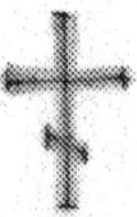

The news struck Strong Ivan and Old Ivan hard, very hard. They'd trapped with him every year for decades and the bond was close. They wept—Strong Ivan profusely. Philamon will hold a funeral service on Saturday. He, even more than others, is horrified that the Japanese allowed Sad Stephan's remains to go unheralded from this life to the eternal. This is a most profound transition in the Orthodox view of the soul.

It is late and I write by candlelight. In honor of my function as scribe, I'm given unlimited access to Philamon's votive candles, but I ration myself to one per week. My "quarters" are now a tiny monastic cell constructed from scavenged tin and wood, an effusive mark of kindness that I repeatedly tried to decline. It is a balm to my guilt that I've made it our infirmary, when needed.

So this explains why the single "Edison" light, even prior to midnight when it is turned off, casts insufficient light into my cubicle.

A storm, heavy with the wettest, largest *blobs* of snow I've ever seen, discharges seemingly tons over everything. The sounds of a freight being formed in the nearby railroad yard are muffled. Occasionally, the wind strikes the barracks harshly, reminding me, and surely the others, of Attu.

I feel terrible, for Osmond and I never spoke to Stephan, or took any pains to extend friendship. We might have invited him specifically into our home; we did *other* adults. Yet it didn't occur to me to invite Sad Stephan. Despite shyness, Aleuts consider an invitation absolute, for they are endlessly social. So, if invited, Stephan would have come.

But we never invited Stephan, even once. And I must take responsibility for this omission, and not pass it along to poor Osmond. Mother was all hospitality! I can still remember her serving tea to the most humble "coolie" and saying in perfectly horrid Chinese, "I do hope the sun rises everyday on your roof." I would try to correct her use of this traditional Chinese greeting, but she never got it right, strictly speaking. She would ask, *so* hopefully, "Oh, Lila Ann, isn't it close enough?"

❧

<u>February 14, 1943. Otaru Barracks. Japan</u>
It is St. Valentine's Day, which is not observed by Orthodoxy. Still, I did my best to manufacture Valentines, and to give them to each child. Last year, I explained it as a custom "in Iowa." Sometime, well, I take shortcuts. This year there is no candy available.

It is a Sunday, so no one worked, and there was church. All remain dejected over the death of Sad Stephan. The treatment of his mortal remains reminds all of the heartless disposal of Anise Sergief en route. "Don't these outrages foretell what might become of us if we were to die here??" No one gives voice to this fear, but I know every adult ponders it.

I speak rudimentary Aleut now, and hope to continue improvement. Friend Annie and her Mike are my main tutors, and I've become their Iowa protégé. My word book grows.

Villagers have come to enjoy my accounts of Iowa. Delbert is at least as foreign to them as Attu was to me, and the telling and listening helps us all—and the children!

The children most of all enjoy my modest accounts of crickets and fireflies, and most are convinced their dear teacher has made up fireflies. It has become a running item of humor with us all.

There is little enough of that.

❧

<u>February 16, 1943. Otaru Barracks, Japan</u>
Drs. Nagai and Takata came today, the former with his nurse. They used my room as a clinic, and during this time Dr. Takata and I conversed at length over tea. This time, I asked more questions than he. Within certain limits, he was refreshingly forthright.

He is eighty-three years of age, and long retired from medicine. Dr. Takata's background is unique: He lived in

France for almost fifteen years. His father was the first Japanese Ambassador to France. After studying medicine in Paris, his specialty eventually became children, and he pioneered that field in Japan.

He was widowed ten years ago, and his two daughters, grandchildren, and great-grandchildren live elsewhere in Japan, but his son's family lives in Sapporo, the central city on Hokkaido Island. It is only an hour distant by train.

"We were all very happy."

When I inquired about the use of past tense, he smiled and went on to one of his favorite topics, anthropology.

Dr. Takata is extraordinarily interested in the Aleut people, who he used to think might be an extension of the Ainu people of Hokkaido Island. Seeing Aleuts, he has changed his mind, astounded (as all Japanese are) how much Aleuts resemble Japanese. Without exception, Aleuts who work at the clay mines are assumed to be Japanese. The mine personnel were furious with the villagers' inability to follow spoken orders. But when they understood the problem, they marveled at how someone can *be* Japanese, yet not speak a word of it and speak *another tongue* so utterly unintelligible!

He had questions about my background, especially my linguistic "half," which I did my best to answer. Finally, I decided to risk our acquaintanceship and raised the issue about our children not having enough to eat, and how it oppresses their parents. I *almost* informed him of the pilfering of foodstuffs en route here from Attu, but did not.

His response was a sad shake of the head and that "he was an old man whose few official connections long ago joined the deceased." Then he added that food shortages were now nationwide. "The war weighs heavily on this country's resources." And that concluded our visit, for Dr. Nagai's duties were completed.

He bade me farewell with a European-type bow and, quite the courtly gentleman, clicked his heels a bit and was escorted

out by Dr. Nagai and his nurse. Mr. Ojiwa [*a constable/guard*]
saw them out and when he returned expounded on a topic
to the accompaniment of proud clucks of his tongue and a
genial smile.

Luna and Mavra, the Chirikof twins, of all the youngsters
speak the best Japanese and since they overheard, confirmed the
gist of Mr. Ojiwa's talk: "Mrs. Smith, Mr. Ojiwa said the old man
is most best trapper in all Japan." Somehow, "physician" came
out "trapper," I'm sure. We translators have a difficult calling!

February 28, 1943. Otaru Barracks, Japan
Constable "Big Jaw" has become a problem, especially with
adults already distraught over nagging food shortages. The
children suffer; Friend Annie's little Titiana is in jeopardy, for if
the mother suffers, so does the infant. Mike gives virtually all
his ration to Annie, and is losing weight. Most are.

Yet problems persist.

"Big Jaw," who refuses to allow anyone to call him by
name, insists on all bowing to him, and if these honors aren't
forthcoming on each and every occasion, there is shouting and
violent gestures with his "wand of office."

He terrifies children already terrified.

But such harassment might be tolerable if hunger were not
its daily, even hourly, companion.

The snows are extraordinarily heavy and the men labor to
clear the roof and footpaths each morning. I've never seen
anything like it.

March 8, 1943. Otaru Barracks, Japan
I have been ill, as most have. A flu has swept through, and
ended the life of Elder Tschigorin, age eighty-four. By blood or

marriage he is related to most, and all mourn and wear black armbands.

The constables insist on removal of his body with official disposition, and the villagers refuse, in view of past circumstances. Services are pending.

Though weak, I collect as much information about Elder Tschigorin as possible. Later, I shall write down what I've learned; such a venerable old man, indeed any of my new family, will not pass from this life without notice.

Elder Tschigorin was Osmond's sole chum. Though their bond was founded on that "foul weed," it was important to Osmond beyond that. Our Ancient one departed this unfair life quietly with his beloved imp Zephryis [*his great-grandson, age 12*] at his side.

<u>March 11, 1943. Otaru Barracks, Japan</u>
To document Elder Tschigorin's "story" was difficult due to his great age. Even "Old" Nicholas Andreanof, now our oldest Attuan (age fifty-nine), says that Elder Tschigorin was almost middle age by the time of his first clear memories. Church records provide another, but fading source.

The church register was destroyed in a fire along with the old Chapel in 1931. Its information now exists only in Philamon's head, though he assures that "duplicates are in Irkutsk." This is where he spent his year (1919) studying to become a church Reader. (Philamon was a member of the last class of Alaska Orthodox faithful to be so schooled prior to the Bolsheviks closing all seminaries.)

So it is mostly these sources that provided the main threads of the deceased's story.

Elder Tschigorin's given name was Peter. He was "born in 1859 during the years of the 'Benevolent' Czar Alexander the Second, who ended slavery in Russia." He was a great trapper and hunter, and at story times told about hunting sea otter for the "Bostons," an old-timer term meaning any fur buyer or trader.

By his youth the otter were virtually gone, so each animal was an accomplishment and was traded for much stock and provisions. He was married twice. First to an Atkan [*Atka is the first Aleut village east of Attu*] named Mary who (in Aleut) everyone called Mary Longnose, and who was quite homely but of a wonderful disposition. They had three children, but only son John survived a terrible epidemic that swept the Aleutians. John is the father of Kusma and Old Ivan Tschigorin, Elder Tschigorin's grandsons.

His second wife was named Anise from distant Akutan Village, hundreds of miles east toward the mainland. The poor thing never adjusted to her strange distant home. It was probably this that resulted in mental confusion. She died very young, childless. Her fate was a deep sorrow for which Elder Tschigorin never forgave himself. He had tried everything to make her happy. Some, however, attribute the misfortune to unskilled matchmaking by a young priest from Russia.

At this time, around the turn of the century, steamwhalers would occasionally stop by Attu headed north, and the villagers came to have fear of them.

Everyone was surprised when Elder Tschigorin shipped with one of these. "Perhaps it was his sadness over Anise" that caused this unhappy decision. Fortunately, he returned three years later, though in frail and ill health.

He never discussed his years away, except to say there were many things best not experienced by Aleuts and this is why God gave them their home in the Aleutians. "This is where we should stay."

After his return, his activities as a trapper and hunter continued with much honor until old age forced him into retirement. He could make any of the great Aleut crafts. He was a valued though demanding teacher for the young men. According to Elder Tschigorin, his brightest protégé was young Zephryis, his great-grandson.

Though Elder Tschigorin died in this far-distant land, all agree that God will return his soul and spirit to Attu.

March 17, 1943. Otaru Barracks, Japan
A quiet sense of outrage and resignation dominated: Elder Tschigorin's remains were taken and his ashes returned in a clay urn. The Attuans, if for no other reason, think their captors uncivilized. "Nobody ever did Aleut people so much bad," admits Philamon.

By resigned, I don't mean they reacted in silence.

Constables "Big Jaw," Ojiwa, and Nasimi, overseen by Mr. Osimi, removed Elder Tschigorin over the most emphatic objections of First and Second Chiefs Alexi and Peter. During the removal, Philamon also protested, even reading from the "holy book." He demanded burial in consecrated ground, such as a Christian cemetery. All was to no avail.

That night I read aloud Elder Tschigorin's "Life Story" and all were pleased at the results of my interviews. Unfortunately, it was in English so I provided long pauses to allow or translations.

Negative facts in a European world-view aren't necessarily the same in the Aleut world-view; therefore, to omit something like plainness or odd-sounding nicknames would be considered poor work. I am learning slowly. My position as "Village Gazetteer" is similar to that in Shansi Province as a girl when I was publisher, editor, and star reporter for the monthly Chinese-language *Mennonite Clarion*. It was my brainchild, and Father and Mother were extraordinarily proud, though only Father could read it.

March 26, 1943. Otaru Barracks, Japan
The life of a prisoner is boredom, routine, and vulnerability, and when such routine is broken one knows at once something bad has occurred, yet for the first time my new family con-ceals. It must be ghastly, for more conversations are in Aleut now, and, knowing of my increasing skill in the language, in *furtive* Aleut.

I hesitated to ask Friend Annie or Mike (they would not lie, for this is considered a sin) but eventually when I did, I was told it "was too much ugly for our Iowa sister's worry."

So I continue to teach, care for children, and mind my business. I find myself oddly hurt to be so excluded. Usually, my counsel is sought, and last night I lay awake fearing they have heard I am being removed to Honshu Island, as was offi-cialdom's original intent. Then I feel terrible guilt for worrying about only Lila Ann.

April 3, 1943. Otaru Barracks, Japan
After almost a week of mystery, I've deduced that one of the Chirikof twins was indecently approached by a constable, and I expect it was "Big Jaw." Twice the men held meetings in the "kitchen," a utility annex built in back that shields the cooking stoves and surrounding area from direct weather. I'm sup-posing there is disagreement about what must be done.

My exclusion is now understandable.

These matters are *never* discussed between Aleut men and women, save only in most extreme situations. They are a *strait-laced* people, Osmond oft observed. In a rare moment of levity, he supposed even his mother would approve of the Attuans, at least in this way.

True, occasionally their humor is ribald, in a respectable sort of way. But, nonetheless, serious situations referring to private matters remain so.

Anyway, tensions have arisen in our barracks.

The Chirikof twins have been virtually cordoned off, with their father Old Albert and brother Young Albert on duty singly or together; usually Strong Ivan is close by. I hope there is resolution soon, and that it be prudent.

April 8, 1943. Otaru Barracks, Japan
Since April 4 was a Sunday, it was observed in peace, yet after services a pall hung over the barracks. But on Monday morning Alexi, Peter, and Philamon directed all of the women and children to the rear of the barracks when the watch was changed. (At this hour the constable coming on duty inventories coal supplies and the one going off escorts the work detail to the clay mine on his way home.)

This morning Alexi informed the watch they wanted to speak to Chief Constable Osimi. "Big Jaw" was the constable coming on duty and Mr. Nasimi was going off—the latter the favorite, the former the unfavorite, as it were. Big Jaw made a ruckus, insisting work schedules be kept. But Alexi remained steadfast. "There will be no work until we talk with Chief Constable."

Mr. Nasimi recognized the "fat was in the fire" and hurried off to contact Chief Constable Osimi after a brief but voluble argument between the two officials.

Big Jaw was furious, menacing everyone with his scepter of office, a stout bamboo rod. This frightened the children, for though a slight man, Big Jaw has a loud, commanding voice and long ago intimidated all with his manner.

Even with my meager Japanese, I understood that Big Jaw threatened to take away or reduce rations if they persisted. I must say that Alexi and Peter remained composed, doing their best to ignore him. Big Jaw continued to rant.

Then, from out of nowhere, Heratina (mother of twins Mavra and Luna Chirikof) stormed forward brandishing the coal prod. This was such a sudden and extraordinary sortie that none of the men stopped her. She squared off with Big Jaw, each vying for an opening to strike. Lord knows what might have happened if she weren't at once taken and physically lifted by Nicholas [*Nickels Chirikof, Heratina's brother-in-law*] while Peter and Alexi called for order.

Poor Old Albert, the most gentle of men, looked on in confusion and horror at his wife. They say opposites attract, and Old Albert and Heratina prove this, for all of us know that Heratina has more "sauce" than any two men amongst the villagers. And Strong Ivan—despite Heratina's struggles and volley of furious Aleut—did banner work relieving her of the coal prod. Anyone in her vicinity was in danger, albeit unintentionally, of being struck with it.

And, the irony of the matter reached its climax when Big Jaw finally retaliated by striking the confused Old Albert across the shoulder with his stick. And this is the scene that Chief Constable Osimi found when he entered with Mr. Nasimi and Ojiwa. A strange thing then happened: as if all were contained in the reels of a failed motion-picture machine, everyone stopped in place.

Quickly, and as if thoroughly rehearsed, all the constables withdrew under the Chief Constable's fixed gaze. Old Albert rubbed his broad shoulders, adding to the strangeness by laughing and shaking his head. Then Alexi and Peter, followed by the Chief Constable, retired to the annex in back and conferred.

In just minutes, Constable Osimi departed with Big Jaw while Mr. Ojiwa assumed the morning shift, busily counting chunks of coal, keeping the routine of the hour. Mr. Nasimi gathered the day's work party and off they went, leaving us non-miners, as it were, behind.

By evening, the situation had become village legend, with events being retold and reenacted, especially by Zephryis, Alfred, and Nicholas, who took Japanese parts, while (quite ironically, really) the Chirikof twins vied between them to take their mother's. Mostly, it has worked into a compromise, and they alternate. The other parts are filled on a rotating basis.

Initially, Heratina was irritated by these dramas, yet after two days allowed this amusement without comment, but those who know her realize her nature will come through. She unfailingly loves to laugh.

The men gently sport with Old Albert about wife Heratina, who attends his bruise, rubbing in an ointment wild-crafted by herself. She is very proud of him, of course. In his youth, I'm told, Old Albert could lift even more than Strong Ivan, and indeed he is still built with amazing bulk and compactness.

There is no further mention or discussion of the incident that resulted in this confrontation. Mr. Big Jaw has been blessedly absent for four days, and I'm guessing his duties have ceased. I thank God for that, and how it all was resolved.

April 22, 1943. Otaru Barracks, Japan
Tomorrow is Good Friday. It seems decades ago that Osmond and I experienced our first Russian Orthodox Easter, or

Paskha. Lent came and went without fanfare, and Philamon laments the difficulty of celebrating Paskha with proper reverence in this barracks. He, like all of the villagers, misses their tiny chapel. It was the cornerstone of village life. Food aplenty is also part of the season, and that is of course absent.

"What is Easter without a feast to our Savior?" almost everyone laments, especially the children.

Faith comes without effort to my friends, but not for me. I would shock all my friends both here and especially in Iowa if they knew this. I've always been part of Mennonite life, and most would assume that my faith is most steadfast.

Indeed I do read Scripture, I do pray, but with difficulty, and often my heart, and especially my soul, is unsure.

Initially there were six of us girls taken and held by General Lon Shi. He hoped to exact ransom from our home governments in the form of modern weaponry. His subordinates thought his plan a poor one. After being ransomed, I told the various consular officials there had been *six* women originally held. Yet American and British sources circulated a figure of *four* as the number who survived the year and a half. It was as if two of us had never existed.

We were all daughters or wives (two of them) of missionaries. Yet our diverse faiths did not mitigate the wretched, slow deaths of the two souls, and the treatment of us four who survived. I remember our nights of prayer—we'd take turns leading our group each day, if possible.

It is a terrible thing to be angry with one's Maker. I remember poor Alice Deifenbakker, who'd been such a pretty girl. One awful evening when our group began to pray she lamented, "Prayers to God!? God delivered His own Son to the hands of murderers, why would He help us?"

<u>May 2, 1943. Otaru Barracks, Japan</u>
Evidently a local service organization has donated blankets, nails, and a modest amount of lumber. Though the blankets are a case of better late than never, the nails and lumber are prized by our menfolk, who constantly cobble together things to keep the barracks whole and reasonably comfortable. Of course, there was a presentation ceremony.

Though late for this ceremony, afterward Chief Constable Osimi asked me directly—in slow, careful Japanese which I now am having limited success with—if I might be willing to do light *day work* (I *think* this is what he meant) for pay if the situation ever arose.

I said, of course, if the pay were in foodstuffs for the children and mothers. He agreed, leaving Lila Ann in a very curious state of mind.

<u>May 15, 1943. Otaru Barracks, Japan</u>
Something dreadful happened at sea during the night of May 13–14. We are a stone's throw from Otaru Harbor, hence the open sea. I was awakened by Friend Annie during the night, for Titiana was fussing and she was attending her.

She pointed in horror out the window, and the entire western skyline was pulsing with what had to be a giant and catastrophic conflagration. Annie awoke Mike. "That is at sea. The open sea."

Mike, possibly more than any other, has become familiar with the geography of the area. He works in the mine—going to and fro each day—but also he purposefully volunteers for work parties venturing beyond the mine. He is curious about all things, and this includes our involuntary home.

We watched silently while the sky, so bright with the distant fires, intermittently cast our shadows on the opposite wall of the barracks. The sky would become positively brilliant in a sudden burst of light, then the light would die down—only to have it repeated. After an hour or somewhat more, it subsided to a dull glow, then was gone.

It was fortunate, I believe, that only we three saw it—others slept, including Mr. Ojiwa, who "watches big time when sleeping," as the children put it. Mike said he'd inform Alexi in the morning, but thought this disaster might well be no accident. Whatever it was certainly involved the destruction of shipping on a vast scale.

The following day our fears were confirmed, for even the constables were late changing shifts, and one (Mr. Nasimi) had clearly been weeping. All seemed emotionally devastated, and at the clay mine, many long-time employees were absent.

Sometimes in our routine of discomfort and worry, I forget there is a World War beyond the confines of our tiny world. The disgrace of war is too easy for me to put out of mind.

ᡐᡝ

May 23, 1943. Otaru Barracks, Japan
Three civilians appeared today during church services. They seemed unconcerned about barging in uninvited, and strode about the barracks, their noses wrinkling from the natural smells of forty-plus people packed into a structure which is, at the *largest*, the size of two schoolrooms. This persists, despite all efforts at cleanliness, which are very admirable. Such is the result of drastic overpacking, with ONE bar of soap rationed per week.

They toured as if in a zoo. But business seemed to be their concern, for two were making a case for one thing or another with the third, who, with a handkerchief held to his nose, didn't seem persuaded toward whatever ends the other two desired.

Then they drove off leaving a hodgepodge of translations of "overheard" Japanese. My eavesdropping had been nil, and those of the children, the real Japanese linguists, wasn't much better.

The Aleut people live on, unconcerned about this breach— just another thorn. I am worried though, and hope to find out what their business was.

ᡐᡝ

May 26, 1943. Otaru Barracks, Japan
The most critical of village needs has improved. Food! Our rice rations are raised, and there was an increase in vegetables and even fish parts (tails, heads, etc.) on occasion, until finally today, an *entire box of herring*!!

The villagers were absolutely distracted—overjoyed—to see not only food, but that familiar to them. Fish! Whole, shiny, gloriously nourishing fish.

There has been more laughter in the last three days than in all the previous months. One ongoing and desperate omission is canned milk. All, especially the mothers, beg the constables for it. But this recent bounty is a wonderful change for the better. With improving weather, I pray it is a trend!

<u>June 2, 1943. Otaru Barracks, Japan</u>
Patience has provided an answer to our "mysterious" visitors in the form Dr. Nagai's monthly health clinic. He was once again accompanied by Dr. Takata.

During the clinic Dr. Takata and I drank tea and talked in French, which affords us privacy. This visit he was attended by two women and a third elderly man, clearly Dr. Takata's domestic help. They set up a low table and served. My old bones take to sitting on the provided floor mats with creaky resolve.

I described the visit of the mysterious civilians, and he told me straight away—in confidence—that it was the manager of the railroad who declined to sell it to the two other men, both from the prefecture seat, Sapporo. They have a business idea related to wartime industry, but the manager declined. This added some relief, and suddenly the good physician said, "I think Chief Constable Osimi's offer to you will offer distinct advantages, will they not?."

When I told Dr. Takata there had been no offer, he laughed, confessing to getting ahead of things due to old age. "Actually, Mrs. Smith, he discussed his idea at our Rotary Club meeting, which when war sadly was declared we renamed the Otaru Wednesday Club"—then he chuckled about that—"but it is the old Rotary Club. Rotary is too American, you see."

I was surprised there were Rotary Clubs in Japan, especially in Otaru. He went on to explain more. It seems, since made aware of our arrival, the members of the Otaru Rotary have become involved in the Attuans' welfare to a limited extent. "It is *one* of our Fellowship projects."

Dr. Takata explained that the war effort brought several special club projects into play. He assured that Chief Constable Osimi's business idea for me would be forthcoming, but that it would be disrespectful for him to broach details now. He then gracefully changed the topic away from war business to questions about the Attuans' way of life. Transitions are a rhetorical device at which he excels.

Late night ruminations resulted in sleeplessness.

Osmond had been a Rotarian, and I believe at one time Uncle Thomas was also. Osmond eventually quit because it was suggested by a member that Mennonites had been war slackers.

And Uncle Thomas? I can't imagine him joining any club, but I do remember that he did attend.

After my talk with Dr. Takata, somehow this fraternal *relationship* (?) between east and west—by societies and governments so *intent* on killing one another—resulted in a major case of the "blues." The irony of the situation's humanity testified to the witlessness of war, and how this flaw-of-humanity visited moral outrage on those I love.

Faith is a difficult course.

My heart continues to equivocate about the efficacy and truth contained in the Essentials of Jesus. I know this is selfish on my part, yet it is difficult to be *selfless*.

During my first twenty years Father and Mother were entirely devoted to those Essentials. And I cannot cease thinking how dubious their devotion was in contrast to their untimely demise. All were casualties of warfare, save poor Emmett [*Lila Ann's first husband*] in the flu epidemic. Mother, Father, brother, friends—now Osmond, a good, honorable man and husband.

<u>June 7, 1943. Otaru Barracks, Japan</u>
The plan for our *non-mining*, stay-at-home work is sewing. Constable Osimi asked if I would "lead" a sewing shop, as it were, for he'd heard my abilities celebrated by the village men. We would be paid, of course, like those who work in the clay mine. He then unveiled two machines in poor condition— yet proudly brought in by workmen—and I recognized two things at once, may God forgive me: One, that I had a working knowledge of both, one a Wilcox and Gibbs, and the other a Singer Commercial. I guessed that few in Otaru did, for espe- cially the former requires experience and some training.

I reminded him (perhaps my heart had been hardened by the previous night's ruminations) that speaking only for me, I would not work on anything connected with the military. He assured me this was not the case; in fact, that it would be on civilian clothes, mostly children's.

I agreed, but then Lila Ann, sensing a bargaining position, persevered.

"I want my pay to be in the form of canned milk. Not script. The children desperately need the nourishment."

The poor man got a sad, almost resigned look, and said that this would be "most difficult." He kept repeating this in slow, clear Japanese. Then he looked at me, drew himself up a bit, and said, "Even Japanese families are without this. All I can do is promise my best, but I cannot promise anything beyond."

So there we were, at loggerheads. I must admit that I knew how beneficial an alternative to the clay mines would be, for some of the younger women would be excused from work there—work they hated and the men hated to see. Certainly Constable Osimi sensed this, and so in the end I yielded, and I am now Chief Threader and Stitcher of the Otaru Barracks Sewing Shop.

This is a strange life.

June 23, 1943. Otaru Barracks, Japan

A busy time is now upon us, and that is good. Summer has also arrived, and is another positive development. The weather here is far better, in my view, than in Attu. Much more sun and warm weather.

So there is gardening for subsistence (we were given cabbage seeds!), sewing as work, and dealing with shortages, though less now because of the season.

I can honestly write that all fare better, though a half-dozen of the men have developed chronic respiratory ailments because of clay dust. Dr. Nagai has not, in the village view, interceded in our interests either enough, or at all.

This is our captive souls' greatest trouble, for the affliction, of course, grows worse with continued work.

Two Otaruites have entered our life: Mr. Seguda, the machinist, and Madam Fukama, Circuit Garment Inspector.

Mr. Seguda attends the needs of the machines when matters get beyond me and parts are needed, which is not infrequent. He is an incurable "sad sack" though a well-meaning soul. There is not a problem he doesn't *at once* deem absolutely and completely impossible to rectify.

Then he goes about resolving it expertly, and within reasonable time limits. He is a tiny, wizened man, a master of the machinist trade.

There is little to recommend Madam Fukama. She arrives every two or three days and inspects the bundles of finished goods, criticizing the work—rejecting some, accepting most.

My co-workers, most still in the apprentice stages, are terrified of her and hide when she comes in with her two woeful servant girls and one elderly man; she treats all awfully. I cannot write any further about Madam Fukama or I shall risk rash, un-Christian words.

And in the midst of improved spirits, a rumor has begun and spread that all will be returning to Attu by the route we came, via ship. When? "Before the year is out," most have decided.

This cannot be true, for even our meager news informs that the war is anything but resolved, though last week Mr. Ojiwa remarked that the warring parties—the U.S. and Japan—have now recognized the might of Japan, and "are coming to terms for an armistice."

But, in truth, the rumor began before this snippet of dubious journalism. I try and strike neutral ground between Mr. Gloomy Gus and Miss Happy Tidings.

June 28, 1943. Otaru Barracks, Japan

Monday, and as usual with our new "industrial schedule," boxes of batch-sewing were unloaded from the wagon by Madam Fukama's people, with her raining invective upon them in the manner of an angry teamster.

I received the batches, which entails the usual Japanese administrative flurry of paperwork, making the Alaska Territorial Schools and Mennonite Overseas Service appear like paperwork midgets.

In the process, I discovered the military uniforms.

Since this violated my agreement, I informed Madam Fukama at once that I would not work on them, and briefly explaining the conflict to my co-workers in a mixture of English and Aleut, I retired to my room. I fault myself for not having explained this before, but I'd assumed my agreement with Chief Constable Osimi stood firm. The sewing day came to a halt and Madam Fukama flew into a grand tizzy.

She insisted that Mr. Toshihara beat me and others for refusing to work, which frightened Mr. Toshihara. He fled across the railroad yard to a switchman's shack, the closest phone. We were left with a livid Madam Fukama. She stood outside my door and heaped abuse on me, I assume, for Japanese at that speed is beyond Lila Ann.

Evidently Constable Osimi was in Sapporo and not available. Returning with Mr. Toshihara, Mr. Ojiwa put in an appearance instead, and implored Madam Fukama to leave off until Chief Constable could be consulted on the issue.

Furthermore, our chiefs were at the clay mine. Despite a mixture of three or four languages, Mr. Ojiwa maneuvered a difficult negotiation, and I agreed to put aside the two batches of military uniforms, which left three batches of adult clothes. So there was work to do.

That evening, Alexi and Peter, along with other adults, listened as I explained how prisoners of war cannot be forced to work on military projects, either directly or indirectly. I *tried* to explain how controversial this had been during the last war, and how it came to be forbidden by international law.

This, I'm afraid, made little sense; sewing was sewing. For the first time I became exasperated with my friends' boundless innocence. As calmly as I could, I said they could do what they wished, but I would stand by international law. Also, I would *never help* the military brutes who'd murdered my husband, an unarmed non-combatant.

I withdrew and lay down, trembling with anger. I have never known such ferocity in myself, and cannot think it but a lamentable development. And so late in life.

Overwhelmed by such an emotional expenditure, I fell asleep, waking with Friend Annie seated beside me. Seeing me awake, she said, "We don't know much except about our home."

<u>July 4, 1943. Otaru Barracks, Japan</u>
Independence day fell on a Sunday, and since this is one national holiday understood by the villagers, it rather served

two duties. They included George Washington and others in their prayers and songs. And Philamon felt sure the Lord would give his blessings to the United States and bring victory to them, "so we can go home."

Since the difficulty over the uniforms, I am viewed as a trouble-maker, with Constable Osimi and *of course* Madam Fukama my keenest critics. I realize the latter lost face, a situation into which I usually avoid thrusting any Oriental. The uniforms, contrary to her wishes, were *not* worked upon by anyone here.

I knew that a significant number of the villagers wanted to work on them—or at least saw no harm in doing so—but without my efforts, the machine work would be impossible.

"Don't let that old woman"—I'm pretty sure that is not the best of translations—"take money and food from your pockets! She is the enemy!" Madame Fukama ranted. I'm flattered to report these words discredited her at once, and she was pelted by "spitwads" when her back was turned. For this, the children were lectured at top volume by Constable Ojiwa, who is all bark, thank God! It is a troublesome skill some of the boys have, but in this case. . . !

But Madam Fukama's rantings disclose a truth:

All the Japanese—military, civilian, and otherwise—view the Attuans as Japanese citizens, and Attu as Japanese territory.

I don't and certainly the Attuans don't.

<u>July 22, 1943. Otaru Barracks, Japan</u>
The pure *busyness* of these long summer days has reduced considerably my literary contributions as Village Scribe and Historian, an unofficial title. Though, when I do settle in to write, I am given respectful solitude. Adults quiet the children, saying, "Mrs. Smith is thinking, don't you know!"

Yet most of my entries are made either after the children are to bed, or before. I have *gallons* of ink now, and could go on like pen-masters Melville or Hawthorne if I desired, which I don't. (If only Lila Ann were even approximately close to their art!)

I am so tired each day, I must write in short entries, but date them all-in-one, keeping content and relative time unified. In short, as village chronicler, I cheat!

The greatest time-consumer is the sewing-batch work, with the cabbage patch a distant second. I start early each morning, except on Monday when Madam Fukama shows up with new batches and to inspect those completed. Plus there is her labyrinth of record-keeping. The villagers have an established Aleut term for her, and it isn't nice. For me, *Madam Fukama* must suffice. She is an overbearing woman, and her *wards* suffer through each day, it seems. On bad days, she supplements spoken invective by striking them across the backsides with her walking stick.

Batches consist usually of used children's clothes, toddler size on up, freshly laundered; next are used adult clothes. Only in recent days did we receive bolts and patterns to make new garbs—strange white robes in adult sizes. I think they might be religious in nature.

My loyal full-time roster of seamstresses are Friend Annie, Agafia Sergief, Anna Tschigorin, and her Auntie Mary; then Heratina and Binni Chirikof, and Lena Ivanof.

Other village women fill in part-time, for in some weeks batches are larger and more demanding than others.

Those part-timers spend the remainder of their hours in the garden and on the demands of domestic work. So these responsibilities have the advantage of completely excusing all adult village women from duties in the clay mine. This is a significant load off their menfolk's minds, for health problems due to clay dust continue.

The children help, but their "help" and our work often conflict, and we are on the verge of appointing Anna Tschigorin full-time monitor. This is especially needed for the *imps*, with Zephryis eternally in the forefront as First and Second Imp.

All water for our cabbage patch must be hauled from down the street—the closest spigot. Our water people have come to be known as the "Walking Clouds" in my poor translation from the Aleut. Whatever the term, it is all hard, time-consuming work, with hindrances at every turn.

Our bane for the batch-work is the sewing machines (and for the garden, not Peter Rabbit, but Japanese gophers). The machines are ancient treadle models (one converted poorly to electric power)—long since worn to exhaustion by heavy commercial work in a *sailmaker's* shop!

My experience, but especially *Master Seguda's* continued miracle-making, enables sewing operations to continue. There is not an original part left on either machine.

Unfortunately, the gophers have no ready solution. The men have fashioned traps from bits and pieces of wire and springs, but despite their long experience in trapping, the gophers prevail. We are, in short, losing the gardening war; this has caused the animal to become reviled amongst the villagers, especially our Walking Clouds, the primary gardeners.

Much of the villagers' pay is spent on tobacco. Aleuts do not understand budgeting and prioritizing of purchased items. It is difficult to witness the children wanting, yet smokers (men *and* women alike) spending sparse resources on that foul-smelling, unhealthy, and costly herb.

The "pay" for our work is just enough to qualify as pay. It is a pittance. I hoard mine in hopes my "agreement" re: canned milk be met. Chief Constable Osimi avoids my glance those few times he's appeared of late, and milk remains absent.

Wednesday afternoons are store days, and Heratina and Lena Ivanof are the official shoppers. Little foodstuff is

available in the store, an establishment closed to me. I'm
absolutely not allowed beyond the confines of the barracks
yard.

One reason for this, I suppose, is wartime security nonsense,
but the other is more understandable. "You would cause a
townwide sensation, and all work would come to a halt," Asst.
Constable Ojiwa points out with great humor.

Few white women are seen in Otaru nowadays—or perhaps
at any time—and there is my height.

One word for me in Japanese is "Walking Crane," or "Old
Woman Who Towers." I am easily almost a foot higher than
any Japanese woman, and a half-foot than Japanese men.

In America, this was a great social disadvantage for girls.
In Japan it seems it is nothing less than fantastic, in a positive
sense, as Americans might admire a splendid skyscraper!!

July 31, 1943. Otaru Barracks, Japan
When all seems tolerable the intolerable returns. Chief
Constable Osimi proudly announced yesterday that through
valiant efforts we are now *self-sustaining*, and no more food
rations will be issued. All staples now, in view of our "afflu-
ence via wages," are to be purchased. Bathhouse, health services, water, and such municipal services, though, will continue
to be provided at no cost.

To commemorate the occasion, and as a reward, all of us
were given slippers for indoor use. (Even after all this time, our
guards view in horror the Attuans' continued practice of
wearing footwear indoors.)

This announcement done, Chief Constable departed with
the two individuals who were present for the occasion,
somehow connected to the gift of slippers.

That evening the adults were not convinced this was a
serious development. In fact, they saw the gift of slippers as a

sign of our hosts' good will. A windfall, as it were. Sadly Alexi, who like the rest, has no concept of budgeting, saw no problem in buying rice and such provisions. We were being paid, after all.

There is no concept of the *amount of all monies earned* vs the *amount needed to buy all supplies*. So they don't realize that this figure must sustain them entirely, including non-food items, such as tobacco.

Friend Annie and husband Mike are the exceptions, including to a lesser degree Heratina and Lena, the shoppers. "Well, they must be going to give us more scrip," Heratina guessed in her mixture of English and Aleut, "for they take all we have each week, and we even owe more, they say."

Lena, in her meek way, is even more suspicious than Heratina. Mike, as is his practice, says nothing publicly. The most worldly of all the villagers, he harbors his knowledge carefully so not to offend. In private, he shook his head and predicted, "I think, maybe, breakers ahead."

Time, I fear, will convey sad news for my misguided, innocent friends.

September 1, 1943. Otaru Barracks, Japan
As my dear Uncle Thomas would say, events went "gunnysack" on August 14, and there was no resolution until August 28, when I was returned to my friends. The span of time re: my absence is documentable, because Philamon keeps strict record of the calendar, albeit a different one than most. I was removed by the authorities on the first day of the Dormition Fast, and returned on Dormition Day of the Mother of God—the village's patron.

[These segue marks (~) make their first appearance in the 9/1/43 entry, and were inserted by LAS, I assume, contemporaneously. Probably they denote a multi-day effort, i.e., some-

what alleviating her "cheating" mentioned, however whimsically, in the 7/22/43 entry.]

August 14 was a Saturday, and there was batch-work to do—Saturdays are work days. Chief Constable Osimi, however, along with all his assistant constables, appeared an hour early in a great frenzy. We were to be inspected by the "High Commissioner" of something like Homeland Defense.

His office was so lofty that Constable Osimi and his staff maintained a constant stream of urgent invectives and hand-wringing, for the Commissioner, and other important officials, would be here at 10 a.m.

We had three hours.

All normal work—anything—was canceled until after the visit. In fact, as added enticement, Mr. Osimi said we'd not only get the rest of the day off, including us seamstresses, but he would see to it there would be fish along with fresh vegetables and *rice candy* (!!!!)—only if all went well, and our premises passed with high praise.

Then efforts became fever-pitched.

While putting our sewing area into tip-top condition it occurred to me my presence would certainly look out of place, but of course, I was *hardly* a national secret!

This was the only foreboding I had, and it fleeting.

~

With great ceremony, a processional of three machines, two quite grand and elaborate, pulled up, and (it was a very hot day) the Commissioner was escorted up the walk, a parasol held over his head by an aide. Their dress was military, and this made me uneasy.

We'd all lined up—on each side of the room—and when all entered, we bowed deeply to them, and within seconds his eyes locked on me and things went gunnysack at once.

It did not take five minutes for me to be whisked from the building; my parting sight was the Commissioner's top aides severely upbraiding Chief Constable Osimi while the Commissioner stood icily by. I was pushed into the smallest of the automobiles, actually a Ford, by three soldiers. At that moment my attentions were shut off from the outside world by a sack being thrust over my head. Then, very roughly, my arms were tied in back of me at the elbows. I began weeping, for I knew a catastrophe had occurred. Clearly, my presence with "*Japanese Citizen*" (I heard this expression repeated several times) was a severe violation of policy—or even worse.

I was driven at such a speed over the poor roads that I thought the machine might disintegrate. I was hurled repeatedly against metal, unable to protect myself, cutting my head. My memory is not clear, save that I was driven for hours and kept in the car, the sack over my head, and refused water or even a chance to answer nature's call.

It was late when I was half-carried, half-pushed into a room, untied, the sack removed, and that is where I remained, save for interrogations, for the next two weeks.

There were no windows. There was a small ventilator over the door, more of an aperture than a door, made of solid metal plate; the door itself was about three-quarters my height. Finally, a thin mat on cement and two buckets in the corner, one with fresh water. It was horribly close during the day, the heat unbearable, not alleviated, of course, by the single light bulb which was always on. I never knew if it were day or night except that I was given a bowl of thin broth in the morning, and rice balls in the evening.

The interrogations, initially, involved nothing less than what I'd term silliness, regarding my possible presence as a spy. They were quite tedious, and conducted clumsily in Japanese. Each session lasted precisely one hour. A gentleman in a three-piece suit stood by solemnly checking his pocket watch and clucking his tongue. His function I cannot fathom, save as timekeeper, which cannot be right.

Soon, this absurdity was dropped, and the sessions became shorter, clearly more cursory, and after a week, ceased.

Then I was just kept prisoner.

~

There is nothing more to enter, really. I had no reading material, no view, and spent the time baking from the heat and, of course, in ceaseless worry over my eventual destiny. Would I be kept in this room for the duration? That was an oppressive thought.

Then a day short of the second week the door was thrown open, a table and chair brought in, a better bed, and an electric fan. Also, a much larger latrine bucket with carbolic to reduce the oppressive stench.

A few hours later Dr. Takata appeared! Two soldiers followed, both meek and clearly assigned to see to his well-being—in fact, the sole task of one of them was to carry a stool for the good doctor.

"I've learned that you've had a most unpleasant experience."

"They've treated me like livestock."

I did *not* weep. Bruised, surely weighing *pounds* less due to dehydration than when I was shut in, and nearly mad with worry, I had steeled myself. I was filthy, and it stank—which did nothing but confirm the level of my treatment.

"You will be returned today. In fact, I will be accompanying you back. What can I do for you now?"

~

My basic needs began with a private visit to a nearby bathhouse; at the same time my clothes were laundered and quickly dried. While I waited, clad in toga-like attire, basking in newfound cleanliness, I was visited in polite but purposeful succession by a doctor and nurse, then by two young ladies with a proper, if Spartan, meal. But better, while waiting for my clothes, the wonderment of peace and quiet while looking out on *life*—real and so delightfully refreshing in the tiny garden next to the bathhouse, complete with small fish pond.

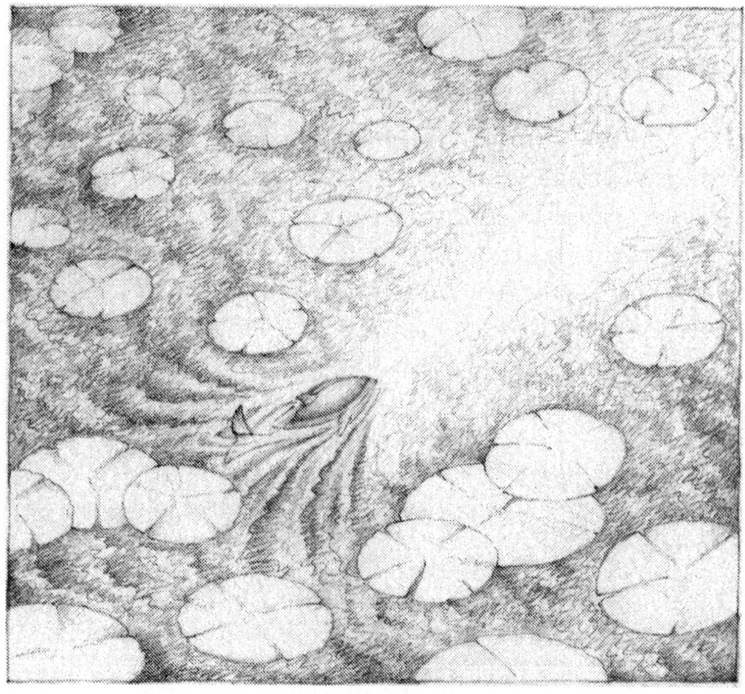

There is no higher praise and worship of God than this tiny patch of life and wonderment. How wonderful this small, humble nook was at that moment—I cannot describe. My prayer of thanks was my most heartfelt in years.

~

The trip back, without the drawback of a sack over my head, Lila Ann enjoyed far more. A vast machine, with an enclosed passenger cab and an open chauffeur's seat, was our carriage. Its interior was all beautiful wood trim and richly upholstered, very spacious. I had never occupied such a luxurious horseless or horse-drawn conveyance.

Dr. Takata and I rode grandly in back, while his maid sat forward with the chauffeur. Preceding *and* following were cars each carrying two military men whose duty it was to attend every need of the procession. (My, but did they excel at bowing.)

Slowly, with *immeasurably* more dignity than my arrival, we drove through Sapporo, Japan, the prefecture seat. It is a very large city. Everywhere were signs, small and large, exhorting the population to sacrifice for the war. Also, these same sort of postings warned of enemies to the Emperor and the grandness of the Japanese struggle in the vast Pacific War. Many of the signs were simply slogans with one or several illustrations.

It seems scarcity has become a part of their war effort. Certainly Dr. Takata knew I could read Japanese, yet there was no effort to hide *this* American evidence concerning the obvious hardship the war is causing in civilian Japan.

We spoke little, for though genial, he is a quiet gentleman. He did seem to assume full responsibility for my mistreatment, which of course is anything but the case.

But after leaving Sapporo City—forced to drive along very slowly because of the poor roads—he talked more. And since we were doing so in French and in the obvious privacy of the *great sedan,* I think he rather relaxed his sense of reserve to explicate current, recent, and not-so-recent events with more candor. Yet I hasten to add that in such a reserved, dignified gentleman, this is done only gently!

He *was* more specific about his medical career, and it was far more auspicious than first related. At the peak of his medical career, he was recalled from his posting in France, where he'd returned to pursue advanced studies and be physician to the Embassy staff. Once home he became the Chief Physician to the extended Imperial Household of the Emperor Yoshihito, a position of august responsibility [*died 1926; father of Emperor Hirohito*]. As with all Imperial families, and especially ancient ones, the extended family is vast, numbering into the hundreds.

"By the time of my retirement in 1934, I had seen much unique to any loyal Japanese subject, let alone a mere physician." And he gestured around him, adding enigmatically, "These are trappings of honored service; nowadays, I wonder if they are to reward or to contain."

I asked nothing at that point, knowing well the cloak which surrounds the Imperial Dynasty of Japan, then and now. Seeing the signs of understanding, Dr. Takata allowed the tiniest of smiles, and added, "Discretion is the highest form of honored service," and then nodded off. It was drawing late into the afternoon, and though the road still was uneven, our motion was more ship-like—a sway, rather than a jolt.

~

My return to the Otaru Barracks was a humbling yet flattering experience; also, one filled with as much emotion in myself (almost) as if I had returned to Delbert [*Iowa*]. Even some of the men (surely Strong Ivan, who weeps readily) came forward and touched me; Friend Annie and I embraced. Oh, I could go on, but it was such a *reunion*. My Attu friends were convinced I was gone for good.

All sewing had ceased, and batch-work had piled up in one corner. Weeks' worth stood undone!! Also, both sewing machines were broken. My services, without a doubt, were required.

Dr. Takata and his entourage looked on, and even they could not help but warm to the occasion. Smiles adorned all faces!

I thanked Dr. Takata with a warm shake of the hand, a western habit not strange to him. And in parting, he allowed a most intriguing addendum: "Mrs. Smith. These are times when human connections far outweigh those Imperial, as it were. So, I look forward to our future talks."

So my interpretation of his departing remark is that Dr. Takata's connections, however lofty with the Showa Emperor [*LAS means Emperor Hirohito*], cannot be tested too severely.

❧

<u>October 6, 1943. Otaru Barracks, Japan</u>
With the increased work load, one positive aspect is that the days and weeks pass like "boxcars do hobos," in the parlance of dear Uncle Thomas.

Routine has returned and events unfold with Japanese exactitude. The Japanese culture is even more ordered than Chinese, and the constabulary—to whom we are responsible—are forever faithful to the clock.

Guard shifts are changed to the minute; business, including schedules at the mine and store, is conducted at the same time—hour, day, and, week. Schedules are unyielding; Madam Fukama and her unfortunate assistants arrive and depart like tides. The Japanese are as attached to their time-pieces as Aleut people are to times-of-year and (somewhat less) their Orthodox calendar.

So, in a way, the two understand each other, at least in respect to a sense or rhythm—or timing.

How I ache for home. It has been somewhat over three years since Osmond and I walked down the gangplank of the *City of Portland*, the Alaska steamship that transported us from Seattle to Seward.

Himself was *so optimistic*, eager to reach our post at Three River Station. And me? *I* already missed home and family, for I did not relish, once again, living and working with people in far-away places.

But I was, even that evening inside that tiny barracks in Seward, happy for Osmond. He had been under his mother's thumb for fifty-eight years, and had finally escaped, may God forgive me for saying that about the poor woman. She loved him dearly, I know. He was the only one of the three children who stood by her.

I prayed for better times at Three Rivers, better times for Osmond. And then Chichigof Village—Attu—and the opportunity so far west. "Why, we'd almost be in Russia, Lila Ann!" And it seemed a chance to recover his early optimism and eagerness upon arrival in Alaska.

I know there is a God, just as I know there will be justice and peace in the next life. But my weakness of faith makes me want there to be more of those virtues *in the here and now.* Sometimes, despite the crowding and the sweet friendship here, I sense an aloneness of nearly intolerable intensity.

October 20, 1943. Otaru Barracks, Japan

This week began with Alexi and Peter formally requesting of Chief Constable Osimi that they all be returned home to Attu prior to winter. They did so in writing, addressing their correspondence to Prime Minister Tojo.

The previous week Alexi discussed this possibility with me, and since I could read and, better yet, write some Japanese, would I help them? I did what I could re: explanation. I reminded, mildly but firmly, that such an action might not be advisable until inquiries were made as to protocol, all important in the Orient.

But the shortage of materials, especially tobacco, has brought the issue to its apex. All perishable supplies, now, must be purchased with wages the villagers have come to realize are a pittance—at best. The villagers' desire for return to Attu and its natural plenty has become the center of all conversation, even the children's. So they remain steadfast in regard to making their request formal.

A friend's request cannot be ignored; hence, I consented and, on our only non-work day of Sunday, did my best. I have been teaching the children the rudiments of writing Japanese, and Constable Toshihara, who it seems is a retired teacher, acquired for us rudimentary supplies. Teaching the children anything Japanese is encouraged.

Monday mornings Chief Constable Osimi almost without exception inspects the premises when the night shift turns things over to the day watch. While thus involved, our leaders presented Chief Constable with their correspondence.

He was stunned, looked up at them, and cutting his inspection short, departed early. Prior to this, he made only the briefest remark to the petitioners, glanced worriedly at Constables Toshihara and Ojiwa, then drew himself up proudly and exited, letter in hand.

At once, Mr. Ojiwa—a very observant man—sat down and cradled his head in his hand. Gathering his composure, he stood and announced,

"What you have done is unthinkable and an impolite gesture toward Honored Chief Constable, whose duty it is to see after you."

He too departed, and *without* leading the day's work detail to the mines. An extraordinary lapse. He left a sad and withdrawn Mr. Toshihara, who would not be drawn into any discussion regarding explanations.

We sewed in silence, the men very uncomfortable with these surprising results—clearly negative. At midday repast, I sat with Friend Annie and Mike. Mike, always a careful commentator, said, in English (a language not often used now), "I think a storm is gathering, Mrs. Smith."

<u>October 22, 1943. Otaru Barracks, Japan</u>
Today a half-dozen uniformed Japanese, the sort we've not
seen before, barged into the barracks. Barking harsh words,
they demanded from a bowing, terrified Mr. Toshihara the
identifications of the petitioners. Then they took custody of
them, pushing poor Alexi and Peter rudely before them.

Their removal took at most two minutes.

Looking outside, we saw a dray with a cage as its rear
compartment, and Alexi and Peter were locked in this. This
ominous conveyance was preceded and followed by cars
adorned with Japanese flags. Standing on exterior rear platforms on the "cage truck" were (each) a pair of uniformed
men, like footman of old.

Philamon, thankfully, had not signed the petition, for he
lacked official status as First or Second Chief. He lamented at
once the letter, expressing guilt in not stopping it. Then,
within minutes, Mr. Nasimi appeared and ordered our mine
detail into line, and marched them off. He too, ordinarily a
genial sort, barked orders and carried his white and red stick.

Left behind were we confused womenfolk.

What sort of police were these? Where were they taking our
chiefs? Would they hurt them? Would they be returned? Where
was Constable Osimi and could he help? Mr. Toshihara finally
lost patience with the virtual *pelting* of questions.

"No more questions! Return to work! All citizens have honored duties. Work!"

And to my recollection, this is the most assertive behavior
the thoughtful Mr. Toshihara had demonstrated.

We worked at the batches in silence and blessedly the
sewing machines gave us no trouble and we had no cause to
draw attention to ourselves.

I cannot lie and say I was not worried about my own
status. How could I not be? I needn't guess what Alexi and

Peter were experiencing, and vowed to pray that evening for them, as I knew others would. Past midday, I began blaming myself. Why wasn't I more assertive when they came to me? Though no authority on the Oriental mind, I'm far more familiar with eastern ways than my dear Attu friends.

Nevertheless, Chinese ways are not the Japanese ways, and the unknown gnaws at me—first off, for my friends who were so rudely trundled off, and then for myself. I remember my two weeks alone in the cell without friends. These are my friends now, and I'm more aware of it today than ever.

I don't think time is on our side.

October 25, 1943. Otaru Barracks, Japan
This morning was Monday morning, and all knew it was time for Chief Constable Osimi's inspection. Would he provide answers? Since Friday, the 22nd, the constables have said nothing, answered no questions, and behaved variously from morose (Mr. Ojiwa) to clearly frightened (Mr. Nasimi), with Mr. Toshihara somewhere in the middle.

But all three said little, and the watches and duties proceeded like movements of a watch. The air about the barracks was strained. The Chirikof and Andreanof families were grieved about Alexi and Peter, as were all of us.

And this morning any diminishment of this pall, any hope of answers, ended when the same officers arrived *en convoi* and called us all into line, adult men on one side, women and children on the other. A small podium was brought in, and a tiny, wizened man, a high official, entered, with Mr. Osimi trailing behind, head bent.

We all bowed, and held, then when given permission to resume upright stance, saw the official poised ramrod straight on his podium holding a scroll. He read in a loud, strident voice, pausing intermittently for the English translator to catch up. Though I cannot, of course, deliver it herein verbatim, the essence I remember well:

He blamed everything on Mr. Osimi. If he were more stringent and observing of policy, our ingratitude and rudeness would not have occurred. From now on policy would be followed precisely. In warfare, all citizens must think positively about victory. They must make sacrifices for the good of all. Complaints are disloyal, and an affront to the Emperor. And this ingratitude was even worse in citizens, such as us, saved from the savagery of an uncivilized enemy.

Here he lowered his prepared text, and in fact used it as a pointer, jabbing left and right. His voice became a menacing shout delivered in an oddly singsong rhythm.

Therefore, he said, he was relieving Mr. Osimi as Chief Constable, assigning him more suitable work elsewhere. He would be replaced by another Chief Constable of his choosing, soon to be announced. Because of the Emperor's love and sense of forgiveness, we would be given today free from work. We would use free time to reflect on the importance of obedience, discipline, and sacrifice to assure victory against the enemies.

Guards then shouted at us—ordering us again to bow down and *hold*. While doing this, the entire procession departed. When given the order to straighten, the last person I saw was an aide exiting, carrying the podium. The text of this dictum was posted to the right of the entrance, a red ribbon hanging from the corner, embossed with a wax seal.

At the same moment the cage-truck pulled up, and Alexi and Peter were simply pushed from the door and sent sprawling on the ground. They were in wretched condition, but without serious injury. As soon as the truck was gone, the villagers carried their chiefs into the barracks.

"These are bad people. These are bad people" was all that Alexi managed. Peter was slumped forward, weak. They had been fed only twice since Friday, and given very little water.

They had not been beaten, just treated roughly. While wife Fekla attended him, Peter looked around and lamented, "These are bad people, and we're never going home."

People retired to their various places and left the two men in the limited privacy of their wives' care.

Because the Japanese had murdered my husband and beaten me, injuring me badly, then twice trundled me about tethered like livestock, I cannot say that Peter's words came as a surprise.

The Japanese common folk are *not* bad, however, but surely are ruled by malevolent and corrupt people.

<u>October 29, 1943. Otaru Barracks, Japan</u>
Though I thought the announcement of a new Chief Constable would occur on a Monday, the Japanese being so bound by schedule, it was today, a Friday.

The new Chief Constable is Mr. Aiko, a dour, cheerless man, older than Mr. Osimi by quite a bit, I would say, possibly approaching his seventies. He walks with a serious limp, uses a cane, and has a patch over one eye. The other eye is very mobile, taking in everything.

After a brief introduction by Mr. Ojiwa, the Chief Constable and our three guards inspected the premises. Mr. Aiko would stop occasionally, ask a question, then move on, even exiting the back entrance to inspect the out-buildings the villagers had constructed out of whatever was available.

Then he reversed path and came back through, stopping, looking about without hurry. Finally, his attentions fell on me, and our sewing "section," with batch-work piled left and right. He gave a bit of a nod.

He then turned and announced in a quiet but firm voice, "There will be no more nonsense. Procedures will be followed; work and obedience are everyone's duty."

And he left. Mr. Nasimi led off the work party, and Mr. Toshihara began his day shift. The end of Mr. Osimi's tenure was as simple and brief as that—briefer (almost) than the time it took me to write it.

Within the hour, Madam Fukama put in her appearance with new batch-work. She had evidently heard of events, crowed openly how she'd long advocated Mr. Osimi's removal and how Mr. Aiko would put a stop to any laziness and slip-shod work.

On this day in particular, I was gloriously relieved to have batch-work business done and to see her gone. I am exhausted by all this, and by all this, I mean *all this* (!). I'm a weary Lila Ann, hardly the woman I used to be.

<u>November 10, 1943. Otaru Barracks, Japan.</u>
Winter approaches and the snows have arrived, with heaps of it being shoveled or plowed everywhere. There is more snow than last year, though last year seems ancient history. Budget and the availability of commodities is a major issue though not the only one, for a new "problem" has come along that enhances the former: For reasons that fly in the face of ordinary common sense, four of the younger women have allowed themselves to become pregnant.

It is awkward and disconcerting to discuss such issues in Aleut society, especially one steeped in Orthodoxy. It was a shock to me to learn that Friend Annie is one of these. *When was there time and place?*!!

But what is done is very done. With our basic subsistence ever worsening, especially in the wake of the requirement we purchase all foodstuffs and the like, winter promises even darker times.

This inexplicable behavior frustrates and (yes) angers me even more that when our infinitesimal resources are squandered on tobacco. If this was not bad enough, now—pregnancies! *New mouths. Nursing mothers.* To witness such heedlessness in adults for the practice of doubtful pleasures is profoundly disappointing for me.

And indeed, the foolishness over tobacco goes on. And the men are the most *addicted.* Fully one-third of our budget is spent on it, for it is dear. Furthermore, accessing affordable quantities is done via questionable sources at the clay mine, dealings of which I've purposely remained ignorant. Father ranked tobacco with opium, though in those early days, few did—perhaps even fewer now. But I've become convinced he was right.

Now, *pregnancies!* The rigors of winter, shortages of coal—even rumors of a possible requirement for us to *buy* coal and charcoal (it is still provided each Monday) loom.

I'm trying to maintain a sympathetic heart with our menfolk, but since they demand sacrifice for tobacco use, and obviously claim husbandly privileges, sympathy for them is difficult for Lila Ann to sustain.

≃

November 21, 1943. Otaru Barracks, Japan
This is the holiest day for Attu Village. [*The celebration of the Presentation in the Temple of the Mother of God (Theotokos), a fixed religious date on the Orthodox calendar.*] Despite being a thousand miles from their beloved home island, Philamon has planned a special Sunday, with several services. There was chanting and singing in the Slavonic language of the church. Listening to it invariably soothes me with its evocative eastern tones. The villagers know and sing it well.

Why can't I share in their faith and sense of spiritual unity with our Savior? All Christians, certainly us Mennonites, practice Christian fellowship and forbearance. It is one of our Essentials, and central to our missionary charter.

But even on this Holy Day my beliefs fail me. This faltering centers on the children, ten of them. They are not well and have either lost weight, or gained little, for between visits by Dr. Nagai and nurse, I weigh them with a Japanese-style scale. [a *balance scale made from two sticks or small boards*]. I am the keeper of records, and update Dr. Nagai's every visit. It has become a sad duty.

I still function as teacher and amateur nurse's aide, though the sewing is central. Classes are about five hours a week, for Japanese teachers (various ones) come in three times weekly to teach the children, or anyone, Japanese. They seem poorly suited to the task. But I will not rant re: pedagogy, for health is a far more critical issue and renders difficult any feelings of optimism.

There are now FIVE pregnancies, the fifth being the *45-year-old* Lena Ivanof! Dr. Nagai does nothing to help, instead commenting that "having babies is fun." In fact, the Doctor has posted a quote from the Prime Minister's wife's speech urging women to become pregnant, which I herein record: "It is the duty of all Japanese women to know that motherhood is a vital part of the national destiny." And the doctor, always a dutiful patriot, praises the wisdom of Madam's words.

To struggle against this tide is frustrating. This Holy Day, then, finds me at an emotional divide.

☙

December 15, 1943. Otaru Barracks, Japan

There has been nothing new or I'm afraid to say, positive to enter; hence, what to write? There have been changes, and those not for the good.

One personal change is I stopped allowing my wages to be paid into the community fund. I collect them directly from the "paymaster" each Wednesday payday at Otaru Barracks.

Since my sewing wages are more than most, my decision was noted at once. There were hurt feelings. I explained to the "shoppers," without effort to mollify, that I could not allow *any portion* of my wages to purchase tobacco when shortages of foodstuffs are so dire. The children are in poor condition, and purchasing tobacco instead of food was blasphemy.

"But we love our children, Mrs. Smith."

"And I do too, Heratina."

I explained with unusual directness that people *must* have food, water, and warmth, but that tobacco was unnecessary for survival. In fact, it can threaten survival if it takes the place of food. Since then, there is a palpable strain between myself and the villagers, particularly with the men. Not so Friend Annie and Mike, friends *always*.

I know there is a black market, and that is how tobacco is being purchased. And this is how I intend to purchase milk solids, or perhaps even canned milk. I must learn the "ropes" of this shady business even if I must *enter the dragon's lair*, as it were, and deal directly with the mighty worm himself.

December 22, 1943. Otaru Barracks, Japan

Mr. A.C. Doyle himself could not write a more suspenseful tale than my quest for milk solids [*powdered milk*] or, better, canned milk.

It ended with *Mon ami le réparateur* [*"My friend the repairman." There is no reason given why LAS switches to French. Perhaps increased security in the event the journal is discovered*], whose knowledge about this activity surprised me. During the conduct of business, my broad hints to all and sundry hit home in this unlikely personage.

Every speck of money I could muster yielded thirty cans of evaporated milk, including an added incentive of a half-dozen custom *monpes* [*a type of Japanese peasant pantaloon, the required everyday wear for Japanese women during the Pacific War*] painfully scavenged by Lila Ann from bits and pieces of batch-work. This latter part of the costs actually carried the day. Ordinary *monpes* are hated by the womenfolk as being oppressively drab. So even the slight modifications I was able to include thrust the wearer into the lofty realm of fashion!!

This adventure of acquiring milk has shown me a source for future purchases, a way around this odious tobacco situation. The milk will be the most *useful* Christmas present I've yet to manage anywhere!

January 3, 1944. Otaru Barracks, Japan

This is a sad day for me, so close to both Christmases, yet so distant in the spirit and mood of our Savior's birth. I'm too disillusioned and emotionally drained to bother narrating a long account of events.

The outrage is brief: some of the men bartered the canned milk back for tobacco with the acquiescence of the women. How I found out is not important. Fact is, I did. To betray one's children, one's friend, one's religious beliefs, for such an odious habit as tobacco is beyond my comprehension, and I will not tolerate it.

Right now, I'm pondering the notion of requesting through the kind Dr. Takata to be removed to a British or Dutch Civilian Containment facility to the south. I've heard of them several times.

The incongruity of these sweet, peaceful people betraying the sacred trust of their children, their responsibilities as loving parents, absolutely confounds.

<u>January 21, 1944. Otaru Barracks, Japan</u>
The last three weeks elapsed almost without mention or discussion of sad events, save for one occasion. I have simply given up. I do what I must daily, and my thoughts are my own.

Friend Annie, seeing my disheartened state, brought up the matter, and even *she* said, "The men must have tobacco, Mrs. Smith."

And I answered, "The men *do not* need tobacco," and perhaps it was the devil *in me* that compelled me to repeat the message in English, Chinese, Japanese, Aleut, then French. "And they all mean the same thing, Annie. *The men do not need tobacco.*"

This talk was occasioned during a break from sewing, and I ended the discussion at once. There's nothing to discuss without broaching the plain facts, which are severe, that the men have stolen milk from the mouths of children, *their children*, which of course I will not do.

And in that same realm, community health is in increasing jeopardy. Two days ago Dr. Nagai held his regular clinic, during which, for the first time in months, it seems, the gentle Dr. Takata was well enough to come along. "I've been ill subsequent to our car trip," then added at once, as if worried about offending, "though not because of it. It I enjoyed."

He would not be drawn out concerning his illness, a most artful dodger! Instead he was anxious that I catch him up on the two and one-half months that elapsed "after your lamentable episode in Sapporo."

After doing so I sounded him out concerning war news, and once again struck a firm surface. *No war talk, please!* Now, he didn't *say* this, but his elusiveness coupled with his old-world charm does an even better job of effecting the same result.

After a brief segue to matters about Aleut culture, he stopped and asked, "I sense that today, you are not in an anthropological mood."

I concurred, but didn't feel I should visit the details on my honored visitor. He took something of a patient breath and asked if I had not seen physical addiction in China during my youth, especially to opium.

Now, since I had not brought up anything about tobacco or addiction, I'm supposing the gentle doctor had foreknowledge of some sort. Admitting I certainly had witnessed addiction, he added that speaking as a doctor, addiction to a drug deprived its victim of choice.

"Sadly, addicts have been known to kill their own parents to sustain their addiction. I presented a paper on laudanum addiction to the French Medical Academy in 1903, and was honored by its being generously received by physicians many years my senior."

I was about to ask about addiction to tobacco when Dr. Nagai joined us, which is very unusual, as he keeps his distance from all Attuans, and especially me. "We will need to return with an ambulance, it seems. The disease is advancing."

I actually understood this in Japanese; fortunately, Dr. Nagai doesn't realize I've learned a little. So I asked Dr. Takata in French, "What disease?" and he responded in kind, "Why, he means tuberculosis." And at that point, all departed, after Dr. Takata bid me a very polite farewell, as he always does.

There was much to consider, all of it ominous.

January 22, 1944. Otaru Barracks, Japan
Today, very early, an ambulance came and took away Strong Ivan [*Sergief*], Kusma [*Tschigorin*] and Walter [*Sergief*]. Kusma, unlike Walter and Strong Ivan, was not required to work in the clay mines, yet as the next oldest male after the death of his grandfather Elder Tschigorin (the eldest, now, is "Old" Nicholas Andreanof, age sixty), everyone was understandably distraught during his departure.

It was explained they must remain in isolation. For the disease, latent in most, is now active in some, hence communicable to those entirely unaffected. Tuberculosis is the disease that is familiar to the Attuans, and indeed all Alaska native peoples. It is their most serious health problem. There is one large tuberculosis sanitarium in Alaska, and Walter had actually spent time there, it seems, twenty or so years ago.

In fact, he seemed most reassuring, saying, "Now I'll eat well. But good smoking will be harder." Which was news I viewed rather with much irony.

Strong Ivan and especially Kusma, however, were understandably uneasy. But there will be the three of them, I assume, in the same isolation facility; therefore, they can share their language, for Kusma and Walter have learned almost no Japanese, and Strong Ivan just a few words.

I felt sad at developments. I did what I could to cheer everyone up by holding a doll-making session for the girls, and even a few of the older women attended.

~

Dr. Takata's discussion about addiction, I think, was intended, perhaps, to teach. Was it to teach me moderation in tendering judgment? Compared to him, my six-plus decades pale.

Opium addiction was a part of life in Shansi Province, and especially Yangquan, the largest town close to our mission. One of my earliest memories is the infirmary beds for those withdrawing from the vile substance. The beds were equipped with leather restraints, and the rooms had strengthened doors and windows.

These unpleasant humanities were pursued by Mother, Father, and the Johnstons, who were co-posted with us. Actually, they preceded Father and Mother to Mennonite Bethel Mission by some years. Dr. Johnston had been a doctor in the Civil War, and Mrs. Johnston a nurse, which is how they met.

Dr. Johnston, in a calamitous yet well-intended action, purposefully allowed himself to become addicted to opium. He did so with the announced and clear intent to prove the power of prayer and clean living to the Chinese, providing them with a demonstration certain to win many over.

According to Mother and Father, by the time of their posting, Dr. Johnston had finally severed his connection with opium, but it had broken his health. He passed on a few years shy of my tenth birthday.

I do remember him, though even better, "Nurse Johnston," who was invariably unsmiling and somber. Then one day, the poor lady had a nervous breakdown and was returned to the States.

So I might have imparted this to the benevolent Dr. Takata about addiction, and how Father honestly thought all addiction, be it plant or liquor, was of the same stripe—loathsome and to be "stamped out *by the honest heel of Christian strength*" was how he put it. And his convictions were sealed forever by both Dr. Johnston's teachings and tragic example.

Our modest clinic came to be known as the "Fair Shelter" hospice in missionary circles. Few took on opium addiction, but ours did. The Catholics at St. Ann's used something like exorcism, Father guessed, probably somewhat unfairly. Baptists had nothing to do with addiction at all, considering it Satanic. Other missions were too distant to know.

Though it was forty years and some ago, I remember the screams of the poor people withdrawing. "Their demon within is dying, praise the Lord," Mother would say, especially when such outcries would scare Joseph and me and she wished to comfort us.

~

It was just a few months after my return to Delbert and the recuperative care of Uncle Thomas when Great-aunt Eunice, from my mother's tirelessly severe Presbyterian side, visited from Maine. Uncle Thomas maintained that his sister-in-law's kinfolk in Maine lived in ice caves (!) sleeping on nail beds, consuming meals of scone and cold mutton pie. (Though perhaps not word for word, that is close to how he irreverently put it.)

"Your dear mother was the only warm-blooded one in the lot," Uncle Thomas concluded.

So when Great-aunt Eunice arrived, I was prepared for cold judgment. But I was not steeled for what she did say, which I shall never forget: "During our missionary work in Africa, if that would have happened, we women would have destroyed ourselves first."

A grand *bake* sprang up between Aunt Sarah and Great-aunt Eunice, and it was humiliating for me during a confusing time. The sounds and smells of that awful General Lon Shi's camp were yet fresh in my mind, and at twenty-two years of age such talk carried lasting hurt. The scene occurred when the men were outside "playing horseshoes," an Uncle Thomas euphemism.

But, despite my youth, I knew what she meant, and the other women did too.

When Uncle Thomas found out about Great-aunt Eunice's comment, even more acerbity was exchanged, but I shall end the incident here.

She was an elderly woman, quick to judge, and perhaps said before me what others said when I was not present. Who can know? I pray not. For those who loved me, I'm sure, it was enough I survived.

February 9, 1944. Otaru Barracks, Japan
Life has returned to its previous state since I've redirected my salary back into the general pool, which I did a fortnight ago. Actually, in truth, I *did* by *not doing*.

On payday, I simply ignored the proceedings, and busied myself. There was pause from Heratina and Lena, until finally

Lena came over and asked me if I did not want my pay, and I said I preferred the matter to return to the way it had been.

There were nods, a few smiles later on, but inwardly I wonder if I've done right by the children. I've *yet* to resign myself to the hardship this hapless tobacco habit inflicts, though.

<u>February 13, 1944. Otaru Barracks, Japan</u>
There are heavy snowfalls, the most I've seen—more than last winter, surely. After a shift in the clay mines, the men get extra work by shoveling snow. On the urging of Chief Constable Aiko (a formal individual, a stickler for rules, though in the end with a sense of fairness), they have formed a "Snow Brigade" and do special jobs around Otaru. So this brings in extra money.

And there are developments in matters financial with us sewing people:

It seems a renowned and very influential *military figure* has a daughter marrying into the foreign diplomatic corps. A Western-style wedding dress is absolutely required and that is where Lila Ann comes in. So "Wedding-dress Negotiations" are in progress.

A discarded box of patterns in the old Wilcox and Gibbs machine (actually, in its heyday, a beautiful cabineted machine) was an unexpected trove. There were a half-dozen for wedding dresses. Since I taught my "Sewing Beauties" (the levity works better in Aleut!) the *ins-and-outs* of patterns by making doll dresses of diverse sorts, we included several wedding dresses. The dolls, enormously popular with the girls, were evidently espied by the keen Constable Aiko. At that point, he brewed this idea.

"It will bring us honor to accommodate such an august personage."

And so important are these pending negotiations that Chief Constable brought along an *English Interpreter* to establish details! I have not seen one of these in a year. She is a meek little thing who is not allowed to give her name. ("NOT IMPORTANT!" barked Chief Constable, when I asked her. Poor thing cringed.)

The sticking point now is the "august personage's" inability to understand that we require his daughter's presence (initially) for measurements, then subsequent several fitting sessions.

I have done many wedding dresses, beginning with the wonderful gown for Mrs. Hadley-Wilkinson in Shoyang; I was not yet sixteen years of age, and Mother had already promoted me to apprentice! I was very proud, for dressmakers didn't come any better than my dear mother. I swear, she could have made a most fetching blouse out of cotton batting!

This business development has potential, if indeed it goes through, which is anything but certain.

February, 28, 1944. Otaru Barracks, Japan
A period of storms and intense work has occupied all. For whatever reasons, shifts at the clay mines have been lengthened. Here, sewing responsibilities increase. We work exclusively producing *monpes* from fabric of the poorest quality. Madam Fukama has increased the batches and decreased the pay, and there is dissatisfaction.

Worse than anything, we now must buy coal and charcoal with our pay, and it is dear and available only in tightly rationed quantities. So our "shoppers" ply the black market. But even there caution is the rule, for penalties are severe regarding coal.

In the barracks we are always cold, and sewing is made arduous because of frosty fingers. Then there's more need for food to provide energy, especially for the children.

Our commissary officers are Heratina and Fekla [*Andreanof*], with Philamon functioning as Minister of the Exchequer. The Aleut people are endlessly practical, and have no difficulty with pride, meaning the person most fit for the job does it.

Heratina is fierce, never compromises, and has more sauce than any of us; however, Fekla is diminutive and shy. Yet she has a strange, photographic memory and an ability to do figures in her head without hesitation or flaw. Since Philamon is financial officer for the church, his present function is a logical extension of the former. So they are a formidable team, learning rapidly on the job.

There are many minor ailments, such as colds and bronchial conditions, though thank God nothing worse has swept through us all. This, more than anything, worries me.

Wedding-dress negotiations have either seriously stalled, or simply failed. The overall idea seemed off-center, to me.

<u>Otaru Barracks, Japan</u> [*One of the few undated entries, though I suppose it is in chronological order, and clearly a winter entry. Her reference to the 1/22/44 entry further indicates its position. No explanation is indicated for the omission of date(s).*]
Otaru is a small and dreary seaport, but I've seen little of it. The men, and those who commute to the clay mine, naturally see more.

Mike and Alexi, though, are our resident travelers. Peter less so.

Mike and Alexi venture weekly, accompanied by one of our constables, to the sanitarium to visit Strong Ivan, Kusma, and Walter. No other visitors are allowed, and Mike goes along for purposes of language (he has come to speak the best Japanese of all the adults), for presence of mind, and to keep Alexi's spirits up. (When it became apparent the villagers were not going to be returned to Attu, Alexi—*of all the men*—began to sink in spirits.)

Also, Alexi is anxious that while *in transit* they'll be seized by military "press gangs" (as it were) and never seen by anyone again. Not an altogether illogical fear, considering circumstances.

Some womenfolk increase anxiety, especially Heratina and Agafia who—though fine and caring women—are whirling dervishes of rumors. Agafia, of course, is rightly worried about losing husband Alexi, but Heratina purely dislikes and doesn't trust *any* of the Japanese. The incident with her twins was proof positive of overall bad intentions.

I pled for Mike to write his own impressions of Otaru and its ordinary people, but he won't, rather says, "I tell about it. Then you write it, Mrs. Smith. You do it better than Mike."

In reply, I say I'm fortunate to write about what *I* have experienced let alone what I have not—and that he must relent! But, thus far, my persuasion, even with the help of wife Annie, will not convince Mike to become a chronicler.

~

Otaru is a poor town by any standards. Passing through it, you see tarpaper and such being used for house repair, and this was as much the case when we arrived as now. This gives many neighborhoods a poor, shambling appearance.

There are still numerous horse- and mule-drawn conveyances, enough to keep tiny men wearing red scarves (insignia of office?) scurrying about on "manure patrol," much like in pre-World War I times in the U.S., and of course China. (I risked indelicacy in explaining to the Attuans, early on, the value placed on *all* manure in the Orient. They were abundantly dismayed by such practices!)

There are also bicyclists and many foot-travelers. Since a bicycle and rider were unknown to Attuans, this impresses them even more than the machines. Yet one could never use the words *busy* or *bustling* to accurately describe downtown Otaru. Also, a "sleepy port," though closer to the truth, it is not. The dockside centers are serviced directly by a network of rails that is always busy—and noisy! The harbor itself is the port for the largest city on Hokkaido Island, the northernmost Japanese island, and this is Sapporo, an inland city of hundreds of thousands of people. It is only a few miles distant.

This center, of course, makes an active, vital port a necessity, for more products leave the island than arrive, due to its still rich endowment of resources. I suppose the war drains these at an increased rate. There are still large stands of timber on Hokkaido Island. Lumber and coal trains are common in the formation yard behind the barracks. Each coal car is monitored by a severe, elderly escort with stout sticks, as all energy is dear.

None of us ever ventures to Sapporo, in fact, my sad foray to a Sapporo detention center (?) makes me the only one to have seen the city.

Men with diverse military or civil uniforms are in evidence in every nook of Otaru life, and no one is sure of their individual meaning, save for us the meaning is simply *Trouble*!!

There are manufacturing concerns in this area, and occasionally the men venture to them to shovel snow. In one, great quantities of cooking and eating ware are made from the clay mined by the Attuans and many resident workmen. This is a business that goes back many years. Twice our *snow crew* visited a tannery, and at other times a vast system of warehouses.

Everywhere, there are few dogs and cats around, and wild songbirds—or birds of any sort—are absent. It is thought that this absence is due to the scarcity of food—tight rationing. Even with my background, I found this not credible. Then, three roughshod men stopped by one day with piles of gossamer nets in the back of their wagon, trying to sell us ordinary songbirds, such as robin-like birds, etc. My doubt in the situation of snaring tiny birds ceased. None of the villagers, of course, could afford *one* of them for even the tiniest of a meal.

~

And the sounds of the railyards are with us all through the night, when most activities take place. In the last year of our captivity there has been a great increase in this activity. For the first months, it disturbed everyone, but now we're inured to it. Perhaps we would be disturbed without it.

Some are wondering if we'll end our days in this strange, drab land.

<u>March 20, 1944. Otaru Barracks, Japan</u>
Though days lengthen as we approach the first day of spring, Otaru Barracks contains a sad group.

Over the last three months, since their removal to the tuberculosis facility, Kusma, Strong Ivan, and Walter have not responded to treatment, and it seems Kusma is worse. For many weeks, our regular official visitors—Alexi, Mike, and Peter—kept this from their kin and friends. But finally Mike convinced Alexi the truth must be conveyed, for Kusma is in dire condition now.

Ann and husband Old Ivan are near distraction with desire to see their uncle, and Philamon, as Reader, to pray with him, or perform needed ceremonies. But no, Dr. Nagai will not permit it, and in the end, his word prevails over all, including Chief Constable Aiko, of course.

Food and heating have become constant problems that have increased since mid-winter. Everyone has one sort of ailment or another, thankfully nothing more than bad coughs due to a cold, or to the clay dust at the mine.

There was, evidently, an ugly scene at one of the two stores our shoppers may patronize, so Heratina is confined to the barracks until further notice. Lena, the other *shopper*, is not too forthcoming, for both were thrashed by a store clerk, then later by police officers who were summoned. And Lena blames Heratina, and even if Heratina had not been deemed *persona non grata*, Lena would not go provisioning with her any longer. "She is a crazy woman." They are half-sisters through their father's side, and old animosities have arisen, it seems.

Troubles are handled by the Aleut people by not discussing them. Heratina will not discuss what happened, the menfolk will not ask, and Lena won't talk with Heratina, of course. Philamon declares the strife a result of a decline in religious observances, and that's the end of that.

I've determined the scene became ugly over a can of fish priced beyond our means, and Heratina took exception. Heratina, if she perceives an unfairness, can be a terror. This cannot be denied.

Hence, the position of co-shopper is vacant, and Alexi is waiting for a volunteer. Provisioning day is now on a Thursday, four days hence.

~

La situation avec commercial clandestinement [*meaning essentially "the situation on the blackmarket"*] has become unworkable, for almost everything is beyond our means. Even basic items, such as rice, charcoal, and coal, require every snippet of scrip. The Attuans now realize our pay is a pittance. It is essentially *pro forma*. Frankly, none of us are much more than slaves.

Additionally, shopping is complex and often risky. Rice is central: It is one price (lowest) at the stores, but often not available. It is entirely another price (very high) *elsewhere*, yet always available.

Everyone is hungry, even I, long infamous for an avian appetite. The children complain ceaselessly, and nerves fray.

Health is declining, and twice I've made formal complaint during Dr. Nagai's clinics. "Your country has taken us prisoner, and is bound by treaty to maintain us humanely."

His response was a shrug and "I've taken no one prisoner. Save for you, these are Japanese citizens. You, I understand, requested to stay here, did you not? So neither are you a prisoner. Food is short everywhere."

I learned two things that afternoon: one, just how dire our situation is, and two that Dr. Nagai spoke a rather rough but effective Chinese, something he had not shared with me until then.

<u>March 30, 1944. Otaru Barracks, Japan</u>
In the midst of unrelenting bad news, Chief Constable Aiko appeared this morning, usual on provisioning day. But when I saw the hapless young lady who is his English interpreter, I knew immediately Lila Ann was the focus of the visit. And I hoped the wedding-dress issue would reopen.

And I was right.

The three of us retired to my cubby hole, sat on my "hospitality mats" (chairs in Japan are a Western item, and my elderly bones do miss them horribly) and at once Constable Aiko announced it was with great joy and honor to *all* of us that I and my assistants had been selected to make the "*august personage's*" wedding dress, or rather—the daughter of said personage.

And, we would be additionally honored by a personal visit by the august personage's daughter, and retinue, in one week's time for the "technical necessities previously mentioned by myself." Meaning, measurements.

I had pondered my response (in the event the work request came true) for many weeks, and was undecided how to respond. But now it was upon me, for the first time in my life I applied un-Christian cunning combined with a downright gamble.

"So our duties with Madam Fukama will be suspended while we make this dress?"

At once our honorable Chief Constable's joy receded, as I thought it might with the name of Madam Fukama and her batch-work entering into the matter. I have learned that Madam Fukama's work, etc., occupies a high priority. I'm not sure why, save to assume it is associated with wartime responsibilities. Also, Madam Fukama is a force not to be tampered with; in short, she's a "pill."

"Absolutely not. This will be an additional duty."

"Then there must be additional pay, and in rice and coal, not scrip."

"Oh! Please don't. I fear what Chief Constable might do."

At once I saw that Madam Translator had lost courage. When Chief Constable demanded to know the essence of our exchange, I understood enough Japanese to comprehend she'd not translated my request and temporized poorly.

Sparing her a potentially threatening situation, I said in simple Japanese that we needed to be paid extra and in rice and coal, not currency.

"IMPOSSIBLE! YOU WILL DISHONOR US!"

And he sprang to his feet, stomped his foot at me, turned, and left us sitting there. After a moment's hesitation, a fearful interpreter trailed after him, quivering, eyes downward— clearly scared witless.

Of course, my village family (those who had not left on work detail) wondered what hubbub Lila Ann had begun, for an angry Chief Constable Aiko was something new, and could mean trouble.

So for the first time I sat my Sewing Beauties down and told them the situation. For having been uncertain about the "wedding-dress situation," Miss Mum had been the word. But now the cat was out of the bag, and all were excited, for an increase in means will result. Word spread rapidly.

This all, of course, was pitted against the risk of trouble due to my bargaining. Lively Aleut everywhere, with Friend Annie leading the "charge" in admiring my pluck. So much did she admire it, she announced in English, "This is so much the good thing, Mrs. Smith. I love you very too much."

So as of late evening, and with work parties home, two main schools of rumor have developed: Heratina and Lena [*Ivanof*] have established the "Wealth and Plenty" theory, while Fekla and Mary [*Tschigorin*] are leaders in the "Mrs. Smith will be thrashed and sent away" school.

I can't claim to be established firmly in either.

March 31, 1944. Otaru Barracks, Japan

A granite-faced Chief Constable Aiko and interpreter put in an appearance this day after the work party had departed. He got to his message at once. Retiring to my cubby hole, he said, "You will make this dress without condition, or my superiors shall send you to a prison camp in the south at once. As to food, I'm doing everything I can."

"There is food and fuel available on the black market, and I refuse to watch dear friends slowly die. As to consequences? I've seen Japanese soldiers murder my husband in cold blood. So tell your superiors anything they might do now pales compared to that."

I think the strangest thing about this unpleasant and potentially harmful exchange is how angry I became (in a *seething* sort of way) and how little I regarded the Chief Constable's ire when he wheeled about and marched away. In my view, he and his superiors are no less criminals than General Lon Shi.

<u>April 14, 1944. Otaru Barracks, Japan</u>
So much happened so rapidly, and our work load has become so heavy, that there has been no time for this journal, which in a way has become my *confidant,* in addition to a village chronicle.

Every one of my sixty-four years [*LAS was born on March 15, 1880*] rests heavily on my bones each evening, and I fall to sleep almost without pause.

After rereading my entry of 3/31, I count myself fortunate that I don't occupy a distant detention center.

Within forty-eight hours after the contentious meeting with Chief Constable, an unscheduled clinic was held with Dr. Nagai on Sunday morning. I was braced for immediate departure, and after much soul-searching had not informed anyone of the possibilities looming.

What good would it do? Farewells are best kept short, and it is enough the sword of Damocles hung over my head alone. Since I'd been removed before, Friend Annie and Mike had developed a standing emergency plan for such a recurrence. The batch-work for Madam Fukama should proceed unimpeded. I have trained Friend Annie and Young Anna as "journeylady" seamstresses, and they've learned much. The *monpes* are routine for them. Though they claim the contrary, they are ready.

So though Friend Annie knew something was amiss, my heart sank when I saw three machines arrive rather than the usual two (one sedan and one ambulance) when there is a clinic.

There was much initial joy when Strong Ivan was escorted in, for he'd unexpectedly been discharged from the sanitarium. This at once turned to sorrow when we learned the small urn he carried contained the ashes of poor Kusma.

Though all knew how sick Kusma was, the Russian Orthodox view of cremation is one of abhorrence. Old Ivan wept for his uncle, and Philamon took the ashes from Strong Ivan, who sat down dejectedly in the corner.

Dr. Nagai and nurses were clearly not prepared for such abject sorrow, for they are as knowledgeable about the villagers' beliefs as the villagers are of theirs.

I was doing what I could to help console Mary [*Tschigorin*], who was Kusma's daughter-in-law via a family network about which I'm unclear. Nonetheless, Mary was Kusma's "guardian angel," which I'm told is what the Russian expression means.

When Dr. Takata entered with two of his house attendants, I cannot describe my relief, for that explained the third machine and indicated my removal was *not* in the offing.

All this mixture of news took place inside of five minutes on a Sunday morning.

~

I have managed a few "interviews" regarding the life of Kusma Tschigorin, plan a few more, then shall write an obituary similar to that for his grandfather. Once I complete it, I will read it at a community meeting. This worked much to ease the sadness of villagers after the passing of Elder Tschigorin.

Though I'm always happy to see Dr. Takata, for he is indeed special and has done much to help, I felt that his presence could be related to recent events. He is frail, and I have a growing sense that he does not wish to travel often.

"It is good to visit you, but I'm afraid there is an ulterior motive," and he spoke in Chinese, a relief for Lila Ann, for I'm far more comfortable in the language of my childhood than in my awful French! So, like the honest gentlemen he is, the good doctor and professor (for he spent much of his life as teacher) would not conceal. "Chief Constable and the Prefecture Administrator requested my humble offices for this diplomatic mission." Then he switched to French (a language which holds fond memories for him), cupped his tiny hands over the head of his ancient cane, and chortled, "The Japanese male is unused to dealing with non-compliant women of any racial stripe."

Then he had another chuckle, popped a mint from a tin held out by his elderly lady assistant after offering me one. This lady and her husband are referred to very warmly by Dr. Takata as his "gentle assistants in life." They are clearly in awe of the elderly scholar.

"I thought I was to be shipped away from here?"

"Yes. But the thinking is that, like so many Americans, you are fond of feigning, or *bluffing*, is the English word? This is my purpose here, to determine this. I told them you were certainly not, but they are individuals embedded in a certain paradigm."

I think it was at that point, when tea was just being served (our visit, as always, takes place in my cubby hole), that something most unplanned occurred. Perhaps it was because of the terrible suspense of it all, the emotions connected with this and all that has happened, that I just wept, unable to talk.

I was attended by Dr. Takata's people, while he waited patiently sipping tea, shaking his head sympathetically.

Why is it that humans throughout my life have demonstrated so much brutality and plain nastiness to one another? It cannot be simple race or religion. It *is* not.

It all came down upon my shoulders at once, the thought I might feign abandonment of my friends—their children—using poor Osmond's calamitous end as a ploy. As a young girl at Bible study, I recall being so devastated that the Sanhedrin and Romans would take the Lord Jesus out and visit savagery upon such a God-given soul.

I remember Mother comforting, I think somewhat taken aback that her lesson (she was teacher at Mennonite Mission) had been more effective than she had anticipated.

"Lila Ann, you have many years ahead of you, dear girl. Prayer will help you bear up."

~

There is so much to impart, yet simple hand fatigue urges me to be brief yet convey the essence. That awful day is two weeks behind me, yet it seems yesterday, for Dr. Takata's words regarding his mission and Chief Constable's wrongful interpretations regarding my words and actions still ring fresh:

Dr. Takata informed me that I had placed the powers-that-be in a position where they either lost face or sent me away. And despite the urgency and honor bestowed in the making of this wedding dress, they would indeed send me away rather than yield to outright deal-making, especially at this juncture.

"You must yield, otherwise you will be sent to the south to some awful place. What good will you do your beloved friends there, Mrs. Smith?"

Key here was the word "outright," yet Dr. Takata held his peace, sipped tea, and added nothing more. It was up to me, for he'd completed his mission.

He was, of course, right. I would do Friend Annie, Mike, the children—all of them—no good at all in some far-flung place with strangers. Yet I've always been a curious creature, and I pointed out that I knew full well Japan held some of the finest seamstresses in the world, and why, of all people, had I been selected?

There was the tiniest gesture on his part, for he saw I was weakening. The information he gave was cautiously presaged. "For these are bad times for free talk. And I have children and grandchildren who benefit from the quirks of fate that have given me influential friends. So, in this matter, you must feign ignorance as to details."

Then, that trust conveyed, he explained:

Indeed, the dress is for the daughter of a prominent minister at the "highest level." Such Western-style lavishments have abundantly drawn the public ire in Tokyo. Ministerial and Imperial special privilege was early-on openly condemned. By doing this at the beginning of the war with China [*in 1937 after an international incident at the Marco Polo Bridge, south of*

Beijing] the ministers created their own quagmire re: taking advantage of their powerful positions. The *official* image is one of public sacrifice and extreme austerity, and it cannot waver.

The remoteness of this prefecture and obscurity of Otaru Barracks are key.

"If you consent, the measurements are to be taken at the Prefecture Administrator's Residence in three days. He is the bride's uncle, the Minister's brother-in-law. A powerful and ambitious man."

In Japan, as in China, *ambition* frequently has pejorative overtones, unlike America. Since the word was in French, I asked for clarification in Chinese, and Dr. Takata reaffirmed my translation. In Chinese, there are many words and expressions for ambition.

Power and *ambition* when used together in an Oriental context were a clarion warning. How sweeping would this administrator's wrath be? I could not ask my Japanese "guardian angel" this, but the thought was unstoppable. I was, and am, *absolutely* a prisoner in every human sense.

~

For *Measurement Day* I was allowed one assistant, and immediately chose Friend Annie. Save for our regular community visits to the baths, Annie hasn't left the barracks, and certainly not baby Titiana, now almost two and a half years old. (Friend Annie is due in July, and is such a tiny wren of a girl, I cannot imagine anything more draining upon her health.)

Prior to our task, we were inspected by Chief Constable Aiko, and four constables heretofore unknown at the barracks. "Our" constables did not participate, but all stood by in uniform, clearly infrequently worn; they were sad, threadbare garments.

But the visiting constables' uniforms were immaculate, and they were groomed with great care.

Instructions for proper behavior were recited by Chief Constable. Evidently the function of this veritable *squad* of constables was that of professional nodders and grunters. During his "invocation and instructions," the four grunted and occasionally stamped a foot!

"Who are they, Mrs. Smith?"

Friend Annie managed this in English when we were escorted into the long, curtained limousine for the trip.

"SILENCE!"

Probably words such as *silence, prohibited/not allowed, obedience, punishment, you must bow*, etc., are the first portions of the Japanese language myself and the others learned.

During our first summer the initial reaction when these words were yelled or barked was to recoil, for the Attuans are, beyond everything else, gentle spirits. They don't shout, let alone use prohibitory invective, and think it uncivilized.

But now two years have elapsed and these words and harsh tone are part of living, and no one even winces any longer. Rather they do as requested, as if the constable or official had requested the same thing couched in a normal, polite voice.

"Their way is not good, because of course they are not Christian," Philamon said once during a Sunday homily.

Friend Annie had never been in a machine of any sort, let alone such a grand *specimen* as this; I believe it was of British manufacture. She carried my kit clutched to her, but remained *all eyes*, the most apt expression to describe her awe.

"Oh! Do you think we'll be all right, Mrs. Smith?"

We were thankfully alone in the spacious compartment, quite darkened because all curtains were drawn. Just before the last curtain was drawn, I noticed that each of the constables traveled on running boards, like footmen of old did upon royal carriages. This machine must have been a regal, important sight passing along public streets with four uniformed constables, an elaborate uniformed driver, with Chief

Constable in his finest sitting alongside of him in a semi-open compartment. All these Japanese officials were every bit the equal of the cast from an operetta by Masters Gilbert and Sullivan.

Seeing that Friend Annie was becoming terrified, I put my skinny old arm around her, and there we rode, in all ironic splendor. She terrified, me holding the wisp of a girl—as dear to me as any daughter might be—and bracing her up with English and Aleut words.

The vehicle was so ponderous and heavy—a *behemoth* of a machine—it moved along like a ship, gently swaying.

~

The Prefecture Administrator's Residence was a sprawling, one-storied structure of old-style construction somewhat out of town—opposite the railroad yard, and in full view of the port. A panorama to be envied. One of authority.

Inside were networks of sliding doors, walkways of finely treated and polished hardwood put down in intriguing inlays of squares, triangles, and such. Of course, we removed our shoes and put on slippers given to us by a trio of young ladies, all dressed traditionally. Despite their formal deportment, they were as in awe of my height as Friend Annie was of the limousine!

At six feet, I exceeded the dimensions intended for occupants, and I had to duck frequently in quite unlady-like motions. I felt I had entered my two nieces' playhouse for their "teatime" in the backyard on Billings Road.

"You will wait here."

Friend Annie and I availed ourselves of the thick floor mats, clearly of the highest construction and quality. At once, the door slid back open, revealing Dr. Nagai and nurse—both familiar faces. He was dressed in his usual, but his nurse was dressed traditionally, including odd hair adornments. He gave us surgical gauze masks and while nurse secured them to us explained we had been heavily exposed to tuberculosis, and these would protect the important personages present.

"Also, I will be present."

We had seen such masks worn, but despite the situation, Friend Annie got a case of the giggles looking at me masked. My dear "guardian angel's" giggling is infectious, so I giggled too, but a far more older, somber giggle, I'm sure.

"What is the meaning of this female nonsense!"

With this burst of Chinese, Dr. Nagai at once cured the outbreak of levity, reaffirming his "cure" with an icy stare as he exited. The nurse remained.

The beginning of action was fast, and clearly planned to the second. We were escorted to the residence's central area—two of the constables in front, two to the rear, all preceded by the three house maids.

A much larger, elaborately embossed sliding door was opened and in a large center room were three officials seated on a slightly elevated platform; to their left was a partition screen, each of its six panels intricately decorated—art pieces in themselves. Before them on a low Japanese-style table was an extraordinarily beautiful tea service.

But above and beyond all this, most impressive was a beautiful young lady with classic "Madame Butterfly" beauty. She stood by patiently, holding white gloves daintily. She wore a simple but effective Western dress, and was "made up" in Western style. Evidently a very Japanese "modern Milly."

After a cavalcade of bowing, our usual young lady interpreter (*"Miss Meek"*)—also dressed traditionally (at first I did not recognize her) —hastened from a side entrance, sat at the foot of the platform and translated the august words of the Prefecture Administrator!

"You will now begin."

Friend Annie had never seen such faultless feminine beauty and was transfixed. The young lady smiled at us, and with the tiniest shrug asked in absolutely flawless "Oxford" English,

"Why are you wearing those outrageous masks? And is it true you two are prisoners?"

"Who told you this outrageous nonsense!! And no talk! This is not agreed to."

At once, chaos and outrage, for her question was translated, and indeed the "man in the middle" was her uncle, for his Japanese was in the familiar, which caused our "august personage" to grouse, "My sister will hear of this willfulness!"

And when the translator put *his* statement into English, one of the administrator's men admonished her blunder, but was cut short by my client.

"Can we begin here? We are wasting time with this talk."

This was said with the healthy good humor that such silly behavior deserves. I liked her at once!

Within minutes, a young girl attendant of hers had been called, and something I had not seen in *months* was brought in. A table and three Western-style chairs!

We sat blissfully, poring over a half-dozen magazines, clearly our client's prized references. It was clear that none of my "discovered patterns" would do for her, whose name is Kimura, who insisted in English that we call her by the familiar. This was her wedding dress, and Mistress Kimura wasn't about ready to rush matters for the sake of the menfolk.

Is this not a universal? Wedding garb is absolutely significant to any female of the species, at least in all portions of the world which Lila Ann has visited.

April 29, 1944. Otaru Barracks, Japan
Kusma Tschigorin was born "two years after my mother, and she was born in 1881," Philamon advised from his records, which means Philamon was Kusma's nephew.

Kusma was born in Chichigof Village, then, in the winter of 1883–84, and was just sixty-one years of age at his passing. It is almost certain that Kusma never left the islands of the far western Aleutians until taken prisoner by the Japanese. These islands remained his beloved country all of his life. He was a perfectionist in the vanishing art of making a *badarki*, the extraordinarily famous seaworthy craft of the Aleut people.

Accordingly, the last one he made—a large, fully constructed sea-going variety—was given as a gift to a naturalist in 1935 who took possession of it in the name of the Smithsonian Institution in Washington, D.C. Kusma's name, along with when he made it, is on the plate as its maker and the people of Chichigof Village as those who donated it.

"He was sad always about the old ways."

Kusma looked back with fondness at the years of his coming of age, and a time when he learned his craft under the great master, his father John Tschigorin, eldest son of Sergief ("Elder") and Mary Tschigorin. Kusma was a wise trapper and hunter, but in the "old style," for he prided himself on maintaining traditional methods. He was the resident Aleut language authority, insisting on precise usage in the young people when learning their language.

Kusma's "great sadness" was in never finding a wife. In his far, isolated village, matchmaking is difficult at the best of times. First efforts were, as with most Chichigof Village men, in the Aleut villages to the east, toward mainland Alaska. At this time two Orthodox priests perished in a ship accident, and one of them was the principal matchmaker and go-between in the island groups. This stopped an already slow process. In the end, a wife was never found, and soon Kusma gave up.

Everyone was impressed with Kusma's ability as an artisan, his skill with language, and limitless information about the old ways. His memory for these rivaled that of his grandfather (over a quarter-century older than Kusma), making the old man very proud.

He was a devoted member of the Orthodox faith, respectful to every aspect of the "holy ways," and very skillful in the language of the church [*Old Slavonic*]. There is not a heart amongst the villagers who will not beat heavier because of Kusma's sad departure from us.

<u>May 2, 1944. Otaru Barracks, Japan</u>
My days will become far easier (and shorter!) when Mistress Kimura's wedding dress is fitted and completed. Her wedding is to the Japan's Ambassador Designate to Spain [*Spain was neutral in World War II*] and is on June 15, in a *Christian* church at Nagasaki, a beautiful, ancient port on Kyushu, the southernmost island about which my father spoke so laudably.

The fine fabric required has slowed things considerably. Even for those of great influence, quality fabric is most dear. At this point the mock-up is the pride of Otaru Barracks. Every day the villagers look it over, awed. I think half, and nearly all the men, think it the *real* wedding dress! Though Friend Annie has explained a dozen times how such fine work is done, to no avail.

The work continues, with the final fittings due in three weeks' time, and only half the fabric is here!

The food situation is better with spring firmly in force. A box of kippers was greedily consumed by the children. One Sunday was spent entirely by the menfolk clearing away all furnishing and trappings, then sweeping up every square foot of floor space for stray snippets of tobacco. Their desperation is boundless.

The tobacco supply is a trickle, and the only source is someone at the clay mines, and it's per *gram*, unspeakably high in price.

I sew for Madam Fukama, sew and fabricate on Mistress Kimura's wedding dress, teach the children six hours a week, and still function as first aid person and occasional translator. I've lost weight, though how much I don't know. At night I collapse into bed.

And work has increased for everyone; shifts at the clay mines are longer. Work parties for duties diverse are more frequent. And all the time, the scrip becomes increasingly worthless, and prices *avec commercial clandestinement* are exorbitant if the item is even available. But we *do* survive, the daily *guiding light* that makes brothers and sisters of all prisoners, past, present, or future.

<u>May 18, 1944. Otaru Barracks, Japan</u>
The "voyage" to the Prefecture's Residence for the final fitting began in the early morning. This is the fourth trip to the Residence, and Friend Annie and I are now "old soldiers." Each trip was identical to the first, including the surgical masks.

But now, knowing the countryside would be burgeoning with spring regrowth, I asked if this time the limousine's curtains could be raised for the three-quarter-hour trip. "Not Permitted" was the predictable reply. This time our "butler/constables" were more participatory in the packing and carrying, because the "real thing" wedding dress was almost on the level of a *holy artifact* in their eyes.

Since Heratina and Young Anna never rode in a machine, their first ride was as pivotal as it was for Friend Annie, though they had benefited from *weeks* of the latter's oral storytelling! Nonetheless, Young Anna had to be comforted as Friend Annie had initially; the sounds and movement of the limousine frighten a first-timer. Yet the entire passage and entry into the residence was all a very grand experience for them.

For the final fitting, the identical undergarments and shoes to be worn on the wedding day must be worn to ensure both a perfect fit and correct length. So menfolk were absented from that portion of the pavilion, for partial disrobing was required. A good dozen women were in the large room. Mistress Kimura had her own dresser/attendant with her this time, clearly an expert seamstress in her own right. They and the Otaru Barracks females were dressed "normally," the remainder traditionally. Formality was at its slackest, and this was not a scene of *occasional* talk.

So the final, elaborate act of this drama and labor was getting a vanguard look at Mistress Kimura. We saw her the way she'll be seen by approximately three hundred dignitaries on the day of the wedding. We worked until the final moment, when we all stared in pure awe, bringing upon this room full of chickadees rare silence: There was the perfectly beautiful Mistress Kimura, reflected in triplicate in the three-paneled, full-length mirror in its rich, bronze-colored wood frame. But most magnificently, before it stood a genuine beauty in the full regalia of maidenhood.

She was a wonderfully life-sized doll-child. Slightly less than five feet tall, not an ounce over "seven stone," as she put it (98 pounds). We all looked on for those moments, then one and all of us—Friend Annie being the first—began weeping, with only the sober but consistently good-humored bride tearless. Oh yes, I'm afraid I joined in. And in her Oxford-style English—all the world in the manner of a British movie star— she smiled and asked playfully, "I say! Why are you crying? It is endlessly beautiful. I am happy beyond words."

<u>May 25, 1944. Otaru Barracks, Japan</u>
It was just a few minutes past midnight when I was awakened by a villager friend who was shown into my cubby hole; I recognized the tiny woman at once. She was clearly frightened.

She bowed, then pushed a slip of paper into my hand and left immediately.

I could hear her coming and going at the rear entrance via the kitchen and out-building area. Her delivery took thirty seconds at most.

The note was a warning, in French. I am to be removed from Otaru Barracks at once, and should steel myself. I would not be hurt, but beyond that matters were unsure. Removal would come at daybreak. My informant would do what he could, but that was possibly little or nothing.

It wished me God's speed, and requested I destroy the note at once, which I did.

My Attu friend was privy to the contents, and clearly had facilitated the messenger's entry and departure so it would be out of view of Constable Nasimi, who at this hour (midnight to 1 a.m.) is brought tea and something to eat by his daughter. It was decided I could not delay a minute in telling Friend Annie about my planned removal.

When she was brought in and told, Annie—poor child—collapsed into the corner weeping silently, Titiana held to her. Alexi then brought in Philamon who avowed he would note the time and nature of my departure; also he would hide this journal with the church records and funds. "It will never be discovered, Mrs. Smith."

So, as I hastily write this entry, it is a dismal, hurried scene.

I cannot reckon why this is happening, save it must be connected with either the making of the dress, or events surrounding it. At the Prefecture's Residence all were profuse with gratitude. Since no extra gratuity in scrip or goods was negotiated or given for our labor, I perceived the economics of this gratitude to be its mainstay.

Though I part from this journal now, I declare my love for these wonderful Attu friends; also, all my family back in Delbert. And I cannot convey in words the love for all those who meant so much to me. Their time in this troubled world is over. If my time, too, is over, it will be God's will and I yield to it.

<u>July 23, 1944. Otaru, Japan</u>
How miraculous it is to be reunited with this old, old friend;
how its rough pages bring back better times. "It would have
never been found," Philamon guarantees proudly. But even
the miracle of reuniting with this tome cannot compare to the
joy of setting eyes on my dear Attu friends.

It has been an eventful, lonely two months. [*LAS was separated from the Attuans for fifty-eight days.*] Yet before I
begin a retrospective, I will catch up generally regarding
events and situations in Otaru.

Most importantly, all the Attuans are surviving, indeed
instead of thirty-nine there are now forty-one, for two infants
have been added, though it would have been three but one
infant died soon after birth. Sadly, this loss is closer to me, for
poor Friend Annie was the unfortunate mother.

Otaru Barracks is no more. A month after my removal, all
were moved (on one day's notice!) to a house on the opposite
side of the railroad yard. Though it was promoted by "our"
constables as an improvement, the villagers' opinions are
mixed. To begin with, there is no more room, overall, and what
there is, is distributed on two different stories.

The ancient stairs create a hazard and a problem.

It *is* closer to the stores, has a greater amount of land, but
like the barracks is without indoor plumbing, and there is a
single spigot. At the barracks, it was a job to keep it unfrozen
in the winters.

Work has increased for everyone, food has decreased, and
hunger is constant. No adult is exempt from work. Everyone is
bothered by hunger and fatigue.

Though during the summer all assumed food, especially vegetables, would be more abundant, they are not. Also, what is available on the *commercial clandestinement* is exceedingly dear. Of course, coal is not an issue during summer, but charcoal or fuel by which to cook is.

No one, especially the children, looks well. Everyone dreads the coming of winter.

~

The theme of my removal and treatment for the first week was humiliation. They waited until late in the morning to take me away, and did so after I was bound, elbows behind my back, as is the custom for criminals. A hood was put over my head, and I was tugged through the barracks by the four unknown creatures who I assume were some sort of policemen.

The last I remember of the barracks was the children and adults crying out in alarm, or weeping, at seeing me so treated. Also, as is customary, I was screamed at by my escorts. Once I was kicked, I assume in full view of all.

The hood remained on throughout the roughshod ride to the Prefecture's Residence. There it was removed, I was pushed out of a police wagon, and made to bow to the Administrator's Residence. He, nor anyone, was in attendance.

Then I was pushed to my knees and admonished, "Apologize for your greed and outlandish demands, besmirching and dishonoring. . . ."

And on and on in that vein. As I guessed, my attempt months before to bargain for food as regards fabricating the wedding dress was at center. Now the dress was done, the "important personages" gone, and it was Lila Ann's turn.

(One strange fact I recall, is they kept raining insults upon King George, so evidently they thought me British!)

I remember bracing myself to do what they said, but never to weep or ask for mercy. In the Orient, officials view pleas and tears as disgraceful. Occidentals, save for Germans, are widely held to be racially incapable of enduring hardship, and in fact, in the view of most Orientals, are simpering cowards. In fact, I never wept or asked for mercy.

This treatment continued for perhaps five or six days. The lowest point of my humiliation occurred when all my clothes were roughly stripped from me, and while I stood naked men laughed and said horrid things. I remained hooded. I have no idea where this took place. Only the humiliation of previous experiences made it possible to endure.

My hands ache from the weeks of labor, and I cannot write any further. But, I am so happy yet utterly tired in body and soul.

July 25, 1944. Otaru, Japan

I get constant questions such as, "Why is it that happened and you don't tell us yet?" This is Heratina talk for desiring a full report. Or, "Will you out loud read bad times?" which is how Binni shyly put it. In short, all are curious; hence my sorely treated hands are forced back to their previous duties as memory writer! But gladly I do this.

Within an hour, or less, after my ghastly humiliation, I was marched along flagstone streets (?) to the railroad station (again, all the while hooded) and put into a livestock car with many people; we were off. My guard was Mr. Kosei, a man in his sixties who spoke little, and when he did so, was gruff and officious to our fellow occupants. When they asked who this extraordinarily tall woman was, and why was she hooded, his dry little voice croaked, "SILENCE. QUESTIONS NOT PERMITTED."

I didn't know where I had started from and did not know where I was going. After dark, the hood was removed. Since it was summer, night came late. Around me burned a single coal-oil lamp, very low, and we proceeded slowly. Great puffs of engine smoke choked us, for the livestock car was slatted, giving free access to outside.

The people were all very poor, and for the first time I met Koreans who, like me, were being transported as compulsory labor, or slavery in my view.

I'm sure everyone in the car was Korean, save for a half-dozen guards like Mr. Kosei. No talk was allowed; facilities were like that on the coal ship that took us to Otaru. Unlike the ship, there were no children, and all the Koreans were far older than middle age.

Several asked for water, and again SILENCE was ordered. Koreans are extraordinary-looking people, resembling my Attu friends so much I almost felt like saying something in Aleut. This feeling was to continue, for I was often "detailed" with Koreans for the next two months.

~

At each stop, we were made to lower ourselves down from our railway car, a *long* drop! We fetched wood from the countryside, or indeed anything that would burn. Bundling it under the eyes of the guards, we'd walk back to the tracks and load it onto the tender car. Here burly little chaps, all black and smeared as hellish gremlins might be, took the bundles.

We were invariably scolded, for it was *never* enough wood, or *never* the right sort. If the guards took our part with the train crew, the words would fly even louder and faster. The work was brutal, for I was not used to it; the Koreans moreso, but still I could see that some were in the same situation as I.

We then were reloaded, each of us helping the more frail back into the livestock car, and there we would stew until the resumption of the trip. These pauses lasted, in some instances, a half-day.

The only advantage to the stops is we were allowed to answer nature's call, plus at the end of each work period, we were fed tiny balls of rice, which we wolfed down greedily. Throughout these two months, I experienced periods of extreme hunger, rare for me.

~

I must admit to great ignorance regarding geography, and especially that of Japan. Hokkaido Island must be quite large, for we traveled for five days through forests, steep alpine mountains—all the world as if we were back in Alaska, or perhaps the Northwest. It was almost identical to the countryside that swept past the delightful Pullman car that was Osmond's and my conveyance to Seattle, hence the ship north.

When the sun was up, I was hooded, but after four days Mr. Kosei allowed me to convert my hood to a makeshift purse. Also, there were fewer Koreans about; in fact only about a dozen remained.

Finally we arrived at the town of Wakkanai, on the north-ernmost tip of Hokkaido, just a few miles across the sea from Sakhalin Island. [*At this time, Sakhalin Island and the Korean Peninsula were under Japanese administration, which ended in 1945, the former becoming a part of the Soviet Union, the latter two independent nations.]*

And it was in this strange, windswept port town where I spent the remainder of my time away from Otaru. We were now a work party of eight, all the oldest, exclusively under the guardianship of a clearly at-home Mr. Kosei. "It is good to be in my home city." And he at once began to imbibe at various tiny saki shops, evidently inhabited by cronies of his. He would have us sit on the street, warning us of dire results if any escape or mischief were indulged. There we drew the high curiosity of all, especially the children—and moreso for me than the Koreans. If the curious became too numerous in viewing this extraordinarily "*long*" woman, Mr. Kosei chased them off with volleys of invective.

My comrades-in-work spoke a sort of Japanese I could only understand with difficulty, and vice versa, sad to say. One thing sure, we were the culls resulting from the long train ride. This meant that along the way the stronger and fitter of the workers had been chosen by municipal poobahs, who I've now learned are Council Chairmen and/or Council Captains. Every Japanese village, hamlet, town, and city has at least one Municipal Neighborhood Council.

~

By the second day in Wakkanai, we were virtually left at liberty, for Mr. Kosei was quite intoxicated, and had clearly given way to what appeared to be chronic dipsomania, the poor devil.

The eldest Korean, a Mr. Koo, had been in Wakkanai before, and since all my comrades had resided in Japan for many decades, they were at home with the culture. Their social status, though, was lowly. Finally, Mr. Koo found a Council Chairman, for now we were caring for Mr. Kosei, not he us. Because there is more than one sort of council in larger

Japanese towns such as Wakkanai, this Council Chairman knew nothing about us or Mr. Kosei, save for the obvious.

My stature and race had gained a following, for Mr. Kosei no longer chased gawkers away. I was something of a public hazard by impeding pedestrian travel.

The Chairman who had "inherited" this problem temporized by putting us in a small empty warehouse. Mr. Koo said to me that this food warehouse, like all of its kind, has been empty for some time. "Food is now scarce country-wide, of course."

~

What comes to memory is that in Wakkanai I realized no harm was going to come to me, and that—as in our removal from Attu—confusion dominated. It took several days to locate the proper authority, someone that knew of Mr. Kosei's mission.

Soon I was assigned as a scullery in a large food-service center where all manner of workers were fed daily. I worked in a basement, a steamy underworld of vats, piping, and such; I cleaned pots, pans, and diverse cooking ware. Well over one thousand people were fed each day.

I slept in a room where straw mats and sacking were stored, a place horrid for its infestation of rats, reminiscent of my confinement in China years before. We were given short clubs, and the four elderly women who shared the room arrived at a system of watches, meaning one would stay awake while three slept, and so on.

When the victims of our vigil were collected in the early morning, I knew enough not to ask about their disposal. Within two weeks, there were few rats to bother us.

<u>August 2, 1944. Otaru, Japan</u>
Friend Annie has fallen into a depression over the loss of her
newborn; emotional lows also plague the other mothers due to
the consistent undernourishment of the children. Friend
Annie's Titiana, an intensely eager, black-eyed doll of a babe,
is much too small and frail for her two and a half years.

Mike provides what he can extra, which is little. This
weighs on him enormously.

Vegetables are somewhat more abundant now, but this
added availability is rendered useless to the Attuans because
prices are exorbitant. Starches and protein are virtually
unavailable, save for rice. Still, despite its availability, the
purchases of rice takes the combined monies earned by all.
During my absence, batch-sewing income lessened, for one
experienced hand absent adversely affected production. Then
there were Madam Fukama's rejections and "secondings,"
which were suspicious. That individual is not to be trusted. But
my return has put an end to her machinations.

This all bodes darkly for the coming autumn and winter,
and it is a topic in all conversations. For above all else, my
Attu friends know about winter hardship. And I'm afraid the
intelligence I've accumulated to the north at Wakkanai does
nothing to brighten those discussions.

Regarding food, the situation here precisely reflects the
scarcity region-wide due to this calamitous war. Oftentimes in
the Wakkanai Port Authority Kitchen, which is where I worked,
there was little kitchenware to clean because that day there
had been almost no food. Those days were easy for us, but
made everyone cranky, and save for a thin broth, we were not
fed. Everyone lost weight.

~

Every day we loaded clean pots, pans, and mammoth
crocks onto a dreadfully unstable wagon and wheeled it

"upstairs" to the kitchen proper, which really meant "upramp," for floors were connected via steep cement inclines.

There we would pick up loads of dirty pots and pans, and more crocks, and wheel them back downstairs to a vast system of tanks and basins. Feeding a thousand people, even as little food as we often had, created a great volume of dirty cooking ware. And this daily humdrum of delivering clean cooking ware, then picking up and cleaning those that were dirty became my reason for existence. There is not much romanticism in such work.

<u>August 4, 1944. Otaru, Japan</u>
The addition of three nursing mothers weighed considerably on the already shabby food situation; however human nature (I suppose) being what it is, two more women are now pregnant. Unlike the former births, these new potential additions are viewed with appropriate gravity, if for no other reason than the sad outcome of Friend Annie's infant.

Philamon, in his official church position, has embarked upon a program of increased prayer and appeals to the Father and Son through an increased discipline of evening devotions. Growing hardship and the accompanying "weakness of the flesh" demands it, he feels. Though prayer each evening and morning in the "Holy Corner" was a part of life, there was general diminishing, in Philamon's view.

I agree an increase in matters of faith is positive, and I do admire them, but daily rigors must be confronted nonetheless. Reality in the form of hunger is unrelenting.

~

My stories about my northern adventure are pure gold in the "Stair House," the villagers' name for their new abode.

None of them had ever seen stairs in a house, save for a few of the men. About storytelling: my dear family does not hold to Mr. Aristotle's view of poetics, especially as regards suspense and conflict. In fact, a story once told may be retold again, becoming a village tradition; furthermore, a story *read* to them is yet another layer of interest.

Prior to my removal to Wakkanai, I had read or told several stories to any and all, if they could manage attendance. The three most popular are "Hansel and Gretel," "Little Red Riding Hood," and "The Boston Tea Party." (I have thrown tea into Boston Harbor at least 150 times!!)

Aleuts do not view children and adult stories as separate. So Hansel, Gretel, and Miss Hood—and all the American revolutionaries—occupy the same storytelling tradition. (Often, in the retelling of these stories, the Attuans will blend them all into one, a most *intriguing* amalgam!) So now, Lila Ann's adventures in the wilds of a Japanese kitchen have joined with Hansel, Gretel, Miss Hood, and the revolutionaries in Boston of old. May the spirits of my professors at Oberlin look down and forgive for me for so *discombobulating* history and folklore.

~

In Wakkanai I learned much about conditions for Japanese civilians in wartime Japan, or, at least this terminus of Japan. Since it was a busy port town, even this *official* kitchen dealt in the black market for food. The head cook, a swarthy old Chinese-Japanese woman whom I called "Minnie Ha-Ha" (I have adopted my Attu friends' penchant for nicknames) would "vanish" when shadowy male figures came in the rear door, but we sculleries knew they were black marketeers. If Minnie Ha-Ha did not deal with them, there would be no wood for the ranges, nor food to serve, for the most part. She held disdain for these sorts.

"Scum. All of them."

Loading and unloading in Wakkanai were merchantmen from all ports of Japan and China. This active interchange with underground provisioners, as it were, amounted to transactions with a multitude of greedy ship's officers; therefore, the dismal business gave us a unique link to outside sources. So our kitchen became something of a regional newspaper. Since three or four languages were common in this culinary mix of peoples, we learned that Japan was getting far the worst of it in the Pacific War. Also, that they were retreating, losing one Pacific island after another. Worst yet, heavy bombing of Japan's biggest cities was expected as soon as the Americans and British secured landing fields close enough to Japan. "Then the rats will be in the granary," opined even the dour Minnie Ha-Ha

Also, there was a wealth of domestic news. Confirmed were my suspicions that Japanese civilians nationwide were short of everything. Rationing was severe, and ordinary Japanese families also depended heavily on the black market, which was almost an open secret everywhere.

"There is even a black market inside the black market," our steward (a Korean) observed. Fuel was just as critical as food. Keeping this kitchen going, a so-called wartime *Hodgepodge Dining Hall*, was an every-hour ordeal. When all civilian restaurants were ordered closed for lack of food, these hodgepodge dining halls took their place for the public. In fact, I think our Hodgepodge replaced most of the restaurants and cafes for waterfront Wakkanai.

Often, our main bill of fare was only a thin porridge with bits of potatoes and radish, and perhaps a bit of snail. Always, there were a few grains of rice in it. We served once a day, at midday. A rare glance out one of the few windows was more than sufficient evidence of the extraordinary long lines of civilians forming several hours before opening time.

If I were to read everything to my village family, it would sadden and scare them even more than they already are. For the situation in far north Wakkanai, I'm fairly sure, is better than points south due to the former's porous merchant trade.

I have every fear that this coming winter, unless the war ends and sanity returns, events will be extraordinarily bleak.

<u>August 10, 1944. Otaru, Japan</u>
<u>Her Return: Reasons</u>
The miracle (best word) and answer to my prayers—the return to my friends in Otaru—began as abruptly as my odyssey to Wakkanai and for reasons equally opaque. One morning two *constables* (an assumption by Lila Ann, for they wore strange uniforms) appeared, and Minnie Ha-Ha said, "These trained apes will escort you to the railroad station."

And that was the entirety of the explanation and preparation time allotted. But this time there weren't group humiliations or confinement, thank God, but a simple direct trip to the station in the company of my escorts; in fact, it was done on municipal transport. They had no machine nor wagon.

My former hood, in which I'd been so abused, was now my only portable item, my converted purse. Begging for two minutes' time, I quickly "packed" and the last I remember were the aged, emaciated Korean women and men with whom I worked weeping for me. To this hour, I don't know if they did so for anticipated sorrow, or the joy of my liberation as a seven-day-a-week, fourteen-hour-a-day scullery.

"I shall pray for you all" was all I could manage before being hustled away. Poor, poor people.

~

Since I was *unhooded* all during the return trip, the two and a half days were filled with sights of Hokkaido Island. I ate and slept on the train, with only brief escorted outwalks during longer stops and transfers. I wore a string label around my neck, every bit like a naughty school child. I was ordered to stay in one car, and was closely observed, initially, by the conductors. After the first day, their scrutiny became cursory. This was quite a contrast to the northward portion of my journey.

Once again, I had a powerful feeling of Alaska, especially that seen around Three Rivers Station, with the intermittent timber stands and wild country, with many miles between towns. It had a distinct un-Asian feel to it: Everywhere was bustle, and especially logging, milling, and mining. Our train, which carried passengers and some freight, was stopped frequently, for the materials for war being carried by laden freight trains took priority.

At every station were signs exhorting the citizenry to wartime sacrifice; these posters included large illustrations of various sorts. My car always was chock-full of civilians of all stripes. There I sat, six feet tall, an old Occidental lady in smock dress, carrying a worn old sack, and wearing a shipping tag! There was always staring and profuse discussion, and the inevitable questions when they found out I spoke rudimentary Japanese.

Old discarded newspapers were easily come by and were my reading material. Japanese in newspapers is very hard for me, but I understood enough to make trying interesting. Once again, there were many messages of optimism, aimed at boosting the morale of the populace, making them aware of wartime responsibilities for saving and making do. That message was everywhere.

The heat was terrible, and all the windows of the train were open, and there was a constant invasion of all outdoor nastiness, including furious swarms of biting gnats (especially at stops) mixed in with harsh clouds of wood smoke when wind and direction were right. Fortunately, the wind killed or drove off the former.

Passengers would hang out the window, attempting to access breathable air at these times, only to have the conductors scream "NOT PERMITTED! TUNNEL COMING!" and bodily seize their suffocating clientele and unceremoniously haul them inboard. Likewise animals, for I assume my car was a class above the "animal-in-hand" category of passenger. When travelers appeared with caged chickens, ducks, geese, or (on one occasion) two piglets, there were even more shouted prohibitions, and the mischief-maker and unwanted companions rudely and quickly half-pushed from our more civilized domain!

After nearly six weeks as a scullery in the bowels of a former soccer (? I assume) stadium (I have not mentioned that, but this is where our hodgepodge was located), this train trip exposed me to an unvarnished view of life-on-Hokkaido. It was a rich and utterly intriguing experience.

So I could write on for volumes, but it came to an end on the third day after a half-day wait in Sapporo for the change to the coast, and Otaru. There, my transport became more formal, and two elderly constables were assigned upon my arrival. But still no hood!

Everything I learned on this trip reinforced what I'd learned in the hodgepodge at Wakkanai: the everyday Japanese were enduring serious shortages of staples, and they too were taking shortcuts, making ends meet.

The last section of my trip was in a rail car with the windows blacked out. I was kept amused, however, by one of the constables (more garrulous than the average constable) asking me about life in Holland. More or less, I *think* he asked, "Why would the Dutch resist Japan? We have always been friends with the Dutch. Japan eats much chocolate and loves tulips."

Perhaps I spoke my primitive Japanese with a Dutch accent? But, since I was very weary, I allowed his error-in-fact to continue "as-is," until his colleague told him to "shut up." At this, an icy pall descended for the remainder of the trip.

~

At the station in Otaru, there stood Chief Constable Aiko and Mr. Toshihara stuffed into formal uniform, despite the heat. The latter could not suppress a smile, while the Chief Constable upbraided my two Sapporo escorts for something about which I'm uncertain. They went away downcast. Chief Constable had prepared a written welcoming statement—two copies, one which he read, the second given to me:

"Your work in the north brought honor to us. Your return is your reward. Also, you will be of great help to our sewing effort. In your absence, production has slowed, and Madam Fukama is troubled. She is a loyal subject devoted to the Emperor."

With me holding my meager purse, Chief Constable dismissed Mr. Toshihara and myself with a nod, and as we walked away from the station and out of view, I was told of our change in domicile. "This new place is quite a mansion. You'll see. Two full stories with window shades!"

Aleuts view weeping for joy as the highest form of welcome, and men and women alike surrounded me, weeping. I too wept. The children wept. All my little friends were so dreadfully frail.

Friend Annie and I—her recent loss still so fresh—were like mother and daughter reunited; we could barely speak. I have not received such a greeting since my return to Iowa after my years in China, on the heels of my experiences in the camp of General Lon Shi.

That night, I was introduced to my new honored quarters in "Stair House," a tiny but comfortable closet on the street side of the second floor.

My first night was spent wondering after Iowa, for the love and care I'd enjoyed that day in Otaru, I knew, awaited me in Delbert. Thinking of summertime in Iowa, so far away in both distance and time, I experienced sadness, and I missed Uncle Thomas and Aunt Delia as perhaps never before.

My old heart endured both joy and sadness on this first night back in Otaru. Thank God, truly, for the gift of sleep.

✣

<u>August 25, 1944. Stair House, Otaru, Japan</u>
We have been extraordinarily busy since my return, and I've discovered that batch-work, teaching, and scullery work demand different sorts of energy. But I write now, because today, a Friday, is the first clinic since my return. As I hoped, Dr. Takata and his two house "assistants" accompanied Dr. Nagai and his nurses.

I had not seen Dr. Takata since April 14, four months. They have been an eventful four months, and matters would be grim indeed for me if Dr. Takata had not continued to function as my guardian angel, for I am *sure* he had a crucial, if not sole, hand in my return.

It was a warm day, and since the Stair House has a front porch, we sat there on chairs provided by his assistants-in-life, as he so pleasantly calls them. (He eschews the word "servant" in any language.)

I quickly and ardently conveyed my gratitude, but raising his tiny, wizened hand from his canehead and moving it back and forth pendulum-style, he said, "It is my way of apologizing. Your treatment is not the Japanese way. You are a linguist, teacher, and scholar, and such disrespect is shameful, of course. Also, revenge is a low vice, usually typical of criminals and their elements."

Any discussion about events during the previous months was over, and for the first time I was annoyed at my benefactor, for there was much I wanted to know. But I, too, dislike ingratitude, and I owe Dr. Takata much, and what he did certainly risked something of his own prestige. So when he blithely moved on, desiring to talk of China, I swallowed pounds of *curiosity* regarding his statement about revenge, and moved on to the topic he desired. Indeed, he *could* be aware of reasons and benefits unknown to me in *not* discussing past events.

My visit and reunion with Dr. Takata ended abruptly and on a distressing note. It was announced by Dr. Nagai that Strong Ivan must return to sanitarium along with two other Sergiefs, John and Agafia. This latter case is even more dreadful because Agafia has a newborn that must go with her. Our Second Chief, Pete, must also go along with his daughter Angelina; the poor lovely thing is so frail now.

Dr. Nagai's manner is not that of Dr. Takata, or even of our three constables—for that matter, even of the Chief Constable. He is a small, waspish man, without grace or diplomacy. Unlike Madam Fukama, he is not acerbic or in any way negative, just without a sense of tact. So this makes it worse. Family members and friends were distressed, and Mother Agafia was beside herself, for initially through difficulties of language she thought her baby (christened Anise, after her deceased aunt) could not go.

But with the situation resolved, I bid the generous Dr. Takata goodbye, and repeated my thanks. While doing so we stepped aside to allow Dr. Nagai's nurses access as they began to escort the patients to an awaiting transport. At that moment, Dr. Takata said to me in French, "Conditions for tuberculosis, I'm afraid, under these conditions, are at their bleakest."

That evening there were many tears and hands for me to hold. Friend Annie continues to be depressed and Mike worries constantly. I do what I'm able, but my concerns for her, and everyone, increase with the shortening of days.

<u>September 10, 1944. Stair House, Otaru, Japan</u>
This morning was the nadir for Friend Annie. Mike rushed in, a crying Titiana in arms, to tell me Annie would not rise and had

wept unceasingly all through that night. He was frantic, and did not want the others to know. In our living circumstances, this is not possible, and within minutes Philamon knew, then Heratina, then everyone.

Moving her to my closet on the second floor was almost stretcher work, but when secured on my pallet, she turned to the wall, weeping.

Anna [*Tschigorin*] looked after Titiana with the rest of the children, and Mike went off to work, and was nearly dragged away by Alexi with great difficulty.

We were then alone.

I served two cups of hot tea, and after much persuasion, she sat up and cradled the cup in her diminutive lap. As is her habit, she used a spoon, raising it up, allowing it to cool, then drinking.

There is no sugar, no saccharine, and since like all villagers she adores sugar in her tea, she sighed in disappointment at the initial sip.

For the first time since his demise forty-four years ago, I talked with her about Joseph, and it was painful.

We were brother and sister and best friends. At Mennonite Bethel, we were the only Occidental children and I looked after him, but he after me too.

Following my capture, in my most humiliated hours, I became bitter with mother and father for letting Joseph down, allowing the rebellion to reach such lethal proportions without evacuating. There were opportunities Father did not take. In the end, I was left alone, at the mercy of that army of brutes.

I took Friend Annie firmly by both shoulders and said with as much emphasis and love I could muster, "You *must not* allow this sadness over your lost babe to rob Mike and Titiana of his wife and her mother. Don't abandon them like my parents unwittingly did me, nor fail them entirely as happened to dear Joseph."

Annie, seeing me so clearly upset with these memories, became at once comforting. And we remained silent until, pulling ourselves together, we resumed the day's Sisyphean labors in our (new) sewing room.

ॐ

September 24, 1944. Stair House, Otaru, Japan
Disaster has struck. The thirty-eight who remain at the Stair House have almost to a person been struck with food poisoning and Dr. Nagai had to be called in. Fourteen-year-old Zephryis [*Tschigorin*] is unconscious in hospital; also his cousin Alfred, now almost eighteen, "Sad" Peter [*Chirikof*], age sixty-three, and lastly poor Fekla [*Andreanof*], age forty-nine.

Others are less sick, including myself, though miserably distressed. Worse yet, for the first time the fellowship and kinship among the villagers is poisoned, for it was Zephryis and Alfred who stole the fish scraps used in the soup, and Mary and Ann Tschigorin who prepared it. Therefore, the incident is seen as the responsibility of that family, and as God's punishment for stealing the fish during a nightly raid. This activity, I've just found out, has been ongoing.

"Next time, you all will die!"

Dr. Nagai announced this to all, both in Japanese and then through a very ill Alexi in Aleut. I am very weak due to dehydration, for it was a terrible disorder. No one talks to the Tschigorins, despite the fact that Dr. Nagai has opined that Zephryis will not survive.

Ironically, to a person, we thought the sorrowful brew a wonderful broth.

ॐ

October 2, 1944. Stair House, Otaru, Japan
Chief Constable Aiko used the provisioning day (Monday) to announce that any future thievery or unauthorized leave-taking from Stair House will be punished "most severely." It

was, he claimed, due to the generosity and good offices of Dr. Nagai and the hospital that all survived. Also, that Prefecture officials have decided that all medical expenses accrued due to "our chicanery" will be paid by us in work-scrip installments. "You will then learn to be responsible for one another, especially adults for children."

Then Constable Nasimi was scolded before us all, his "wand" of office removed and given ceremoniously to his replacement, the awful Mr. Big Jaw of earlier times.

"You will obey all rules and be obedient to the constables."

Half our scrip was deducted this week, and will be through October to pay for medicines "ordinarily used only by personages vital to the Pacific War effort." This was the first public mention of the war which has brought the Attuans so low.

It is cold now, or colder, and we cannot afford coal. Events do not promise an easy winter. I am still weak, and sewing is difficult.

❧

October 22, 1944. Stair House, Otaru, Japan

At Sunday services, which I sometimes attend also as "guest" since I'm not of Orthodox cloth, Philamon did an unusual thing. Normally he reads the Holy Gospel in Russian, then there are Russian prayers, a scattering of Aleut, and services are concluded. But today he took his privilege as Reader and sermonized. He was uncomfortable with this function. He simply presaged a prayer in Aleut with a simple homily on forgiveness, and how recent events have divided families. "Bad feelings are not holy in the eyes of Christ. If we cannot endure without anger among us, what does the future hold? We are prisoners, held against our will. We are treated badly, but we can't treat each other badly."

This in his clear and distinct Aleut, the translation double-checked by Friend Annie, transcribed here as closely as possible. After it, he led us all in a prayer of forgiveness.

This did wonders in clearing the air which had been heavy with bad feelings for the previous month. None of us need reminding about poor Zephryis, who will never be the same child again.

[*LAS never gives details about Zephryis Tschigorin's permanent malady resulting from the food poisoning episode of 9/23/44.*]

<u>November 2, 1944. Stair House, Otaru, Japan</u>
The weather has settled into dreariness: light gray skies, with frequent chilly rains, often windy weather, and few sunny days. We have experienced several snowfalls. We all work six days each week, save the youngest children. In the sewing room we both look after the children and keep up with batch-work. I am always tired. I now weigh 104 pounds, quite the beanpole at five foot eleven and one-half inches!

There is talk of Sunday work opportunities with private homes in town, and this will be seized upon if offered.

There is scarcity or absence of all necessities, and nothing extra. Two of the leadsmen at the clay mine took pity knowing the plight here. Two weeks back, they provided one-half case of dried herring, some cured kelp, and black, wonderful tea leaves. This from those who I know are also struggling.

This time, the menfolk (and Heratina!) were waiting for the initial signs of Big Jaw's *liberties*, and they were not long in coming. Alexi went at once to Chief Constable, and for now Big Jaw's masher tendencies are squelched. If he resumes, there will be trouble.

Our only two "community times" are on Sundays during church services and the weekly escorted trip to the baths. The Aleuts have not only gotten used to these, but look forward to them. Village fellowship has returned to its former conviviality despite enduring such deprivation.

<u>November 5, 1944. Stair House, Otaru, Japan</u>
Without notice or warning an urn containing the ashes of
Strong Ivan Sergief was delivered by Constable Ojiwa. This
time, he knew the dismay this task would cause. All despaired
over Strong Ivan's death, for he was loved by everyone;
equally, that his Christian remains are so blasphemed.

The last visit to the sanitarium by Alexi one week ago did
not reveal that Strong Ivan was in dire straits, though he'd
been getting weaker. Worse, this horrible news comes in the
form of ashes, placed clumsily in an urn, the lid not even fas-
tened—the urn itself not large enough. No word of solace; no
explanation. Nothing. Just the urn.

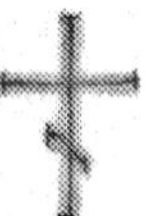

Though Philamon keeps meticulous records, he worries that
facts be recorded in two places in the event his are found or
lost. So I herein oblige:

Since our capture on June 6, 1942, six have died or been
killed: Osmond Smith, Kusma Tschigorin, Anise Sergief, Ivan
Sergief, Elder Tschigorin, and infant Korovin, Annie's baby.

Three have been born, two survive thus far. Total number
of us now: There are forty-two souls, with thirty-seven in the
Stair House and five in Sengo Sanitarium.

<u>November 23, 1944. Stair House, Otaru, Japan</u>
Thanksgiving Day, though only I am aware of it. I do not share
this fact, for Aleuts do not observe it, and it would be too
ironic to even give voice to the *word*.

There is little to give thanks for, and as gloomy as that sounds it is true. I am weak and tired, with no energy, and my lack of vitality renders me unwilling to couch the situation.

There was a bitter scene on Monday, the 20th, "provisioning day." There turned out to be only a half-sack of rice to distribute, nothing else. *For the entire week*. What began with complaints over this tiny ration graduated into much more. Walter Sergief accused Chief Constable Aiko for responsibility in his brother Strong Ivan's death. Thus emboldened, and in the same instant, Alexi declared in Japanese, "You took us prisoner; you work us. You should feed us and give us coal."

Chief Constable is a taciturn person; anyway, he didn't expect this, which seems somewhat surprising. At that moment, Big Jaw responded, brandishing his club and screaming; Heratina and two of the other women joined in, and seeing things spinning out of control, Alexi became the peacemaker, along with Constable Toshihara (this occurred at change-of-watch time). Their intercession resulted in a begrudging peace.

The entire time, Chief Constable stood planted, completely confused. He left, hunched over, escorted by his two constables.

Since then, work details have come and gone—I sew, we all carry on. And every tedious second of the day and night is fraught with hunger and cold. There is almost no rice, and there is *no* coal.

The men scavenge some wood, and burn it in one of the two stoves in the Stair House. The mothers with infants, and the children, huddle close to this one source of heat through the night. In the mornings, they huddle vainly. The stove is simply an ice-cold artifact, for what little fuel there was was hours ago consumed.

I see no let-up in this hardship. If thanks are due to higher forces, it is because no one else has died since Ivan. But I dread the inevitable if these conditions continue.

<u>December 6, 1944. Stair House, Otaru, Japan</u>
Something is terribly amiss region-wide. At the clay mines
Mike and the others have noticed a change in the Japanese
workers. Their friendliness, helpfulness, has been replaced
by polite silence. "I notice this maybe a week ago," my
most devoted reporter Mike observed. The other clay mine
workers reaffirm this, including the women who work in
assembly.

There was much speculative talk about it.

It is indeed real. I too could feel something during this
week's visit from the usually voluble, compulsively deceitful
Madam Fukama. She didn't try and sneak in rejections and
seconds amongst uncut batches, nor did she harangue her two
assistants as much.

Furthermore, all Japanese everywhere are even more close-
mouthed about events. During the day, more machines carrying people rumble by the house, for unlike the barracks, this
house is located on a through street. The only clue occurred
during this week's *unofficial* provisioning (the more elegant
term for the obvious!). For the first time no rice was for sale,
but instead abundant potatoes and dozens of presentable
heads of cabbage. Heratina and group bought the maximum
with funds available, which was little. The sight of plenty was
cruel for those so hungry.

But our callous "back-door" provisioner is a gossip. He
bragged that his change in inventory was due to his keen eye
for business. "There are many well-off people now coming to
the north island from the south. They think they will outwit us
bumpkins and make money by selling produce from there. But
their tails are between their legs, and we know it."

And this was our only clue. But we see no military, only
civilians (many children). And they are carefully packed
together, comparatively cheerful, and, true to the Japanese
way, organized. The skies and surroundings are blessedly
without sight or sound of conflict.

Our curiosities itch! Everyone tries to find out something. Of course, all hope that it *might* be a sign the war is about to end. If this were true, the timing could not be better.

December 9, 1944. Stair House, Otaru, Japan

In the midst of all this hardship, Stair House has developed its own *cacher et l'escouade de poignard* [roughly, cloak-and-dagger squad].

It is our Hollywood drama, something like a *particularly* shocking picture show with Ms. Garbo [the 1933 Garbo vehicle *Mata Hari*]. Our sole movie house in Delbert would not show it, for the owners are strict Baptists. Uncle Thomas, therefore, was forced to load up any "brave hedonists" and drive the dusty thirty-seven miles to Tildon, where they did show it. "Wouldn't miss old Garbo doing a hootchy-kootchy for the world" he proclaimed

Of course, Aunt Sarah completely disapproved, but went along to "shop" (although it was a Sunday and all knew shops were closed). So rather than sit in the Ford, she attended.

"Oh, she knew shops weren't open on Sunday. At center, she's got a bit of the devil in her, that girl does!" Uncle Thomas opined at a group gathering during our monthly "clan dinner," with Aunt Sarah clucking away in disapproval. Those two prove the point that opposites attract, much like myself and Emmett.

But so far, Stair House's *cacher et l'escouade de poignard* has not provided the answer for the change in mood amongst our Japanese neighbors. But Mike and Alexi allow cleverly that "to be known soon. Soon. Yes! We have a good way."

It is too easy, sometimes, for me to forget how far away from home I am, and how much I miss everyone in Iowa. My mind refuses to bring it forth.

It aches they have not allowed me to write letters home, despite international agreements. Perhaps I might have sneaked out something whilst in the north. But if caught, matters would have gotten even worse. I could trust no one save perhaps the Koreans, but we shared the same predicament.

They say the villagers are not prisoners of war, but Japanese citizens. Except me. I'm told by Dr. Nagai that my status is that of a visitor in Japan at time of war, which is different than a prisoner of war.

"Do you generally execute visitors?" responded Lila Ann, referring to Osmond, and with that, there was no more talk about the matter save "that is the official status on the records. I can do nothing."

I have not heard any word from Delbert, nor they from me, since February of 1942. I constantly wonder after their welfare.

December 15, 1944. Stair House, Otaru, Japan
I have been hesitant to open this chronicle, for there is much confusion.

It seems that events on the south island of Honshu, in Tokyo and vicinity, if our information is to be believed, have turned fantastical. American bombers have commenced bombing the city, setting it afire. The bombers come in high, and there is no defense of merit.

Thousands die unspeakable deaths in the fires—women, children, old people—the killing is indiscriminate.

The information is from dozens of sources, including the national radio station, newspapers, and ships' crews. Our sources about these are credible, but their information is *in*credible.

I cannot believe the United States would do such a thing. They did bomb Japan in the Doolittle raid, but they bombed military targets, and few of those, they say. These bombings, by contrast, are by hundreds of planes many times *each week*.

Civilians have fled the cities, and continue to do so. Almost all venture to areas where there are relatives. Adults who must stay in the city make sure their children evacuate. This explains, finally, the influx even here.

They say millions have fled Tokyo. This all seems absolutely the stuff of war rumor, always exaggerated vastly. I tell my Aleut family about war zones, how I lived through them, and how wild rumor flourishes and gains believability through the telling.

They too cannot believe their nation would do such a thing.

"Americans are Christian people, perhaps not all Orthodox, but Christian."

And with that pronouncement by Philamon, all have dug in their heels regarding these fantastic reports.

[The U.S. bombing of Japan's densely populated urban areas via B-29s began in late November of 1944 and continued with increasing intensity and effect until the end of the war, August 1945. An accurate total of civilian deaths will never be known, but most international military scholars agree they exceeded 500,000 during that nine-month period. This includes the atomic bomb attacks on Hiroshima and Nagasaki. One hundred and sixty square kilometers were entirely burned out in five main cities, including twenty-five square kilometers in Tokyo on one night, March 10, 1945. In excess of ten million civilians fled the cities for the country-side in organized evacuations after January 1945.]

<u>December 26, 1944. Stair House, Otaru, Japan</u>
Heavy snows have fallen each day this week, and the entire population struggles at snow removal. "Regular" Christmas

has come and gone, and like all other holidays save Orthodox ones, passes entirely without note. At least my Aleut friends celebrate Orthodox holy days modestly with special services and prayer, thanks to the continuing attention to church calendar by Philamon.

The management of household affairs pushes everyone to the extremes of endurance: *if* we buy enough "secret" rice, *and* are issued even a little "honest" rice, we aren't so hungry, but absolutely ice-cold through the week.

If we hold back a little for coal, then the hunger of all increases, including the children—which is extreme enough— but the awful cold is less. For at least one stove can be kept going for a just few hours a day, and the growing number of sick and weak benefit this way.

The children do not play and there are no longer any attempts at classes for them. Story times do not stem this growing lethargy. Friend Annie yesterday told me, "We will all die here and never be heard from again. God has forgotten us."

I'm afraid she would get little argument from her fellow villagers. I tried to explain that God certainly has not forgotten us, but just misplaced us, and will soon find us again. She held Titiana, who is now under thirty pounds, and wept. The four of us who sew (myself, Friend Annie, Anna, and Mary) struggle to keep moving.

There is little sleeping apart now, and most huddle in groups of a half-dozen or more at night. As I write these lines, the winds have increased and work furiously at the Stair House. I have the darkest foreboding about the coming months.

<u>January 1, 1945. Stair House, Otaru, Japan</u>
The coming of the New Year (modern calendar) ushered in our darkest hours. John Sergief and Innokenty Andreanof ran away from Stair House two days ago; also, the infant daughter of

Mary Tschigorin died on December 31, and late the same day (after dark) a distracted Mary disappeared carrying the body of the infant, just turned three months of age.

Her husband Leonty was frantic. After suffering through a night of inactivity enforced by the constable on watch, in the early morning he too bolted, of course to look for her. But his departure was seen, and Constable Big Jaw followed him, brandishing his bamboo stick, screaming stupidly that unauthorized departures were NOT PERMITTED.

Big Jaw returned within the hour, sans stick and with a great knot on his forehead; he was livid, and took it out on everyone. But his rage didn't last long, for shortly our home constabulary arrived, along with Chief Constable Aiko and three regular Otaru police. They had begun hunting for the boys early on the previous day. Now this.

Chief Constable lined everyone up, and before the resumption of the search (now for four people and a deceased child) he repeated his earlier threats of severe punishment, and how we had not listened. "Now I will use my full authority to exact punishment when all this wasteful trouble is settled."

The search continued through New Year's Day, and though all of us expected Leonty and Mary to be quickly found—after all, they would rather stand out, and hardly be organized— they were not returned. When Philamon and Alexi inquired of the constable on duty (a morose and sore [!] Big Jaw left behind and doing a double shift; perhaps this was a disciplinary measure for allowing Mary and Leonty to run off), Sir Big Jaw was in no mood to impart information, even if he knew any.

This day ended with young and old restless, rife with speculation as to the whereabouts of their fellow villagers and/or blood relations.

I dread the passing of the hours, for everything now has joined the unknown.

Sunday, January 7, 1945. Stair House, Otaru, Japan
Today is Orthodox Christmas, and a most somber and emotionally clouded day it is. There is no word or sign of
Innokenty and John, nor of Mary and Leonty. Questions are no
longer permitted, and the most petty punitive measures are in
force, I assume, via the orders of Chief Constable.

So the joy of this holiday is almost absent for there was
"starring," but it lacked the verve of even previous years in
this terrible imprisonment, (despite what officials term it). This
is the third Christmas spent in Otaru, Japan, by my unfortunate
Aleut friends, and me with them. Fellow prisoners, all of us.

Night came and with it brought a frightful wind storm,
with an abundance of slushy snow mixed in. A few candles
burned, and even inside this old house their tiny flames
wavered with every gust that swept over our residence. I'm
sure that all of us, without speaking of them, thought of our
wayward villagers with each powerful gust of wind.

January 11, 1945. Stair House, Otaru, Japan
The truth has come out about the motives behind John and
Innokenty's departure. It seems that Innokenty formed a
romantic attachment with a Japanese girl at the clay mine
who, when the situation came to light, was shipped off to her
home in a small village somewhere north.

Innokenty was broken-hearted, vowed she would become
his wife, and went off in pursuit, knowing the name of her
home village. John went along because they are fast chums,
and like all the young people, miserable; plus he wanted
adventure. Lastly, John speaks the best Japanese of any of the
men, having something of a propensity for languages, and
will be a pivotal help for Innokenty.

The romance was sworn to the utmost secrecy months ago within the circle of John, Mike (of all people!!), Old Albert (Chirikof), and last but not least, Alexi. "None of the women-folk knew," confessed Mike, including his wife Annie, which put her off somewhat for a day or so.

The truth came out during the investigation by Chief Constable, who got to the bottom of it. One of the kindly potters at the clay mine found out what Chief Constable knew and told Old Albert.

The Sergief and Andreanof clans do feel a *little* better. To begin with, Innokenty at twenty-five years of age is a seasoned trapper, and winter travel will not involve risk. Since authorities now know where they're going, their capture will be sure, and perhaps has taken place already. Since he's a young man long in need of a wife, Innokenty's motives make the situation more logical, certainly forgivable. Of course, what continues to worry the families are the ominous words of Chief Constable.

Innokenty and John have been gone twelve days now.

But there is still despair over Leonty and Mary, who have been gone almost as long. Mary wore no cold-weather clothing, and Leonty could have incurred serious injury from Mr. Big Jaw during the struggle over the latter's baton.

Neither speaks Japanese beyond the most rudimentary level, and such a duo—if indeed Leonty found Mary—would have stuck out like the proverbial sore thumb. There is speculation, but no information at all. As a group, we are almost completely shut off from all news save for a few stalwarts at the clay mines.

Head counts are now every six hours. Our leash has been noticeably tightened. Shoppers and work detailers are absolutely escorted by a constable. About food and fuel, there simply is no good news. And it is the children who suffer most, and the direct reason for Mary's infant death, for malnutrition had made her unable to nurse.

There are special prayers morning and evening for our missing villagers.

<u>January 15, 1945. Stair House, Otaru, Japan</u>
When Dr. Nagai arrived with Chief Constable just prior to the work details leaving in the morning, we knew the news was grim. They stood side by side at the entrance, and I don't recall the Chief Constable being ill-at-ease before, nor Dr. Nagai attempting to be considerate by keeping his language slow, simple, and with some sign of sympathy.

Dr. Nagai explained that Leonty and Mary Tschigorin were found dead beneath a building adjacent to a warehouse several kilometers distant. They had dug a shallow grave for the infant, buried her, then evidently fallen asleep. Dressed lightly, they died of exposure subsequent to that. They were found days after their actual passing. Dr. Nagai personally examined them and said they had clearly been alive for some time after the burial.

He then, with much clearing of the throat and awkwardness, explained how cremation was policy for *all* Japanese now, and that wartime required sacrifice. Yet, because of our loss, today would be a rest day, for he and Chief Constable knew there would be Christian ceremonies.

At that, two urns were removed from a small box by Dr. Nagai's nurse and placed gingerly on a tea table. They then departed.

Zephryis, Leonty and Mary's only surviving child, we think comprehended the news, as he did their being missing, but demonstrates nothing further than simply nodding. He did pray at services. His physical health is not good at all.

The weeping was very quiet; all did what we could to comfort the Tschigorins. There is no word of John and Innokenty. Spirits have sunk in the Sergief and Andreanof families, a result of this awful news.

There were no questions, yet there remained a hundred questions, not the least of which was, did the urns contain the ashes, also, of the infant Alina?

~

Mary Tschigorin was not born in Attu, but far east in the town of Ivanof, which is actually on the Alaska Peninsula. Her father was a Reader at Ivanof. He and Mary's mother were Nikolski residents, which actually is a different group of Aleuts, hundreds of miles east of Attu, on the large Aleutian island of Umnak.

Leonty and Mary's marriage was arranged by the "wandering" priest Father Mikhail Lieskof, famous for his circuit ministry to the entire Aleutians. His skill and indomitable spirit at matchmaking in these lonely, tiny Aleut hamlets has made him a legend. Mary was just fourteen at the time of her marriage, and Leonty was thirty. Their marriage celebration was a time of great joy in Chichigof Village.

Leonty was born on Attu, a tireless trapper famous for his endurance and instinct for following and trapping foxes. Furthermore, he had learned the skill of actually tanning fox hides, and though all pelts were transported to San Francisco, Leonty was an advocate of tanning at Attu, or the very least somewhere in the Aleutians. Their trading value, then, would be higher. He was considered a forward thinker.

Somewhere, Leonty had traded for a violin, and despite hours of practice with a tiny book that had evidently come with it, could never play it even tolerably well. This brought much mirth to the village, and Leonty himself built upon it. He was a great jokester.

Leonty and Mary were admired for their many attempts at parenthood, which resulted in so few children surviving. Mary was a tiny woman, and always had trouble going to term and in labor. They were devout, and Philamon rightly lionized their dedication to their religion, families, and traditions.

Like the others, the ashes will be kept safe, transported back to Attu whenever we are freed, and the proper religious authorities consulted on precisely what to do concerning interment.

I can personally testify to Mary's intelligence and skill in learning the sewing trade. She was a kind, good friend and I shall miss her terribly. I am a wiser woman for knowing her.

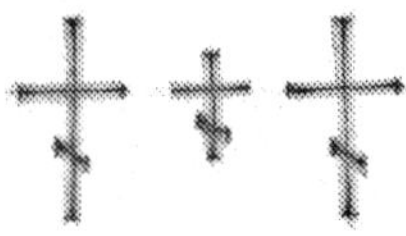

January 24, 1945. Stair House, Otaru, Japan
Finally some word concerning John and Innokenty, however meager. They were finally caught by authorities many miles to the north over a week ago, according to our *confidant*, who is absolutely reliable. And that is all.

Any information regarding the circumstances of their present situation and health is unknown. Again, this has resulted in some increase of the families' spirits, but perhaps more anxiety as well.

I cannot help but think that several of the children and a few adults are close to death. I am familiar with death by starvation; in China, victims of region-wide famine would come to Mennonite Bethel by the hundreds. For many, it was too late.

Adults, children—everyone. It was, and is, a pitiable sight. The little ones are the worst.

The greatest of poets or writers could, *and have*, put pen to paper for an eternity of lines. Despite these lofty efforts, though, they have never captured the tragedy suffered by ordinary folk when those in power partake in the heartless folly of war.

<u>January 26, 1945. Stair House, Otaru, Japan</u>
However belatedly, Dr. Nagai and nurses removed those cases of starvation to hospital. I underscore those who are children or youths:my Friend Annie, her daughter *Titiana*, Old Ivan [*Tschigorin*], Alfred [*Tschigorin*] , *Zephryis*, *Mavra* Chirikof, Peter Chirikof, *infant babe Andreanof* with mother Mary, and *Dimitri Andreanof*.

The nurses at the direction of Dr. Nagai refer to the evacuees as "tubercular," and in most cases they are positive for the disease. But to dismiss or deny malnutrition as root cause is simple nonsense, and for the first time I hold Dr. Nagai's actions as unethical. If officialdom, always prominent in things Japanese, forces him to suppress our situation, then omission would be better than falsehood.

I am angry and beside myself; my best friend in the world has gone to the sanitarium, and her husband Mike cannot deal with the removal of his wife and daughter. He has fallen into an awful depression "Is there nothing I can do?" he keeps repeating.

Including newborns, subsequent to our capture in June of 1942, ten have died, thirteen are in sanitarium, and two are missing.

Two seamstresses remain, myself and Binni. Through the grace of God, we both remain reasonably healthy. Heratina was helping and learning, but now is required at the clay mine.

Only three young people remain in Stair House. True to its ancient pattern, hardship deals most unfairly and severely with the innocent. They cannot defend themselves, nor are they of an age to decide their own fate. I am so tired of this all.

Any prophet who did not advocate an end to this blasphemy with all his eloquence, spiritual powers, and total sacrifice is false.

༄

<u>February 3, 1945. Stair House, Otaru, Japan</u>
John Sergief and Innokenty Andreanof were returned by a trio of railway policemen early this morning. The waywards were trussed up like a pair of holiday geese. Since John's father Walter had not left for work, they embraced and wept for joy, along with everyone else, including Lila Ann! Innokenty wept too, both at the joy of reunion and that his sister, nephew, and little brother are in sanitarium.

But they are alive, and aside from terrible treatment, and a missing finger (?!) from the left hand of Innokenty, now half-healed, they are our Prodigals. Leaving Constable Ojiwa and Big Jaw waiting, Philamon called everyone together at once for prayers of thanks, and a chant. I don't think our Japanese constables had heard Orthodox chanting, and they looked on with great curiosity.

Our returnees were forgiven a day's labor, and we women-folk attended. The poor youths showed an abundance of gouges, scrapes, and diverse wounds, not the least of which was Innokenty's missing finger, an ugly remnant of this adventure. The sight of it initially caused me some queasiness, for it is not completely healed.

Not much sewing, or anything else, was accomplished this day, and most blessedly, the joy did something to abate our hunger and cold.

We got bits and pieces of their adventures during the day, but much of it will wait for group story times, for "to begin at the begin and then to stop all alone not here" is something Innokenty and John will not tolerate. Somehow, their English makes much sense, for when they do employ it, there is a uniqueness to its syntax.

I've become used to it.

Story times will be important. Aleuts enjoy a social, group-oriented visit and, most of all, any story. I've come to admire them greatly.

<u>February 4, 1945. Stair House, Otaru, Japan</u>
It is late Sunday, actually very close to Monday as I write. There was no work today, and due to the generosity of several clay mine workers, scraps from kippers were given, and a fish broth made for all, plus a little rice. A great welcoming feast!

Innokenty and John are definitely the men of the day, and after church services there were special prayers of thanks for their return. Innokenty feels better that the truth about his motives is public knowledge, and every other question from the womenfolk is about his girlfriend, the only topic where he modestly demurs.

In the afternoon, all present listened to their account, told jointly by Innokenty and John entirely in Aleut. I followed, with the greatest difficulty, this time. I had no Friend Annie to help, though Mike tried to take her place. Unfortunately, Heratina would contribute her translations at the same time, and that made for difficult going. As it is, Aleut is not an easy language, especially when the conversation becomes rapid.

I had to ask sets of questions later to fill in wide gaps. In these, Mike was an enormous help. There are so many side trips and asides to the main story, I suppose I'll never have them straight for posterity. Enough to keep to the basics!

The main objective of going to his "sweetheart's" village and bringing her back to Otaru was half-met.

This outward-bound portion of their odyssey was greatly aided by the fact that Japanese think Aleuts are Japanese. They were able to move freely about, so their method of travel and navigation was the simplest possible: They walked, with John asking directions at every point where there was confusion. Aleuts are born great hikers, and this strength came into play during their foray inland.

If Innokenty had not been of military age (John is not, at age fifteen), all would have gone well; but after one scrape with a local official who wanted some sort of identification papers, they took more clever tactics. In the next village, John—who is a resourceful boy, as I found out in my classroom many times—got the idea of Innokenty feigning deafness. "You can't be a soldier if you're deaf."

While playing these roles, they encountered the outskirts of Sapporo.

~

Sapporo was something that any Aleut would find astounding and certainly frightening, and John and Innokenty were no exceptions. Because of their frequent movements in and through Otaru, a modest-sized port town, our travelers assumed themselves prepared for anything modern. Sapporo disproved this at once, and made apparent the flaw in their plan.

How to navigate on foot through this maze? Where did it end, and like a fox's burrow, where would they pop out? And would that be in the proper direction? How would they drink and eat? Hiking through the countryside, they either asked at houses, or took opportunity that came along, regarding water.

They had conserved a little "real" money for their escape, being familiar with tiny purchases at the tea-shop/commissary at the clay mine (where, it seems, Innokenty had been smitten). Twice they'd bought a rice-ball, and shared it in village shops.

Unfortunately, Innokenty made a poor thespian in the city. On the streets, wider and busier than anything they'd ever seen, he'd react with great fright at the loud noises. This dramatic flaw in Innokenty's drama, John and he saw as a source for great humor. And in the midst of all the urban strangeness, it wasn't long before they were hopelessly lost.

Practical to the letter, they saw the single most familiar sign, and that was a cross atop a church. Not realizing there were Christians in Japan, they viewed it as something of a miracle and immediately went there. This Christian church was evidently not in present use—and what denomination I could not determine, save it was not Orthodox. Yet here lived an elderly sexton surviving in poor circumstances, faithfully keeping the building from going altogether to pieces. He gave them shelter, and sometime during their stay determined they were certainly not Japanese. Lastly, he knew the village Innokenty sought and put them on the proper road to it, with clear walking directions. "Like us, this good old man walked everywhere, for he had no money."

By now, roughly a week had elapsed since their "escape"! Time is not too vital to our villagers, so making account for every day is of little consequence in their narrative of events. More important was their continued freedom. I'm sure they did not know how lucky they had been.

~

They reached Innokenty's sweetheart's village within a few days and, guilelessly asking for directions to her house, were at once detected by the village's neighborhood association, which had been alerted by Prefecture police from Otaru. They were arrested and confined.

The ugliness began at once. The village had one constable, and during his absence "bad men not in uniforms" appeared brandishing stout poles with fabric wrapped around the end, rather like unlit torches. With these, they proceeded to beat both senseless. Though Innokenty fought to protect his beloved friend, in the end it did no good.

They kept repeating, according to John, that "such punishment is what happens when 'savages' bothered their womenfolk." In fact, they began their visit by haranguing them about this. But instead of only venting, they became more enraged and went further.

Somewhere during this terrible onslaught Innokenty lost a finger, and I can't determine precisely how, save through violence—either during his attempted defense or when he was unconscious via an act of revenge. Upon his return, the constable was horrified, and their first memory was of his panic. He ran about in circles, then out the door, then back in, and wept. Through their criminal action, the villains had disgraced his office, of course.

Eventually, medical help arrived, and the boys were judged to need immediate attention. They were transported by a horse-drawn wagon, then by machine, to an infirmary. Despite their state, it was their first ride in both, for in Otaru they walked everywhere.

Beyond this, their memories, hence narratives, are vague, for it isn't the material for proper storytelling, which traditionally must contain joyful or adventurous material, like their trip out. Essentially, the remaining days of their absence were spent in the infirmary, though one high point was that a line of bound men was brought in, several of whom they recognized as their assailants. One of the nurses commented proudly, "They will go to jail. Japanese people punish mindless hooliganism."

Their last adventure was the truck ride to the railway station, being turned over to officials, bound, and put in a railway car "full of grass" (straw?) they shared with three pigs in crates being escorted by an elderly man. They had never been on a moving railroad car nor seen a pig. Their guard could whistle loudly, and the pigs would squeal, and this above all else during their "French liberty" was the high point!

"Miss Smith. There be food out around here, and in some other places too," Innokenty volunteered to me in English. This observation had the effect of elevating the villagers' fears that we are being especially singled out for starvation. Alexi now claims he will reopen the provisioning issue with Chief Constable, though I hope he does not. No good will come of that, and frankly, good-hearted Alexi didn't appear to emphasize the idea much.

He's had one ugly experience via the "complaint department" and doesn't need another. [*See October 22, 1943.*]

February 21, 1945. Stair House, Otaru, Japan

The continued hunger and cold coupled with the common assumption that food and fuel are available amongst the Japanese has created hard feelings. Those in sanitarium are still quite ill. Alexi and Philamon's visit yesterday resulted in a gloomy report regarding not only any villagers coming home, but simple survival.

My opinion that staples are not freely available to Japanese civilians wears thin, and I've given up. Because of my almost two-month experience in the north, I *know* there is much hardship, but the "then" pales in contrast to "now."

Yet I know the situation cannot have improved since summer, but only worsened.

Grousing or outright disparagement is aired every provisioning day, and Chief Constable has taken to not appearing often.

And Lila Ann finally had enough of Madam Fukama's petty cheating and created a scene; it seems there is something of the harpy in me. Binni and I feel like Mr. Custer at his infamous last stand, though at least that disaster, if memory serves, occurred during the summer. The situation had become intolerable.

More and more batch-work comes in with increasingly poor supplies—for *less* scrip and *more* spurious rejections and seconding from the *good* Madame Fukama.

So when I threatened my own labor rebellion, Madame Fukama struck me with a bag of batting. I astounded even myself when I pushed her backwards. Since she's a foot shorter than I, her descent to the floor was a short one.

This fiasco became the proud talk of Stair House. Yet ceasing sewing would mean that half of our income will stop. Madam Fukama has sworn intervention, possibly up to Emperor Hirohito himself, of course. At least, that's the last I heard from her.

I don't worry. Even Constable Ojiwa took my side, and worse yet, laughed at the good lady's indignity! I'm too weak and filled with foreboding to care any longer. I am indeed a strange Mennonite.

<u>February 24, 1945. Stair House, Otaru, Japan</u>
Angelina Andreanof and infant died today in sanitarium, the infant preceding the poor child by only a few hours. Angelina was fifteen years old, her infant just several months. I must report that the father of Angelina's child is not discussed here, for the facts would serve no constructive purpose to the bereaved family and I agree.

Angelina was a shy, retiring twelve-year-old when I arrived at Chichigof Village in September of 1941. Back then she was mother Fekla's chief assistant in collecting, drying, and pressing the tiny flowers that abound on Attu. Each Aleut name would be inscribed in phonetic Russian in a great two-foot-long scrapbook provided by Commodore Deery.

Angelina would search ceaselessly for missing flowers her mother knew were present but not yet found. She was a cooperative student if prone to dreaminess! Angelina, above all, was a devoted sister to little brother Dimitri, a second mother, in effect, for Fekla was "provided by God with Dimitri" somewhat late in life.

Angelina's child was a girl, unnamed, two and one-half months old. Their remains, like all our dead, were cremated and returned in a single urn, once again compounding

profound sadness atop tragedy. The official cause of death
was tuberculosis, but the villagers, as am I, are confident it
was malnutrition.

<u>March 1, 1945. Stair House, Otaru, Japan</u>
Another "provisioning" day has passed, which routinely
includes an escorted visit to a local store. No foodstuffs were
issued or purchased save sixteen ounces of dry-measure rice
per person for the next *seven days*.

This is somewhat over two dry ounces of rice per day,
which is completely ridiculous. "You are starving us to death
and God shall punish you."

Philamon made this public declaration abruptly but
deliberately to Chief Constable Aiko—to his painful chagrin.
Moreover, he said so in Japanese, a difficult thing for
Philamon, who has little patience or use for the language.
So when Chief Constable replied that "the war effort against
the Imperalists is requiring sacrifice for all," I don't think
Philamon understood or heard a syllable of it, but in fact
turned his back on Mr. Aiko while he was in mid-sentence
and walked away.

Though all agree, hence are proud of their beloved
Reader, I'm uncomfortable, knowing that visiting such humiliation on Chief Constable Aiko before others has potential for
serious retribution. We are prisoners, nothing more.

~

It was late on provisioning day (a Thursday) when Friend Annie returned via ambulance to us carrying the remains of Titiana in the familiar, ghastly clay urn. All joy at seeing our dearest friend return was utterly ruined, and Mike is without limits in his dismay. He and Annie sit together as I write, he weeping, she—half his size, and now so frail—patting his arm and saying a word here and there.

Friend Annie is cried out, as she puts it, and had steeled herself for this day so she could be strong for husband Mike. The innocent had died almost four days previous.

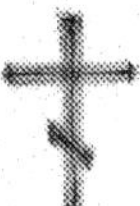

Now Mike Korovin is a strong man in every way save witnessing human pain, and he does not hold up before it in adult or child, let alone his own dear daughter.

My life is replete with examples of powerful people raining cruelty upon those less powerful. Faith was a potent force with Mother and Father and it helped and guided them. But can such faith misguide? Once when he was reflecting bitterly over his favorite brother's demise—*my* family's demise—Uncle Thomas criticized his brother and sister-in-law thus, though at once retracted in the face of Aunt Sarah's torrent of "Blasphemy, Husband! You blaspheme before this child!"

I was only recently repatriated from China. That was forty-four years ago almost to the day. Four decades worth of years have not provided me with insight on what substance I have to counter Uncle Thomas's view. If the truth is blasphemy before the Lord, what good is our faith?

<u>March 9, 1945. Stair House, Otaru, Japan</u>
The winds are driving torrents of slushy snow in piles during the day, then glazing them to the surface of glass at night. Our primitive water system froze weeks ago. Yet these intrepid Aleuts endure, for now at night there is warmth!!

"A miracle from God," Philamon claimed at evening prayers, and he leads prayers of thanks. Well, perhaps so, but much of the Almighty's methods rely on His faithful's timing and tactics.

I know, as fact, that the strategical situation at Stair House changed the week the dreaded nightwatch was foisted upon the hapless Constable Ojiwa. His genial and slack policies coupled with extreme shyness are a blessing.

At each change of watch, a white baton of office, painted red on both ends, is surrendered, one watchstander to the other, much like a relay race. The likes of Mr. Big Jaw loves the feel of its presence in-hand: held before him, one hand on each end, swung by a lanyard laced through one end, or tapped absently against a leg—these are just a few of the numerous actions the baton yields to Mr. Big Jaw.

But this scepter is without function to Mr. Ojiwa. He reports precisely 9:58 p.m. Then after signing in and out in the logbook, he takes the baton. Monsieur Big Jaw departs, and Mr. Ojiwa sets up shop just by the front door, and never goes in any farther—does not perform head counts *at any time.*

"Well, I'm not going to complain about not being counted" is Alexi's observation, and not-too-subtle warning for all of us to be close-mouthed about such laxness.

So firewood appears just after midnight, not from the heavens, but from below, via a hatch leading down into the crawl space. Handed up by the brothers Innokenty and Nicholas [*Andreanof*], the stove in the rear room is soon pulsing rich, lovely warmth. All those not under blankets gather around, and even a few of those. This wood, then, is Philamon's declared gift from God.

Either Mr. Ojiwa does not notice the unusual nighttime warmth, a hardly believable assumption even for his studied state of ignorance, or he dismisses the matter. In any event, about an hour before change of watch in the a.m., the stove is allowed to die down, the house cooling to a Spartan level.

I worry for the well-being of God's "messengers and providers." An occasional painted insignia on some of the wood tells of less than sacred origins.

The number of railroad cars temporarily sided in the nearby yard each day yields a small quantity of fuel for us. At first, our messengers worked their wonder two or three times weekly, but now, alas, it is every night. Prudence has yielded to need and comfort.

The Japanese are nothing but thorough and keen of detail. Therefore, through Heratina (who is of the same mind as myself), I've sounded a note of high caution as regards detection and the consequences it would bring.

March 10, 1945. Stair House, Otaru, Japan

Dimitri Andreanof died at sanitarium yesterday. He was almost five years old. His father Peter, being a patient with his child these past weeks, was with him, but mother Fekla was not. The fact that Fekla was denied visits with her gravely sick child for almost three weeks due to typically unyielding regulations caused the ordinarily placid woman to break.

According to Friend Annie, who was already downstairs, the instant Fekla was presented with the all-too-familiar urn in the hands of Big Jaw, with Mr. Osimi on his heels (it was change of shift, so both were present); she became hysterical, knocked the urn from his hand and set upon the astonished man.

I heard the commotion, and went quickly downstairs. What I saw was the two constables restraining Fekla on the floor. It was a chaotic scene: Mr. Osimi was both holding Fekla and pushing away Big Jaw, who brandished his baton. Mike and Alexi struggled to intercede—in fact, Mike grabbed hold of the baton.

Perhaps it was this divided effort that enabled Fekla to squeeze out from underneath all and go running out of the house screaming "Murderers! Murderers!" in Aleut. Big Jaw was delayed in the pursuit, for there was a brief tug of war between Mike and him over the baton, but Mike, remembering the order of things, let go, and off Big Jaw went, and within seconds they again restrained the miserable Fekla.

They were now outside, in a dirty, slushy bank of snow. At the moment I reached the porch with Friend Annie, Big Jaw punched Fekla in the head, then kicked her.

Both of us cried out in protest, and again Mr. Osimi pushed away Big Jaw, who scowled down at Fekla, wrathful and spewing vehement Japanese.

Since it was in fact Big Jaw's watch, and to the Japanese, *who has* authority and *who does not* means everything, it was he who took action. He began by yanking the poor woman up to a sitting position and yelling, "This is your punishment," or something similar, and ordered Mr. Osimi to watch over her.

When I protested, Big Jaw became vituperative, calling me names, only a few of which I understood. Then he ordered Friend Annie and me back inside.

"But sir, she will freeze in the snow," Annie protested, not realizing she was doing so in Aleut, to which Big Jaw brandished his baton to perhaps strike her. At that moment Mike stepped outside. There was a charged *energy* of eye language between the two men, and Big Jaw lowered his baton, using it instead as a vigorous gesturing device to signal us inside at once, which we obeyed.

Now Innokenty and Nicholas hurled themselves into the breach at seeing their mother so treated. I think they would have seized Big Jaw if he had not jumped back and, raised the baton, but at that moment Alexi, Mike, and the other menfolk interceded, coming physically between the potential combatants and pleading for peace.

Big Jaw at once retreated outside, slamming and *locking* the door behind him, an amazing act since none of us were aware it could be locked from the outside. Also, the intent failed. For without pause, Innokenty and Nicholas ran out the back door, and at that moment I realized that Heratina and Binni [*both Chirikofs*] were on their hands and knees weeping. They made a hapless scene; they tried to sweep up Dimitri's ashes, alternating with making pathetic prayerful motions yet being unable to bear actually touching the ashes. Nearby, also on her knees, Lena [*Ivanof*] picked up the fragments of the urn, and she too wept. Philamon stood, looking down with complete resignation, repeating a Russian expression which I did not understand.

When Innokenty and Nicholas reached their mother, I— along with most the others—was at the window and saw that Big Jaw stood close by, baton at the ready, and somehow Mr. Osimi had availed himself of a short-handled pitchfork. Both constables were at the ready.

Thank God, despite their mother's sad plight—unshod, and squatting down in that dismal, gray-sooted snow pile— her sons did not throw themselves to certain maiming or worse.

Instead they worried the two constables verbally, then fortunately a wagon happened by with four townsmen. Seeing the goings-on, they jumped out. Big Jaw, in the confusion of arguing with these men simultaneous with confronting Fekla's sons, gave opportunity for Fekla to stand. Innokenty stepped forth, took his mother around the waist, and returned into the house via the back door with the distracted woman.

Since Big Jaw's argument with the newcomers was gaining in volume, and knowing well his constables, Innokenty counted on Mr. Osimi's pitchfork being a bluff. He was right, for the elderly man stood by and watched the young men take their mother away.

Outside Stair House the fracas between Big Jaw and the others continued unobserved as all went to greet Fekla, hoping she was not injured. Thankfully she was not, save a terrible chill combined with the loss of her Dimitri.

~

I almost cannot bear to write on after describing the scene. There were my dear friends kneeling over Dimitri's spilled ashes—not sure if they should touch his defiled remains or not. They wept silently while Philamon, as always, was prayerful and stalwart in his ancient faith.

And Fekla, wretched soul, virtually out of her head, instead
of being comforted was punished. I dread chronicling the
immediate future, for more death awaits, I fear.

And the originator of this journal, the person whose idea it
was, is gone from me. Poor Osmond, on our first night aboard
the *Northern Supplier* four years past, out of the blue
declared, "You know, Mrs. Smith, you ought to keep a record
of this great adventure to the dateline. You have a way with
words and an eye for the little things."

If he were here I would tell him that his idea has worn thin,
oppressive, and I am reliving ugliness best forgotten.

May 14, 1945. Stair House, Otaru, Japan
I am suspected of abandonment by none other than Friend
Annie, who noticed that I hadn't entered anything in my
journal for two months. When I do not require this journal for a
period of days, it is hidden by Philamon, so when long periods
of non-entry pass, it is noticed. I make excuses, "I'm waiting
for good news."

Our gentle exchange took place, as most do, over sewing,
when there is time and function to chat, for the work is ceaseless and tedious. Since Fekla has remained in a terrible mental
state, we really have only three seamstresses.

Anyway, there was a week of guilt, and finally I asked for
this tome's exhumation from wherever Philamon and company
hide things.

It is a struggle to find news that isn't sad and entirely foreseen.

Old Ivan Tschigorin, forty-nine years of age, died in sanitarium March 18, several days after baby Dimitri; soon following was Zephryis, nephew of Old Ivan and son of the
deceased Mary and Leonty Tschigorin. Now that branch of the
Tschigorin family is gone from us.

There were no further deaths until April 10, when Vasha Ivanof, age fifty-one, unmarried sister of Philamon, died here at Stair House.

I would deem, as most would, that the deaths were due to starvation, but they are all—save Vasha—listed as disease-related, the disease being tuberculosis. The miserable Vasha, always a confused, simple heart, was not eighty pounds, and even in full flesh was a tiny thing. Philamon, who looked after his sister, "blessed with the simplicity of an angel," was devastated, and the struggle over her remains was bitter but pacific. Much resentment is harbored, naturally, over Japanese officialdom's continuing inability to understand how necessary it is for the Aleut people to deal with their departed in their own way.

I swear upon the most high that if the Japanese hierarchy decreed that everyone should go about with a shoe in their mouth, they would, so hidebound are these people about rules.

Since we were embarked for Japan that September day in 1942, fifteen of the Attuans have died and Osmond's murder makes a total of sixteen fatalities. There are now twenty-eight villagers remaining, though one infant born here still lives! She is the entire Stair House's joy, but clings to life week to week while all watch and offer profuse prayer. Both mother Agafia [*Sergief*] and infant Fervrovnia (Fern!) returned from sanitarium the third week of April.

Infant Fern is now five months old, and special effort is made to provide Agafia with some extra food each day. Two people's lives depend on it. By someone who somehow learned of infant Fern's fate (most likely via her father Walter, who is the most *durable* of our clay mine workers), provided two large kippers to him, who smuggled them past Big Jaw. This reviled man, to the annoyance of all, has the watch when the men return from work.

Another rule, that nothing can be transported from the town/work into our area of confinement, was until a few days ago indifferently enforced. But not so by Big Jaw.

He tirelessly enforces this rule, of course entirely in his own interest. Fortunately, he is not a bright man, and is readily decoyed, usually by Heratina who enjoys so hoodwinking him! Therefore, if there is something to smuggle in at the end of day, it is easily done. The villagers have come to learn the Thespian trade far better than before.

~

Sometimes my old "scratchy" pen is restless.

Strange ideas come to me, selfish in nature. I am an old woman now, and wonder if there was a time when I was ever an attractive creature? Emmett [*Emmett Slater, Lila Ann's first husband*] was the handsomest man at Oberlin, with a vast handlebar mustache and a rakish way about him. It was 1903, and as used by our then President, the exclamation *"Bully!"* was in, and Emmett did particularly well with both the timing of delivery and intonation.

I remember one of my classmates—of course, all younger women than I—gossiping, when they thought I was not in earshot, "Whatever does Emmett Slater see in that hopelessly bony Lila Ann?"

Finally, one night at the Punch and Judy Dance, I asked him, "What do you see in me, when there're so many attractive young women at school?"

He looked me up and down, as if I were quite mad, and responded, "You are the most attractive woman at school. Anyone can see that."

And for such a charming, bold lie, I loved him at once.

So these are old thoughts of better times. Possibly it is my weary brain's avenue of escape, to drift back to those decades whether I wish it or not.

I can't say I mind them, those memories.

<u>May 19, 1945. Stair House, Otaru, Japan.</u>
Old Ivan Tschigorin was born either late in 1895 or early 1896, during the trapping season. According to his wife Ann and sister Binni (a Chirikof by marriage), his father, Zephryis Senior, was a great wanderer. He signed aboard a steamwhaler not long after Old Ivan was born, when Binni was just seven years of age. She can barely remember Zephryis Senior.

His mother, Olena, was from Atka and "always lonely for her people," for Aleut people east of Attu are of a different type, language-wise. When husband Zephryis did not return after five years, she went home to Atka Village with her children.

After some years in Atka, and as a very young man, Old Ivan returned to Attu. He lived in the household of his uncle Kusma and plied the family trapping trade.

A momentous day in Old Ivan's life, which he told rarely but well, was the return of his father. One day he was preparing fish when a strange, elderly Aleut man approached. "What do you have there?" the man asked in awkward but clearly good Aleut. By this time Ivan was grown and was married to his first wife.

The man had one arm and smoked an enormous bone pipe held in a nearly toothless mouth. "Well, these are fish," and then Old Ivan looked a long time at the man. He asked, "And I suppose you are my father finally home these many years from wandering?"

They then sat and talked, for Zephryis Senior had many questions, especially concerning the whereabouts of his wife Olena and daughter Binni. Though brother Kusma and Elder Ivan remained angry with their brother and grandson respectively, other villagers celebrated his return.

He told his son many stories of great adventures, for very soon they became quite a team. The old man even returned to trapping despite some problems over family trapping territories. It is his father, then, who soon passed away, that was directly responsible (according to wife Anna and sister Binni) for Old Ivan having "the wanderlust always in his heart. But he was a good provider and never left."

At the village, he had an old Russian atlas which he would pore over. This would "help him wander the world," said daughter Anna, "and we would travel with him as he pointed out to us the grand places where our grandfather had wandered."

At these times, their mother Anna "would worry after his spirit which was so much like Zephryis Senior's."

Old Ivan was a spirited hunter and trapper, and was most resourceful, especially in predicting the ways of animals and the sea. Because of this uncanny ability, it is thought he was able to communicate with specific sorts of sea birds, a great gift.

~

Vasha Ivanof was born on Attu in the summer of 1895, a few days after the Holy Day dedicated to Our Mother of the Holy Dormition. She was the first born of Sergief and Mavra Ivanof, then a large and dominant family on Attu, according to brother Philamon, a historian *par excellence* of all things in Chichigof Village.

"I was fourth-born, but Vasha was first and a blessing of our Holy Mother, everyone knew."

It is absolutely agreed that Vasha Ivanof was the village's prettiest, most eligible girl. She was of lively and intelligent character prior to the epidemic of 1911.

According to Old Nicholas Andreanof, the oldest villager, save for Sad Peter Chirikof who is in sanitarium and unavailable for interview, Vasha could already weave baskets superior to almost any of the other women. "But she was young, and they had a hard time to sit her down."

No one knows what caused the epidemic of 1911, save that it was of short duration, afflicted only young people, caused high fever, and killed almost everyone it struck. In fact, Vasha was the only survivor. Subsequent to that unfortunate time, Vasha withdrew into her own "Holy World" and became a different person entirely.

Her health was broken, and she rarely talked anymore, though she would perform womanly duties always and with skill. She was a devoted sister to Philamon, who like herself, was one of the survivors of the Ivanof clan, rendered so few by the epidemics of 1911 and 1916.

In heaven, God will make a special place for Vasha Ivanof, a faithful and persevering soul. Missed by all, of course, and especially by her beloved brother Philamon.

<u>May 24, 1945, Stair House, Otaru, Japan</u>
This was provisioning day, which is almost in name only, for most of any purchasing we can do is done through a *different vendor*, which would be the most delicate term for it.

We get very little rice, and sometimes a few greens, and perhaps millet. So this was also the day when Mr. Seguda stopped by to repair one of our sewing machines which is breathing its last. So, with the men who conduct provisioning present, it was during this unusual social scene when Chief Constable also visited. These days, after cruel events with Binni, that is rare.

Chief Constable declared that he bears me good news! There will be a hearing on my status at the Prefecture Court. My Japanese was not equal to the details of his explanation, in fact not even to the central topic. But with John and Friend Annie, plus Anna pitching in, two or three languages sufficed! Within a half hour, this rendering was reached:

Since Attu belongs to Japan, the law of Japan applies. And the law is clear. All Europeans must have a *Status Certification*! Since the Attuans are born Japanese, they do not, of course.

The first category for Europeans is as an INVITED visitor to Japan, caught unawares at the start of the Pacific War; the second is that I am an UNINVITED visitor. The third is the simplest, that I am a PRISONER OF WAR. The final and most inauspicious category is that I am a SPY.

Chief Constable assured me this final category was a mere formality, for the court was extraordinarily thorough, and absolutely considered all official categories, no matter how unlikely one might be. All knew, he reassured, I certainly was *not* a spy.

Quite proud of himself and Japanese officialdom, Chief Constable Aiko departed amidst the usual bevy of bowing. My hearing will be Monday and I will be picked up by himself and/or his representative(s) at midday.

This evening there was a thorough discussion concerning all this, for my friends honor me by being my "Daddy and Mommy" in the absence of any family. Innokenty proclaimed very thoughtfully that "we would not want them to shoot our teacher." At which point, he was scolded severely by Heratina and company for being insensitive. "If they shoot her, we should not discuss it."

This, in the interest of easing my misgivings!

Actually, it is all nonsense. I've been in Otaru for almost three years, have been in "trouble" with officialdom several times—all this, without having *status?*

Nationality is not confusing to the villagers: They are American citizens, loyal to the last. Only God prevails over their feelings for America. "After all," explains Philamon, "the Americans purchased Attu from the Cossacks, who were very bad to us in the old days. They destroyed all the otter and used us as serfs."

If the Japanese think the Attuans are Japanese citizens, Alexi dismisses this, saying, "Well, they are foreigners, and not smart about America."

So rests the nationality issue with the villagers.

~

Zephryis Tschigorin was the only child who survived infancy of his late parents Mary and Leonty Tschigorin. He was born at salmon camp in 1929. According to his aunt and cousins, he was always remarkable for his strength and wile.

It was decided by Elder Tschigorin that Zephryis was his soul brother and he must function as guardian angel to the child. They became thick, great-grandfather and he, and remained so until Elder Tschigorin's death.

I can attest to Zephryis's great intelligence, and his sense of humor and impishness! He played tricks on quite a few, the most famous being gluing his grandfather Kusma's boots to the floor.

He could count backwards in English from one hundred to one faster than any of the boys, and most of the girls, and faster than any of the children in Aleut.

Philamon maintained that God gave special dispensation to Zephryis for his impishness; and that due to his sunny disposition and youthful faith, God was always on his side, and that the Almighty possessed a sense of mirth.

He was entirely too young a soul to be writing these lines of farewell about, and it is absolutely certain he rests with his mother and father in heaven. And certainly along with them, Elder Tschigorin.

May 26, 1945, Otaru, Japan. Stair House
Disaster has struck just when winter was behind us and warmer temperatures were returning. But when people are starving, hunger knows no season.

For a long time (at this writing no one knows or will say how long) there have been night time raids seeking edible garbage. All the menfolk knew who the "raiders" were, and even Alexi looked the other way. I am not clear who benefited other than the participants, but it was none of the womenfolk, including mothers with children.

Under the leadership of Gregory Prokopeuff, certainly no child, John Sergief, Alfred Tschigorin, Innokenty Andreanof and his brother Nicholas were the "food raiders" who have encountered a bad end. They were apprehended last evening when three of the five became suddenly and violently ill *miles* from Stair House. In fear for their lives, they sought help.

The survivors are confined either in jail or a hospital other than the sanitarium. Gregory clings to life, but John and Alfred are gone from us. Innokenty and Nicholas are evidently not affected, but under arrest.

"Innokenty saved their lives by getting help," Alexi and Philamon reported, who themselves were both escorted off in the early morning hours. They were present when the young men passed away, though the poor misguided souls were unconscious. Philamon was able to deliver last rites, or its Orthodox equivalent.

But religious observance wasn't on Chief Constable's mind. He was completely out of temper with this recent gross infraction. He certainly has no pity on the wrong-doers, and attaches all blame to Alexi, who is Chief. Hence, he will stand trial along with the survivors when it is time. "And maybe you all will be beheaded!"

Worse yet, he has threatened to throw the remains of the two deceased boys into the sea unless EVERYONE complicit in this criminal conspiracy comes forward.

Alexi and Philamon, of course, did not share the ugliest facts with the womenfolk after their return. But Mike generously let me know details.

The families, however, know the essentials, and Walter and Agafia are absolutely crushed, she—though his stepmother—had raised John from a young age and loved him dearly. Walter endures death badly. He seems thoroughly distracted. On our removal to Otaru, Walter's sister-in-law Anise's death hit him hard. He was her Guardian Angel and felt responsible for her death and scandalous disposal at sea. Also he and younger brother Strong Ivan were inseparable. And now son John.

I fear he will not survive this, nor Agafia, for both are feeble from starvation, Agafia even more so as she is nursing infant Fern.

I cannot bear to contemplate the devastation Ann [*Tschigorin*] is enduring at this moment, and in fact all family members. She is now eldest, and has lost a total of seven family members—her youngest son Alfred is the latest. Now, with her recently departed husband, she has been left a widow with two surviving children thousands of miles from home.

Friend Annie is with her now, as are others, but one woman can only be so strong, can bear only so pitiable a series of disasters. I will now quit these lines for despite the hours, villagers are mostly awake, wondering about the answers to a dozen questions, yet lamenting the answers fate has already so cruelly provided.

The feelings sparked by this day's horrors, I'm afraid, will not grow dimmer with time. In heart and spirit, this is not the same people who in 1942 looked forward so much to evacuation.

✑

<u>May 28, 1945, Otaru, Japan. Stair House</u>
I have minutes before this journal is hidden, for there is word of a reprisal search for "stolen goods." It seems that many stolen items, either imagined or real, have been randomly attached to our food raiders' activities by Prefecture officials. It is nonsense, of course. The men took nothing but foodstuff contained in garbage.

Bless the soul of those who alerted us. My so-called "hearing" is either delayed or simply forgotten.

I don't know how long this nonsensical recrimination by Chief Constable will go on. Obviously, his stature has undergone a severe public blow, and he will have his due.

✑

[*The next five entries, as explained by LAS were short, made opportunistically as later explained, and added when she finally had access to her journal once again.*]

<u>May 30, '45</u>
Gregory Prokopeuff has been moved to sanitarium and though alive seems disoriented. The search was chaos. Confiscation of "illegal" devices such as kitchen knives, etc.. General humiliation. No word of Innokenty or Nicholas. Prayer vigils almost constant.

✑

<u>June 9, '45</u>
Today at clay mine Mike was told America has won over
Germany. General joy for our lot is thought to be related to
this.

Gregory Prokopeuff remains in a semi-conscious state.
Today 2nd Chief Peter Andreanof returned from sanitarium
after five and one half months absence. Much joy. Peter con-
firms Mike's intelligence re: Germany! Even more joy.

<u>June 12, '45</u>
Innokenty and Nicholas returned by Chief Constable this day!!!
Former tells story tonight of "big raid and bad times."
Celebration services by Philamon.

<u>June 18, '45</u>
My hearing has been re-scheduled. Date, place unspecified.
We are informed that Gregory has regained consciousness.
Much grim war news about Tokyo and Honshu Island. News in
general, more forthcoming.

<u>June 22, '45</u>
First provisioning day where provisions were actually available. More rice and vegetables. Broth powder. Peter Chirikof
returned from sanitarium after four months. Celebration services by Philamon.

<u>June 29th, 1945, Otaru, Japan. Stair House.</u>
Much has happened since I've had access to this journal. In the interim I made very brief factual notes in diverse languages on the reverse side of the labels our batting comes in, hiding them on my person. "Not half bad for poor folk just making due," as Father used to explain when he improvised.

Now coal, or lack thereof, is no problem, and everyone is healthier because of it. Provisioning, either because of an official guilty conscious or increased abundance, is somewhat better. Perhaps a combination of the two.

Because Gregory is conscious, the date of the legal proceedings for their "crimes" has been moved up: He, the "hooligan" survivors, and Alexi will stand. It was with great surprise to learn that a lawyer will be provided—grandly announced by Chief Constable via written memo read boisterously by Big Jaw. It seems, of the three Constables, Big Jaw is Chief Constable's favorite, a sad thing.

Work is back to normal: The sewing continues, and work parties go daily to the clay mines, and more often now, to miscellaneous details about town. It is the clay miners and work detailers who now bring in more news daily, for it seems civilians are more forthcoming with the Attuans. Reasons for this? Unknown. But news is welcomed.

I have spent time explaining the in's and out's of lawyers to my villager friends, which of all matters "down below" (how they refer to the United States) confuses them the most: *Will he make Chief Constable return the remains of our dear boys? Which side will he be on? What sort of pay would he expect? Will be speak Aleut, or at least English?* And then, first, uppermost and primary, "Mrs. Smith, do you think they will really chop the heads off those bad boys for just garbage taking?"

These and other questions keep me busy during the evening hours. Plus I re-read some of my obituaries ostensibly for those who were not here, but really, Friend Annie says, ". . . because we like to hear them even though sad to us."

They cannot know how complimented I am by this, for I feel more useful than I ever have prior to this.

❧

<u>July 3, 1945. Otaru, Japan. Stair House.</u>
Professor Takahashi Saburo appeared today, professor of "Law and Culture" at the University of Sapporo. He spoke no English, so had the same translator (always a nameless, shy young lady) as Chief Constable and Prefecture officials have employed with us.

He would only meet with the defendants. "This is no procedure for women!" he scolded when Alexi suggested that I sit in. So, after Professor Saburo left, there was general despondency. He told them (Gregory being absent) they must plead guilty and leave their fate to the mercy of the Emperor. Simply put, all evidence absolutely established them as thieves and Alexi—as Chief—a co-conspirator. "To deny it would be stupid," he concluded.

There is a confusing mix of Aleut and troubled English in transmitting the above; hopefully, I've captured the essence.

My friend's English is rusty and deficient, and I humbly add that it wasn't their prime suit before capture. They benefited from translation into English only minimally. No clarification or repetition was permitted. The Professor was a "Too much angry man" according to Alexi. When asked if they were going to be beheaded if they so pled, the stern Professor shouted, "Don't be stupid! Such punishment for petty thievery is the talk of very ignorant people."

Their attorney would not enter into a discussion on what punishment they might receive, only that whatever it was, they deserved it. This session confirmed almost everything my beloved Uncle Thomas thought about lawyers!

~

Our only surviving infant, Fern Sergief, is the prime benefactor of improved health, and all survivors dote upon her.
You would think that some of the women who had lost infants
and children would perhaps hold back, but not so. Or perhaps
I'm cynical, never having been a mother.

But all attend Agafia and infant Fern, and in view of her
awful fortune, all of us experience joy when we look in the
child's dark, Aleut features. "She will be a great beauty and
master weaver," claims father Walter, who is showing some
signs of recovery, both emotionally and physically.

The days are long now, and there is considerable work for
those who wish it in the gardens around Otaru, the pay being
in left-over produce. This is a new and excellent source. I have
begun taking in non-batch sewing from the town. I'm very
proud of my seamstresses. They still talk of our wedding dress,
of course.

This victory seems long ago.

<u>July 15, 1945. Otaru, Japan. Stair House.</u>
It was a most momentous Sunday. Alexi, Innokenty, and
Nicholas were led off by Chief Constable himself during the
early morning. They returned mid-afternoon under escort by
our constables with one added member, Gregory, helped into
Stair House by Alexi and Constable Ojiwa.

All held their breath as Alexi announced that they had all
been found guilty, sentenced to three years at hard labor, but
excused from punishment due to the mercy and benevolence
of Emperor Hirohito to compensate for the hardship his subjects have endured.

"This Hirohito I think is a just leader," Philamon concluded,
adding, ". . . plus they were only stealing what people threw
away, and two died because of it."

At the once, Philamon proclaimed a day of thanksgiving and prayer, which was held this evening with wonderful singing.

Gregory Prokopeuff has totally regained his senses, in a manner of speaking, and unfortunately his attitude. He is Lena's *[Ivanof, wife of Philamon]* brother, and they never speak. All think him responsible for leading the young men astray, and to their deaths. This, though, remains unspoken.

Since my arrival in Chichigof Village, September 1941, he has never spoken to me (or Osmond, prior to his demise).

According to Mike, who knows Gregory best, he is a strange man who lives with many ghosts from old Russian times. He is, though, without equal as a trapper.

~

I have not written of Dr. Takata, because since late summer of last year, so little has come to me about him, despite my attempts. Furthermore, what little news I get is not good. Last winter, according to the tiny lady who has the misfortune to assist Madame Fukama, he suffered a stroke. Her brother does gardening for him.

"The wise old man is not himself anymore."

And that dismal information is all I know, despite efforts: Questions to Dr. Nagai and the constables are shrugged off. Week to week, I thought I'd come by news through various contacts. But no.

Now I've made serious efforts through Mike. Friend Annie has the most resourceful of husbands, and he is *THE* fountain-head for information at Stair House. He said he will do his best.

<u>July 18, 1945. Otaru, Japan. Stair House.</u>
The ashes of John Sergief and Alfred Tschigorin were finally returned to their relatives this afternoon. I don't think anyone

ever believed what Chief Constable had, in temper, declared he would do [*i.e. throw the boys' ashes into the bay*]

That evening Philamon led everyone in prayer for the young men. Gregory, who almost never attends any sort of religious service, remained consistent, and absented himself. His decision weighed heavily on the proceedings.

~

John Sergief was born in 1927 at Attu. He is famed as being one of the few Attuans—other than Mike—to have gone to Seattle. The Coast Guard took him there when he was a young-ster because ". . . there was something wrong with his head. And he would have died."

He stayed in Seattle for the entire winter, and returned the following summer aboard the Coast Guard cutter that had taken him. John talked extensively about Seattle, and how it was the sort of world he would not desire. "But, he was happy to see it," explained Young Albert Chirikof, for they were fast friends.

The one "Seattle thing" that impressed John most, were juke boxes. His grand goal in life was to trap enough fur to purchase a juke box for the village. A jukebox, he claimed, was the greatest invention, almost as good as the rifle.

To have entire musical groups at one's command—to be able to dance anytime (and Aleuts love dancing!) would be grand beyond description. Mike tried to keep our young friend's feet firmly on mother reality by explaining, "There weren't enough foxes to ever buy a jukebox, for goodness sakes, in all the islands."

But John had faith that he would someday buy one, have it installed in the old store, and then everyone "would dance all night."

John was Philamon's chief assistant, and he was praised for his knowledge of Orthodox scripture. He never learned to write because of a strange "mixing up" of words and such when he attempted it.

But he could draw wonderful figures of animals and people using charcoal and heavy paper. Though he lost his mother early in life, he prayed for her always. But he also remained obedient and respectful to his stepmother Agafia, who said often that "He was my very good son from God."

There is a wonderful voice gone from our village with the early departure of John Sergief to heaven.

~

Alfred Tschigorin was born in 1925 while mother Ann was visiting her people in Nikolski, Umnak Island. It was that year when Commodore Deery's ship *Western Flyer* went aground in southeastern Alaska and was unable to meet its fall schedule. "So this is why dear Alfred was born in Nikolski," explained his mother Ann.

Alfred was a popular young boy if somewhat given to impishness when he was young. His fame as a climber, though, began early. At the age of five he climbed to the very top of the *Western Flyer* nearly giving his mother, and everyone else, heart failure. He gave no reason for doing such a thing, and it was then understood climbing was his gift.

Very early, he was able to climb and gather sea-bird eggs in the most inaccessible places, even those of the __________ [Whiskered Auklet {*Evidently Lila Ann meant to insert the Aleut name for this bird, but for some reason, never did. Ed.}*] whose eggs give valuable nourishment to developing babies, plus strengthens the blood of the mothers.

But the greatest advantage his gift provided was to climb the steepest cliff faces high in the mountains early in spring. Here a plant grows that still holds dormant its powerful juices before summer regrowth.

When dried, its roots possess a curative ingredient ten times the amount found in any other plant. According to Binni Chirikof, the village herbalist, this source is almost never available to Aleut people.

In 1938, the villagers traded one-half pound of this medicament for a skiff made by Old Sarlov in Unalaska. Because of these valuable contributions and of course his pleasant and outgoing personality, dear Alfred will always reside in the sweet memories of his family and all villagers. As Philamon said at his service, "If heaven is on high, then certainly our Alfred is there."

<u>July 25, 1945. Aboard the *Naha Maru*; Port of Kushiro, Hokkaido Prefecture.</u>
Though it has only been a week since my last entry, it might as well be a year for the catching up I must do. And developments have been fast paced and complicated.

To begin, my heart is broken, for I have been separated from my dearest friends once again, this time apparently for the duration of hostilities.

I shall make brief reportage of how this all began—that is, what was Lila Ann's *Listening* and not a *Hearing:* Two days (20th of July, a Friday) after my last entry I was picked up without notice in the middle of what had been an ordinary day by Chief Constable. "Good News! Your hearing is to be in one hour."

I'm certain no individual had a *hearing* with less chance to be *heard*. I was driven to a western-style office building that had housed a European company prior to hostilities and escorted into a conference room by Chief Constable. I was given almost no time to tidy up, straighten my hair, etc., yet served tea in a polite manner by two young ladies. And Chief Constable and I waited nearly a half hour, drinking tea.

Chief Constable conversed with the young women, conducting himself quite paternally all the while. Finally three men in Army uniforms walked in, and there was extensive bowing. The flanking two sat, while the remaining one stood and readied himself to read from a prepared text.

When a translation was handed to me the recitation began.

He wore thick-lensed glasses with heavy tortoise shell frames. Because he barked his proclamation, the glasses would hop down the bridge of his nose with the start of each sentence, requiring him to pause, and poke them back in place before resuming.

Their decision was concise:

They'd determined my status to be that as a *Prisoner of War* with all the legal standing thereof. It was then incumbent—as Japan was the host nation—that I be transferred to a proper Prisoner of War camp at once. Once there, I would be processed according to procedures germane.

"A ship is leaving three days hence for Yokohama. There you will be transported to a Prisoner of War facility for female officers and diplomatic personages, which must be very luxurious," beamed Chief Constable proudly, as if I had been given an award.

I had until early morning of the 21st to make my farewells and prepare. On the return drive to Stair House, Chief Constable, continuing in this new tone of benevolence, informed, "You may take up to 30 kilograms of personal belongings. Your trip will be in two stages: First by train, then by ship to Yokohama. It will be quite an adventure."

From the boot of the machine, he removed a stout, compact sea chest, superbly made, itself a priceless item upon the "gray" or "black" market. "This was my eldest son's. It is my gift to you, Mrs. Smith."

Then we bowed to each other and he pivoted and returned to the machine. It occurred to me as he drove off that I might not see Chief Constable again. I felt grateful for his gift, despite our troubled past.

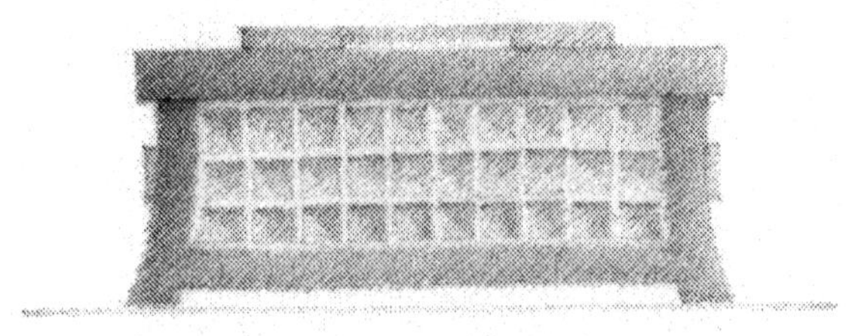

~

The word of my departure got out prior to my return, and throughout that day the sadness of this news built. When all villagers had returned that evening from work details and the clay mine, Philamon called a special devotional service of safe travel and farewell.

Friend Annie, now a very weary 22-year-old woman, is so unlike the one who came into my life nearly four years ago. Together we helped prepare my trunk. We talked hardly at all, save for necessities this first evening. Her dark, oriental features, so frail by nature, are now enhanced by starvation, despite a recent return of somewhat better rations. She is a fragile wren of dusky porcelain.

I studied her features as we decided what to take and what to leave. I reflected that Friend Annie was my own true daughter, just as close to my heart and spirit as if I'd given birth to her. We were not chatty friends, our talk had always a practical bent; long silences between us were frequent but comfortable. But add a Heratina or Lena to the mix, and we could chat away, make no doubt!

That night, she and Mike stayed by my side as others dropped in. There was, after all a day and a half before actual departure. Removal, as I saw it.

All of us, to the person, 28 survivors of the original 42, have noted a change in both attitude and treatment by the Japanese. I noted it today, most strikingly. Ironically being shipped away to parts south was placed in the context of a "reward," or perhaps "leg-up."

Then there was the generous gift of the trunk from Chief Constable.

Mike has concluded (and he is our resident policy theorist and analyst) that the Japanese are about to sue for peace and want to maintain the best official face to all things prisoner-related.

"The war goes real bad for those guys for long time, now. Everybody thinks and talks about it."

~

The last day was frustrating and sad. Though it was a Saturday, hence a workday, there was talk of all taking off. But I urged the men not to, "There would be trouble, not to mention the lost funds." But when it grew time that morning, Alexi told the constable that their teacher and "Wise Woman" was leaving, and they needed the day for all to make a proper farewell. Again, in the changing (softening) of the official attitude, there was no recrimination, for the constable was none-other than Big Jaw.

The afternoon was spent reading some of the "Goodbye Stories" (*I think the villagers often just translated directly from the Aleut into the English, and this is one example*) from my journal of those departed, something all love to hear read. For it is *absolutely mandated* I take this journal with me. It is agreed by all, that the favorite Goodbye Story is of Elder Tschigorin. I am so flattered by these opinions—every minute of each entry now seems abundantly rewarded.

On this last full day at Stair House, I learned nothing more about kind Dr. Takata, who helped me so much. He suffered a stroke last winter, late, and "is not himself." The only additional news Mike could come by, was that "not himself" meant that his keen mind is no longer so, and is likely to remain so.

That was one farewell I could not make.

It is not overlooked by anyone, least of all Alexi, Philamon, Peter and Mike, that a benefit of my transport to "big-time Japan" will be the potential for written communication with the outside world. Therefore, I will be able to inform the Alaska authorities what became of the Attuans.

"Tell them what happened and where we are, for goodness' sakes. Otherwise, we'll rot in Otaru."

~

I have commenced this entry the morning of the July 25, and now it is very late in the day, and we are weighing anchor. My cabin is small but comfortable: On one bulkhead (I do remember my Nautical jargon!) resides a simple pull-down desk and reading light, in a corner alcove, the tiniest of WC's. The entire other bulkhead is occupied by two bunks; the top accommodates my newly acquired trunk. My cubicle is inboard, hence without portholes.

All this is luxury compared to the previous three and one-half years.

Food, fair portions of rice and fish, are brought to me. I am, though, under strict orders to remain inside, unless specific permission is given. My society is this journal, my surest, oldest friend on board.

Lila Ann's Sad departure:

On the morning of 22nd July it was not Chief Constable who came for me, but two strange officials, I think Neighborhood Associations captains or functionaries. I had been correct, for the giving-of-trunk was indeed the last time I saw Chief Constable.

It is the greatest of challenges to maintain composure, to allow me to write in proper detail about these minutes, how I felt—what others seemed to feel, and what was said and done.

Friend Annie and I had endured an emotional collapse the night before. She has Mike, who is devoted to her. I reassured her that, "The end of this stupid war is near. Soon you will be home in Attu."

How I hope these words find truth.

The women and youngsters were lined up on one side of the Stair House, the men on the other: While the puzzled officials looked on, my Attuan family said a farewell prayer. When they finished, I managed to keep voice and say what I'd carefully planned to say in my best Aleut: "As God is my witness and upon the memories of my Father and Mother, I vow to make every effort to see you all again." Then in English, " May God bless you all. You are my friends forever."

And at that I left, Mike carrying my trunk.

July 26,1945. Aboard the _Naha Maru,_ North Pacific

It has occurred to this mariner that I have not seen any co-mariners of late, nor heard same.

My arrival was by horse-drawn wagon in the early morning hours of 26th July. I had spent a day and a half, or thereabouts on the train from Otaru to Kushiro, with many—countless—stops. Kushiro is on the east coast of Hokkaido Island, a port on the open North Pacific, unlike Otaru which is on the Sea of Japan.

A very gremlin-like chap by the name of Mr. Yoki, or something close, was my official escort beginning at Otaru Station. When I asked why we were leaving from such a distant port rather than the closest, he offered an impish grin, and tapped his head with the tip of his index finger several times.

One day, perhaps, I shall determine what Mr. Yoki meant, but for then—as well as now—there is no rhyme or reason to it.

The railway trip to Kushiro was completed on ordinary, bone-cruel seats, and frankly most of the line seemed badly tended—cars weaved back and forth as if at sea, and twice we de-railed. Here and there, we changed lines and trains, often not for any apparent purpose. The one demonstrable difference between my ride this year and last, especially the return [*from Wakkanai, also Hokkaido Prefecture, 8/25/44*], was the absence of people. We rode a ghost train, and at each stop, there was an absence of both bustle and travelers.

Most of the ride found me in a mood of introspection. Is it that trains have a manner of both transporting one to their destination and also back in time? As a Mennonite, for that I am and shall remain, I cannot think of war as anything less than blasphemy. A perversion of the human spirit. Osmond did not see it this way, though in so many ways, he was a more committed churchman. He was forever helping the underprivileged, despite his mother's close-fisted approach to money. Few knew this about Osmond.

But he maintained unflagging belief that Mr. Hitler and his Nazis must be eliminated through warfare, though strangely, he had never waxed so intense about Japan. That ceased with Pearl Harbour, of course.

One night a half century ago, I sat with Father roasting chestnuts outside in the mission "quad," as we called it. It was

October 3rd, 1895, his 50th birthday gathering. Most guests had retired. The Sino-Japanese war had just concluded, and Father and Mother had been involved with many of the evacuees in various ways, and I, an earnest 15 year old, had too, of course.

Quite abruptly, he looked at me and said, "You know I served in the American Civil War, don't you Lila?" Well, if there was one rule Mother taught me, it was never to ask Father about the Civil War. She looked at him, and he just held up his hand as if to assure, "It's all right, Mother. Never fear."

While we opened the chestnuts, he said he had been an Infirmary Orderly—had traveled everywhere with the Iowa Regulars. It had been his first exposure to the world, begun when he was only 15.

It was simply told, about as long as it took to open a few of those awful nuts; then he told me, his voice dropping into that very *educational/teacherly* cadence, "and I learned there is not a foot of ground nor a drop of ink upon a treaty worth the outrage of taking human life. And this is what we stand for, Lila, and shall always."

[Without the presence of the Attuans, LAS ceased all but the most pivotal journal entries. She often mentioned the relationship of her journal keeping in reference to the Attuans, and in fact in the following entry, she states it. Between July 26, 1945 and August 17, 1945 LAS was transported to the Yokohama Internment Facility, a yacht club prior to the war. As she was told, it held Occidental women from military and diplomatic families; also, it included a large number of Dutch, British and Australian nurses.]

August 17, 1945; Yokohama Internment Facility.
They are calling August 15th in America and England, "VJ Day," Victory over Japan. It is the official end to World War II. I

don't feel victorious over anything, however. I do feel gratitude and joy that there is cessation to these outrages. The very
fact that war can end on the very day men decide, logically
establishes proof that wars *begin* when men decide them to.

There is thorough exultation in the Yokohama Interment
Facility, of course. Today several United States Army Officers
arrived in a "jeep," a curious wartime machine, small but agile.
They were accompanied by four soldiers carrying weapons, and
at once dealt with turnover from the Japanese authorities.

According to Lady Cadwaller [*Wife of Sir Walter
Cadwaller, British Trade Counsel to Singapore when it was
captured by the Japanese*], processing will take some weeks,
but already fresh provisions have been dropped into the
facility via parachutes. This reminded some of us of the "flying
circuses" so popular in the decade following the great war.

Slung beneath the parachutes were food and "niceties"
aplenty (including *real* tea), and there is now United States
Authority over everything. There is so much news each *HOUR*
that my head spins trying to distinguish between the true,
semi-true, and straight-forward "camp rumor." Now, I will
discover if my communications of two weeks ago to the
International Red Cross about the disposition, condition and
location of the Attuans reached the proper authority, or indeed
any authority at all! Everything is happening with extraordinary speed.

~

One thing sure, since I have the dubious distinction of
being eldest in this facility, "You'll be first out, my dear, if I
have my say, and I will," assures Lady Cadwaller. In my case,
this means my repatriation to the U.S. mainland. My second in
this lifetime, and I'm sure it will be my last.

This journal now has become quite unnecessary regards its
record of my Attu friends and their sad plight—and sadder

fate, for nearly half are departed from this life. Their fate, and the facts surrounding them, remain central to me. My concern is they not be overlooked during this chaotic time.

My letter to the Red Cross, hand delivered by Lady Cadwaller in the regular "humanitarian pouch" via the Swiss Embassy made detailed report about the Attuans. Most important, is the location of their internment. Then I explained their origins, all details leading up to and including the summer when the Japanese captured Attu. Of course I have learned that the island of Attu was central to the bitterest of fights to re-capture the island. I can only imagine the worst for the village structures.

[*Two thousand, three hundred Japanese soldiers were killed trying to hold the island of Attu, and 1,480 Americans and Canadians died while recapturing it between May and August of 1943. The entire village, including the chapel, was destroyed.*]

Without my report, I'm sure authorities would not know American civilians were taken prisoner in Alaska and removed to Japan. In fact the two American staff officers I talked to this a.m., I think, doubted the truth of my account. Perhaps they think I'm a madwoman, but Lady Cadwaller put them straight on the spot, bless her soul.

~

I meant every syllable in my declared intentions to Friend Annie and Mike, that I would one day meet them again along with all the surviving Attuans. Wouldn't it be wonderful if this reunion took place at Chichigof Village.

Beginning with Osmond, then my Aleut friends now gone from this life, before them, poor Emmett—and of course Mother, Father and Joseph, I declare that I look back on 65 years, and without doubt state that mankind's greatest and most persistent flaw is itself.

❧

<u>Seattle, Washington, December 18, 1945</u>
I arrived in Seattle from Delbert, Iowa, five days ago at the
invitation of the Territorial Indian Service. My avowed purpose
was for my long-requested reunion with my beloved Attuans,
which I assumed, would be at my own expense. Their repatriation from the Pacific had been woefully lengthy subsequent to
their liberation from Otaru in mid-September, 1945.

For my first day and a half in Seattle, my dear friends were
en route there from San Francisco via railroad. This wait was
contrary to my understanding. Instead, I was welcomed at
Union Pacific Station by Mr. and Mrs. Lawrence, the former an
official of the Territorial Governor's office. He informed me I
was the honored guest of the Territorial Governor's Office, and
I would be entirely compensated for the expenses of my stay,
for which I was surprised and grateful.

He explained that the Attuans were not being returned to
Attu due to the dangerous munitions—mainly Japanese mine
fields—left behind after the infamous battle to recapture that
island. Instead, those Attuans surviving would be absorbed
into the village of Atka, several hundred miles closer to the
Alaska mainland.

"Isn't there some other portion of the island, other than the
old village site, not so fraught with dangers?" was my initial
reaction. Mr. Lawrence, though, pled ignorance about
specifics, saying such was not his understanding.

"In fact, Mrs. Smith, I assumed the survivors themselves
preferred being settled in an established village, for they are
now fewer than 20 souls, hardly a village I'd say."

Immediately I feared for my adopted family, for there had
been 28 souls surviving upon my departure. I concluded there
had been additional deaths, and my heart was fearful and
heavy thinking who they might be. A person worries most
about which they love; hence, selfishness compelled me to

worry mostly about Friend Annie and husband Mike, though I certainly remained fearful about the welfare of the others.

And time was not on my side.

My prompt return to Delbert was obligated—for I am now the sole care provider for Aunt Sarah, a duty I am honored to fill subsequent to the passing of my dearest Uncle Thomas during my incarceration in Japan. Cousin Ginny, who fills in during my leave, has her own family, it too tragically diminished by the war.

So I was torn between being anxious to go home, yet eager—and then some—to reunite with my friends and to learn about who indeed survived.

The reunion occurred at the Union Pacific Station in downtown Seattle, December 15th, very early in the morning. I sat there waiting, and distinguishing my Attu family amongst those getting off the packed train was no challenge: They are so different (*ancient, in the best sense!*) in appearance, compared to the bustling European hordes scattering to the four winds—busy to reach diverse destinations, some greeted by loved ones, some not.

Words cannot capture my joy when I saw Friend Annie holding onto the arm of husband Mike, with my other dear friends close at hand. Though ordinarily shy and so reserved, when Friend Annie saw me she just rather leaned into this "tall pine tree" of a friend, and I held her like I would my own daughter. Mike wept, along with Philamon and Lena—all of us, formed a fond circle of reunion on the platform between the tracks.

Close at hand were two representatives of the Territorial Native Service, and to my dismay, I learned the Attuans were to embark this same day from Pier 50 via steamship for Dutch Harbour, via Seward, Alaska. Once in Dutch Harbour, they would somehow access transport farther west to Atka. In short, I had nine hours with them.

We were escorted into a government reception area at Union Station. While Alexi and Peter, as village chiefs, conferred with officials in a nearby office, I was "caught up" in quick order—in his ordered and logical way—by Mike. Listening, and correcting small details, Friend Annie remained at my side. Also, Philamon was consulted for accurate hour and date, the calendar and time-of-day his specialty.

I shall here summarize:

All remained healthy during the three weeks between the time I left them and "VJ Day" arrived. When they found this out, there was exultation on everyone's part. The first and most conspicuous change was, "They brought us more food. Also, they had free-run of Otaru, and no longer had to work." And we began to take foot trips here and there. On one such outing, they found an ancient Orthodox Church at the far end of town staffed by an ancient Russian man. "But he had forgotten most of the good words, and lived there with his Japan wife."

This upset them (especially Philamon) to have had a church so close the entire time. Still, they began holding weekly services there.

By September there was no sign of discovery by American or allied authorities, and the Attuans remained uncertain what efforts Otaru officials were making to notify anyone of these Americans' presence. Also, they could not be certain if I had been able to notify anyone of their presence.

However, they did notice many American airplanes; finally, Mike—in a wonderfully inspired moment—thought to write mammoth letters in whitewash upon the roof of the Stair House. "On one side Philamon and John wrote POW, and on other me and Peter painted HELP."

Later it turned out POW was actually *PWO*, but the HELP *was* 'help,' and that *same day*, "A big plane came over, circled and circled, then left. We knew it was looking down at us. But we prayed anyway."

Whether it was sharp eyes, prayer or both, within two days, the American military arrived at the facility and liberation was official. It was a great day and I only wish I could have been there.

American officials were stunned to find out the villagers from Attu had survived, at least in part, and more—had been transported to Japan from Alaska as prisoners.

From there, their path became complicated: They flew from Otaru to a base near Tokyo—the first airplane flight for all villagers. From there, after the most basic health inspection, they were again treated to an airplane flight to Okinawa, the official headquarters of the Red Cross processing center for Prisoners of War, both civilian and military, it seems. (Frankly, a fair-share of this information came from a Territorial Official who had escorted the Attuans from San Francisco, riding on the train with them.)

It was in Okinawa that most came down with measles and were quarantined for nearly a month. "We were sick so big, very awful." This is Annie's syntax. Because of this, Heratina and Anna continued in a very weak state, "though we thought they was better." Finally, the doctor lifted the quarantine and they all were flown to Manila, Philippines!

It seems, to the Attuans—and Lila Ann also—that this return route was very strange. At first my adopted family did not appreciate how strange, until Mike got-hold of an Atlas and deciphered it for everyone. In the Philippines I herein quote from Mike: "They kept us in a place so hot it was like the banya but all the time, not just in the banya. One guy came with camera fellow and most had hard time talking, like when we had measles. He gave me map."

The villagers' English skills, in three and a half years, called upon so rarely, diminished badly, something about which I feel guilty. Why hadn't I noticed?! But it was in this untoward heat and humidity that Heratina's and Anna's weakened state caught up with them and they were taken to a military hospital. In fact, these are the two who remain missing, but we are informed through officials that they will follow by several weeks. Yet, they are sorely missed. (So the number arriving in Seattle is 23, not less than 20 as conveyed to me earlier.)

Eventually—after about a month—those healthiest enough to travel were put aboard a military transport ship sailing to San Francisco. There they were feted like royalty by the military and a priest of some influence in the local Orthodox community, which is quite significant in San Francisco. Then, after a week of sight-seeing and feasting as the guests of the Orthodox faithful, they were put aboard the Union Pacific's finest passenger train bound for Seattle, compliments of the Alaska Territorial Service. And here, I met them.

~

Never have I experienced a shorter, more emotion-filled nine hours than those between arrival at Union Station and departure at Pier 50. Most prominent was learning that my dearest friends, so long and forcefully absented from their Island home, did not know they were not returning there. They learned this in the receiving center at Union Station. Why the tardiness in informing them—of all people—of this sad decision and necessity confuses and upsets everyone, including Lila Ann. Especially Lila Ann.

"Atka people not like Attu people," was repeated by almost all Attuans. Interceding, I explained to Mr. Lawrence that indeed it was a different language group, but there seemed to be no help for it at this stage. In fact, he informed me, the Territorial Service had already sent construction materials to Atka from which new houses would be made. Most assumed that eventually they would be returned to Chichigof Village, an assumption that is ill advised, I feel. In fact, in the ensuing hours this fact—the shipment of house-building materials to Atka—was also conveyed with sad tardiness to the Attuans.

The hours, meanwhile, slipped away, and I had my own priorities, very dear to me, and long intended: I reminded Friend Annie and Mike that they were welcome entirely and without condition in my (now mostly unoccupied) house in

Delbert. I knew it would be difficult to adjust, but especially now that they were not returning home, my intentions and present offer were especially heartfelt.

I knew, of course, that they longed for their native land—that of sea and winds, the plants and creatures—that was indeed in their blood and spirits. "*This* is where God lives." And that was all Friend Annie and Mike needed to say, for I knew it. But I reminded them that my offer always—always—stood. And that we must—absolutely must—write often. And lastly, that I loved them as my own dearest children.

Nothing more important could have been imparted in this tiny sliver of time allotted us. And in confusion and rush, with all these facts and unfortunate developments still fresh on their shoulders, I saw them aboard the Alaska Steamship *Northern Supplier*. The irony that it had been Osmond and my conveyance to Attu was not lost on Lila Ann, Friend Annie and Mike.

As they ascended the gangplank, I hugged each Attuan, and from each received a farewell blessing in their ancient church language. "We shall always pray for you," Philamon assured, for Lena was beyond words at that point.

Frankly, I was also. And remain so.

~

I write this entry somewhat less than a day out of Chicago where I will change trains. This journal's job is complete and I reflect what I might do with it—of who might want to use it. And nothing springs to mind. I shall keep it safe, of course. As my mother was so fond of saying, "It is a tried and true expression, Lila Ann. But time—time will indeed tell."

It seems God has provided me with several families during my life, and I hope I am the better for it. I try very sincerely to remember the increase his gift provided in my life, and not the sadness of decrease.

LAS December 21, 1945.

Editor's Afterword

It is not known if Lila Ann Smith ever met with any of her Attuan friends again, for the journal ends here. The surviving Attuans were never to return to their native Attu . On Atka they all lived out their lives, and only two ever again set foot on Attu, and only for brief expeditions lasting a few days. The only surviving part of Chichigof Village on Attu Island is the bell from the Chapel of Our Lady of the Holy Domition, *recovered by U.S. military authorities subsequent to World War II. It is now stored in the village of Atka.*

Appendix

Des Moines *Register*, 10/15/1902;
Lila Ann Howland, China Survivor
By Wilson Beasley Jr.

Orphan of adversity

Miss Lila Ann Howland, daughter of the late Reverend Paul and Miriam Howland, has recently returned to a jubilant family in Delbert. She was held hostage by brigands for almost eighteen months in Northern China. Miss Howland, age 22, was born in China while her parents served in the ministry of the Mennonite faith. She is a fluent speaker of Chinese.

As reported contemporaneously by the *Register,* savage Chinamen called "Boxers" rebelled against the lawful order in 1900. True to the ways of such bloodthirsty rebels, they murdered and pillaged, especially targeting the Chinaman's most faithful friends, the missionary community.

At the Mercy of Brigands

Lila Ann Howland and four other daughters of missionaries were held hostage by "General" Huog Lon Shi, a brigand leader of the lowest degree. He coldly negotiated for arms and ammunition with numerous European nations and the Empire of Japan during the entirety of the unfortunate young women's confinement. Fearful of rewarding and even promoting such loathsome acts, the countries whose citizens were prisoners naturally hesitated to provide arms or monies.

"I do understand provisions were offered, and other such non-military items, but they were steadfastly refused," Miss Howland explained to this reporter. Finally, desperate to repatriate the unfortunate young women, cash ransom was provided to the villainous rabble, and they were released to officials at a demarcation station between Hong Kong and Old China.

Nomadic Confinement

"We never remained in the same location more than a few days," said Miss Howland. Fearing European powers, or those loyal to the weakened Chinese Mikado might free them, the brigand commander and his henchmen moved the women often. "Sometimes we had to walk, other times they used mule or horse drawn carts."

Traversing the vast wastes of China, constantly moving from one hiding spot to another, was extraordinarily hard. Eventually all the women had nothing more than what they could carry, ". . . in a bandana, tied with string."

The rigors and humiliation wrought by such a life can only be imagined. When asked if she thought it possible to recover completely from such an ordeal, Miss Howland said, "I think, with God's help, I can."

Though this reporter could not steel himself to ask if Lila Ann Howland would ever return to the Missionary Life, her strength in surviving this ungrateful outrage is testimony to an invincible Christian faith.

Reclaiming a civilized Life

Lila Ann Howland will reside with her Uncle Thomas and Aunt Sarah Howland of Delbert. "Doc" Howland, longtime veterinarian in Staunton County, and former State Senator, assured *Register* readers that his beloved niece, daughter of his eldest brother, "would never know hardship again." Her immediate plans are to reestablish contact with her extensive family, then begin studies in Oberlin College. "I was supposed to begin studies two years ago, but the troubles in Shanxi Province prevented it."

There will be a community "Welcome Home Lila" pot-luck at the Delbert Grange November 1st. Several surviving missionaries of the 1900 rebellion in China will also be in attendance.

ALASKA
Anchorage
Kodiak
U.S.S.R.
Bering Sea
Unalaska
Aleutian Islands
Atka
Attu
Kiska
Hokkaido
Otaru
JAPAN
PACIFIC OCEAN

Books from *Pleasure Boat Studio: A Literary Press*

Note: Caravel Books is a new imprint of Pleasure Boat Studio: A Literary Press.
Caravel Books is the imprint for mysteries only. Aequitas Books is another imprint which includes
non-fiction with philosophical and sociological themes. Empty Bowl Press is a Division of
Pleasure Boat Studio.

UPCOMING: *The Woman Who Wrote King Lear, and Other Stories* • Louis Phillips
UPCOMING: *The Shadow in the Lake* • Inger Frimansson • Trans fm Swedish

Dream of the Dragon Pool: A Daoist Quest • Albert A. Dalia
Good Night, My Darling • Inger Frimansson, Trans fm Swedish by Laura Wideburg • **a caravel book**
Falling Awake: An American Woman Gets a Grip on the Whole Changing World—One Essay at a Time
    Mary Lou Sanelli • $15 • **an aequitas book**
Way Out There: Lyrical Essays • Michael Daley • $16 • **an aequitas book**
The Case of Emily V. • Keith Oatley • mystery • $18 • **a caravel book**
Monique • Luisa Coehlo, Trans fm Portuguese by Maria do Carmo de Vasconcelos and Dolores DeLuise
    ISBN 1929355262 • 80 pages • fiction • $14
The Blossoms Are Ghosts at the Wedding • Tom Jay • ISBN 1929335351 • essays and poems • $15
    an empty bowl book
Against Romance • Michael Blumenthal • ISBN 1929355238 • 110 pages • poetry • $14
Speak to the Mountain: The Tommie Waites Story • Dr. Bessie Blake • ISBN 1929355297 / 36X • 278 pages
    biography • $18 / $26 • **an aequitas book**
Artrage • Everett Aison • ISBN 1929355254 • 225 pages • fiction • $15
Days We Would Rather Know • Michael Blumenthal • ISBN 1929355246 • 118 pages • poetry • $14
Puget Sound: 15 Stories • C. C. Long • ISBN 192935522X • 150 pages • fiction • $14
Homicide My Own • Anne Argula • ISBN 1929355211 • 220 pages • fiction (mystery) • $16
Craving Water • Mary Lou Sanelli • ISBN 192935519X • 121 pages • poetry • $15
When the Tiger Weeps • Mike O'Connor • ISBN 1929355189 • 168 pages • poetry and prose • 15
Wagner, Descending: The Wrath of the Salmon Queen • Irving Warner • ISBN 1929355173 • 242 pages
    fiction • $16
Concentricity • Sheila E. Murphy • ISBN 1929355165 • 82 pages • poetry • $13.95
Schilling, from a study in lost time • Terrell Guillory • ISBN 1929355092 • 156 pages • fiction • $16.95
Rumours: A Memoir of a British POW in WWII • Chas Mayhead • ISBN 1929355068 • 201 pages
    nonfiction • $16
The Immigrant's Table • Mary Lou Sanelli • ISBN 1929355157 • $13.95 • poetry and recipes • $13/95
The Enduring Vision of Norman Mailer • Dr. Barry H. Leeds • ISBN 1929355114 • criticism • $18
Women in the Garden • Mary Lou Sanelli • ISBN 1929355149 • poetry • $13.95
Pronoun Music • Richard Cohen • ISBN 1929355033 • short stories • $16
If You Were With Me Everything Would Be All Right • Ken Harvey • ISBN 1929355025 • short stories • $16
The 8th Day of the Week • Al Kessler • ISBN 1929355009 • fiction • $16
Another Life, and Other Stories • Edwin Weihe • ISBN 19293550117 • short stories • $16
Saying the Necessary • Edward Harkness • ISBN 096514139X (paper) • poetry • $14
Nature Lovers • Charles Potts • ISBN 1929355041 • poetry • $10
In Memory of Hawks, & Other Stories from Alaska • Irving Warner • ISBN 0965141349 • 210 pages
    fiction • $15
The Politics of My Heart • William Slaughter • ISBN 0965141306 • 96 pages • poetry • $12.95
The Rape Poems • Frances Driscoll • ISBN 0965141314 • 88 pages • poetry • $12.95
When History Enters the House: Essays from Central Europe • Michael Blumenthal • ISBN 0965141322
    248 pages • nonfiction • $15
Setting Out: The Education of Lili • Tung Nien • Trans fm Chinese by Mike O'Connor • ISBN 0965141330
    160 pages • fiction • $15